CU00706320

Good Luck
Michael

Jane Scott

MY TEACHER
SAYS
YOU'RE A WITCH

MY TEACHER SAYS YOU'RE A WITCH

JANE SCHAFFER

Seven Arches Publishing

Published in June 2007
By Seven Arches Publishing
27, Church Street, Nassington, Peterborough PE8 6QG
www.sevenarchespublishing.co.uk

Copyright © Jane Schaffer 2007

The moral right of the author has been asserted.

All rights reserved. No part of this publication may be
reproduced or transmitted, in any form by any means,
electronic or mechanical without prior permission from the publisher
in writing.

All the characters in this book are fictitious and any
resemblance to actual persons is purely coincidental.

Cover design, scans and typesetting by Alan McGlynn

ISBN: 978-0-9556169-0-7

CONTENTS

One

Training – Liverpool September 1966

Part Two

Inspection of Beswick Street Primary School, Liverpool

Part Three

Inspection of Higham Primary School, Scarborough

Part Four

Two Inspections, Coventry and West Yorkshire

Part Five

My First Lead, Home Farm Primary School, Birmingham

Foreword

"Are you one of our suspectors"
(a child's question to a team member on the first day of an inspection in a primary school on Merseysde.)

When Jane Schaffer first became an inspector, a school would wait to receive a much dreaded brown envelope from Ofsted announcing an inspection visit. Now it is through a phone call. It is a call that notes a key moment in the history of the school. It promises a very public judgment on the effectiveness of the institution and all who work in it and for it. Invariably it signals a period of stress ahead and while the impact on the headteachers and their colleagues is well documented, rarely is the experience of the inspector explored. Jane does that in this very honest account of her own journey from the teacher's desk at the front of the classroom to the inspector's chair at the back.

Reviewing a school is all about people and Jane's concern for people, especially younger people shines through this book. As the head of one of the inspection companies that asked Jane to lead inspection teams, I recall the self-critical care she took in drafting her reports. That care and the child-centered commitment to improving schools that led her into this work is here in these pages. There are more laughs and more tears in it than would be allowed by the official critical report-reader and it is all the better for that. She reveals the pain, pleasures and panic that lie behind the clip board and the Handbook for Inspections. I enjoyed reading her reports. I enjoyed even more reading her description of life as a 'suspector'. I hope you do too.

Chris Glynn
Former head of Nord Anglia School Inspection Services

For Angela, Louise and Georgina

Introduction

"A good inspection report must demonstrate a clear understanding of the different groups of pupils educated in the school and how the school supports their learning and other needs. Inspectors must take account of diversity among the school's pupils and evaluate how well the school responds to it."

Guidance for Inspectors on Writing About Educational Inclusion in Inspection Reports: Ofsted reference number HMI 745 Crown Copyright 2002

Number 113 Bus Stop Stainer Street, Birmingham – January 1997

Joffrey had been afraid for a long time. The fear was with him in the morning and when he closed his eyes at night. He was afraid now. He wanted to hold his mother's hand but she wouldn't let him. They walked through the cold streets and the eyes looked at them. They stopped and waited at the place where a large bus would come. Some other people waited there. They didn't push Joffrey and his mother or attack them, but perhaps they would, perhaps they were just waiting for the time to be right when they would get out their long knives and cut them into pieces. Every day he and his mother came to the bus stop. They stood at the bus stop with the other people and then got on the bus with them. He didn't know these strange people, with their pale blotchy faces and their lumpy big coats. They looked down at the ground or smoked a cigarette and the women folded their arms. His mother never folded her arms. In his village he had known everyone. After the village was burnt there was no one he knew. Even his uncle who came to the place with the tents, and took them to the plane, he didn't know. His mother said he was his uncle but he had never seen him before. His mother said they would never have got on the plane if it wasn't for his uncle. They wouldn't be alive now.

At the bus stop, his mother stood very straight and very still. He tried to hold her hand again but she shook her head. "No you must be a man now," she said. They got on the bus and sat down on the seats. He sat as close to his mother as he could. He liked the bus. When they were on the bus he sometimes felt the fear in his stomach go away. He felt safe here, sitting next to his mother with the big back of the seat in front hiding him from all the other passengers. He always sat by the window, but he didn't look out. He looked down at the floor. He liked the bumps and rattles and the sound of the engine, strong and powerful. He wished they could stay on the bus all day.

When they got off, they were nearly at the school. He knew that they had to turn down the next road and then they would see the school. He had done this ten times now. He was not a stupid boy – he could count. His father had taught him to count. His father, who was chopped to pieces the night the village was burnt, he had taught him to count up to a hundred. Joffrey would know when he had been to this school a hundred times. He would never forget what his father had taught him. They didn't know that he could count at this school. They didn't know anything about him. All they knew was his name. No one knew anything because they didn't speak to him in his language. Some older children spoke his language. He had heard them outside when they were playing football. He knew how to play football but nobody asked him to play.

When they got to the school gate, his mother said: "Be a good boy Joffrey. I will come for you when it is time." He gripped the fear tight inside his tummy. He said his 'goodbye' to his mother very quietly. He wanted to scream. He wanted to shout 'don't go, don't leave me', but he walked through the gate and onto the playground until he found a place to stop. He stood at that place looking back at his mother. He could see her watching him through the iron bars. She would stay there until the lady came and led him to a line of children. For a few days, after he had first come to the school, the lady used to smile at him and take his hand so that he could walk beside her into school. Now she would come up to him and say his name and lots of other words in the language he couldn't understand, and sometimes she shook her head and looked at him a little crossly. She would take his hand and lead him to the line of children, but not in such a kindly way as she had done at first and sometimes she gave him a little push. Then he would follow the child in front of him into the school. And he would start the long wait until it was time to go home and his mother would be at the gate again.

PART ONE

TRAINING – LIVERPOOL,
SEPTEMBER 1966

Chapter 1

The summer holidays of 1996 were very different for me. I had no need to go into school during August, something I had done ever since I qualified as a primary school teacher. Those few extra days of holidays were such a bonus – no lesson planning, no marshalling of resources and no new work schemes to organise. The reason for this freedom was that I had applied and, to my surprise, been accepted for a year's secondment to be a school inspector with the Office for Standards in Education. As from the second week of September, I was to receive two weeks of intensive training in a hotel on the outskirts of Liverpool, accommodation provided at Her Majesty's expense.

During August, sundry large boxes had been delivered to my house from government central supplies. There was a most wonderful combined telephone, fax and answering machine that in addition could produce a photocopy, albeit rather faint and crumpled, on its fax roll. It came with strict instructions, as did all the equipment, that should one no longer be employed by the government, it must be packed up and returned in its original packaging. One of the boxes contained a small Compaq laptop. This clumpy little computer seemed to me to be the most up-to-date piece of technology known to man. I was a very early stage IT user, but then so were most of my colleagues.

We were also supplied with stationery items, including an enormous pile of brown envelopes with the following commanding message printed in blue across the top:

On Her Majesty's Service.

I found it difficult to imagine what it was I was going to send in all these envelopes, but I was very pleased to have them; they had such gravitas and anything sent in them must surely be of singular importance. We were informed that unused stationery items need not be returned which is why I can still send someone a letter 'On Her Majesty's Service,' should I be so rash. There had also been the extremely gratifying matter of signing the Official Secrets Act - a requirement for all government employed persons of our level. What secrets could I possibly come upon in a primary school that would be a matter of national importance? I could not imagine. But never-mind, it was very gratifying to think that there might be such a possibility.

On the appointed day at the start of the two-week training, I got up very early. I made strenuous efforts to make my rather plain, mumsy appearance look business-like, said sundry good-byes to the unmoving lump under the duvet in my teenage daughter's room, stowed suitcase and shiny new brief-case into the boot of my much dinted Vauxhall Astra and set off. As I drove through the early morning motorway traffic to Liverpool, my mind was only partially on the road. Despite the need for full attention to speeding vehicles and dividing motorway lanes, thoughts about what lay ahead of me intruded. Teachers, myself included, had been given a rude awakening by the new inspection process that had been set up following the 1992 Education Act. Ofsted, it seemed to us, stalked the country like a mighty megalith brought to life in order to terrorize unsuspecting staff rooms. The inventor and puppet master of this many-headed monster was Her Majesty's Chief Inspector, Chris Woodhead. He was the arch-enemy of all teachers. Tapping into the already present public envy of all those long summer holidays, not to mention Easter and Christmas, he had convinced government and populace alike that teachers had been derelict in their duty; schools needed to buck up their ideas. And now I was about to join this monstrous organisation. What was I thinking of?

I arrived just in time to check into the hotel for the nine

o'clock start. I was not late, but my name was one of the last to be ticked off on the receptionist's list; most others having made sure of an earlier arrival. I was handed a name badge and ushered through to join the hundred or so other would-be inspectors milling around in the hotel's main conference room. Smart hotel staff offered coffee and chocolate biscuits. I was tempted, but reluctantly thought better of it as some of the others, the early birds, had already started to move towards the seating area. I looked about me at the gathering of confident well-heeled persons and felt a mixture of pride at being there and anxiety at not quite matching their caliber. Shortly everyone was seated and waiting in anticipation for the opening address. It was to be given by a senior HMI, a lady whose reputation and ranking was second only to that of Chris Woodhead. To anyone within education, HMI are as a breed apart. For a start, they come from London; they might have been born, bred and even be currently domiciled in any of the English counties but without question, they come from London, the capital city. They are government. They travel first class, stay in five star hotels and always transfer from the station to wherever they were going in taxis; there is an unassailable air of authority in everything they do.

Our speaker exuded HMI mystique from every inch of her petite, elegant figure. Her suit was one to hanker after, definitely not purchased from M & S, as were most of the suits in her audience. The speech she gave was impressive. It made you feel that you were the few, selected from many, to be the elite fighting force of the educational world. She spoke eloquently of Ofsted's partnership with schools and how this would be deepened by the infusion into the inspectorate of recently serving headteachers and deputies such as ourselves. She made a particular point of praising the addition of deputies, citing their recent classroom experience for this praise. As I was such a one, it gave me a warm feeling of being special – it didn't last for long and was never repeated in all my time of working for Ofsted.

The next speaker was more down-to-earth, an energetic sort of chap who explained the manner in which we would fulfil our training in the weeks ahead of us. Often eliciting a burst of laughter with a timely witticism, he nevertheless got across the message that if we did not live up to expectations we would be promptly dispatched back to where we came from, whatever the inconvenience. These two played the good cop/bad cop roles. We were being welcomed into the fold, but we mustn't get complacent. You worked for Ofsted – they gave you the badge that schools held in such awe, but put a step wrong and you were on your own. This approach engendered steely determination, so that we silently vowed that we were going to meet the challenge which, of course, was its purpose. We were there to get as much out of as possible but to give little to in return. Because we came from the hierarchy of school leadership, our egos where flattered and temporarily we were allowed to think ourselves pals with these rarefied beings.

After these two speeches the usual conference pattern ensued: disperse and look for your name on a list that assigned you to a group from A – K, and then follow a plan of the hotel to find your group in a smaller room, tucked away on one of the many silent, thickly carpeted hotel corridors.

As usual, my map reading skills let me down. I turned left instead of right on one of the upstairs corridors. In addition, I diverted momentarily into a nearby toilet. As a consequence, I was the last one of my group to arrive. When I pushed open the door, I found that everyone else was already sitting round the table chatting to HMI Henry Calderbank, our course tutor. They had the appearance of having been ensconced for a good while and were getting on famously, as people do who want to make a good first impression. (Had none of them needed the toilet?) On my entrance, the HMI looked up, smiled vaguely and motioned toward the one empty chair by way of acknowledging my arrival.

"Let's get our meeting started," he said, picking up and scrutinising a piece of paper that was in front of him. As I squeezed past two people, in order to get to the vacant chair, I managed to knock over someone's bag and had to loudly whisper my apologies. The tutor paused with an amused but not unkindly smile on his face while I tried to get seated without any further disturbance.

"I am working from my crib sheet." He held it up and waved it, as if we needed convincing of its existence, "which, I hasten to add, is what I will be doing all week. It says here that I must ask you to introduce yourselves. You know how this works – go round the table and say your name and a bit about yourself." He smiled across the table to the man sitting next to me. "Perhaps you would like to start Phil?"

"Sure," the man smiled back. Even in just that one word you could detect an interesting, soft Irish tone to his voice. "I'm Phil Docherty and I've been a headteacher of a primary school on the Wirral for eight years. I was beginning to get stale – you know how it is. I applied for the Ofsted training because I felt I needed a new challenge. My aim is to go back after the year a wiser and more…" he paused a moment as if searching for just the right words, then came out with exactly the right ones, " a more effective head, able to lead my staff into the twenty first century." He was an attractive man and spoke with easy confidence and his slight Irish accent was beguiling. As he finished speaking, I looked around the table at the others; these people were to be my working companions for the next few months, how much more qualified for this job they all appeared to be. The next person, a woman spoke up purposefully.

"Mary Stewart. I've been working for the Bolton advisory service for five years. I've supported schools in my district to improve their development planning and assessment procedures." Mary had a warm attractive smile which she flashed to everyone the minute she stopped speaking. I thought that I would probably like her, though I was not too sure about her somewhat grating, upper-class, home-counties accent. It immediately conferred on her a level of status, which was not at all reflected in her dress, as she had on a rather baggy wooly cardigan that had seen better days.

The next person to speak, introduced herself as Abby Martin, her real name, Abigail she said she never used. I had a sudden jolt of recognition, and I remembered that I had heard her talk at a Greater Manchester schools' conference on special educational needs. She had been the deputy to a charismatic headteacher in Oldham called Marcus Mann whose new methods of helping children from ethnic minorities learn to speak English often grabbed the headlines. Abby Martin had then gone on to her own headship in Rochdale. She said that she had been a headteacher for five years in a very deprived inner city school and briefly described some of the most pressing problems in her school. She was modest and very self-contained. Her contribution so interested me, I almost missed the next person to speak.

"Trevor Barnes, I've worked in most areas of education, including teacher training. Currently I am responsible for the placement and assessment of students on teaching practice at Edge Hill – very rewarding," he added after a long pause which left you wondering if he was going to say any more. Trevor was a slightly over-weight individual but his features though heavy were pleasant. He was clearly less at ease than the others. After he had finished speaking, I realized that there was only one person to go before it would be my turn. Suddenly I felt nervous. What was I going to say? The person on my left started speaking. He was a tall man, probably the youngest in the group and he was full of confidence.

"Nigel Theakston, I'm a deputy headteacher of a very large school in Blackpool. I've a special interest in IT and over the last year I have been on secondment to the LEA for part of the week to work with a group of schools to improve the use of IT across the curriculum." Nigel Theakston had a squeaky voice that did not quite go with the rest of his very personable appearance.

I noticed Henry Calderbank smiling. He had said nothing in response to the other members of the group but now he spoke. "Well Nigel, I'm sure we will be coming to you for advice, because we're all having to grapple with the IT revolution, aren't we?" He looked round at everyone and nodded at the murmurs of assent. Nigel Theakston looked pleased at this recognition of his skills, but he didn't smile. He just straightened his shoulders a little and inclined his head. I thought Henry Calderbank was going to carry on speaking, and that my contribution would be overlooked. But, he turned to me suddenly and indicated that I should begin. I started speaking a little too quickly, feeling a most unwelcome and unnecessary rush of nervousness.

"Jane Schaffer, and I'm a deputy headteacher, like Nigel." I gave him a quick smile, but there was no responding smile or even eye-contact. It turned my mild nervousness into full-blown panic. I needed to add something but my mind seemed to have gone blank. "My school is in a very deprived area" – that was what Abby Martin had said; it sounded trite a second time. They all seemed to be staring at me with the expectation that I would say more. I desperately searched my mind for a point of interest in my recent work. "I've been very involved in developing parental involvement." The ill-formed sentence made me flush with embarrassment, but at least I had finished.

Then I heard Mary Stewart say in her loud upper-class tones: "That's one of my great interests as well Jane; a good relationship with parents is so important for a school." I gave her a grateful smile, even though her compassionate encouragement was exactly what she would have dispensed to a child fumbling over their words in a class assembly. I was relieved to hear the tutor speaking again.

"Thank you everyone for that. The quality and depth of experience that you newcomers are bringing to inspection is exciting. Many people in inspection at the moment, myself included I have to say, can hardly remember the time that they spent in the classroom. The Additional Inspector project, of which you are now part, has been set up to get new people into inspection who understand the current problems facing schools. I think it is a very good move." He stopped and looked down at the papers on his desk to find the crib sheet.

He started on the business of the day, detailing what skills we would be learning and how much theory we would cover over the next week. Then mystifyingly, he seemed to be explaining that the plan was for us to undertake a real inspection, under his guidance, the following week. As this became clear, a ripple of shocked surprise spread round the group.

"Surely we won't be up to carrying out a real inspection in just one week?" squeaked Nigel.

Henry smiled: "You didn't think Ofsted would feed you for free for two weeks did you?" No one answered his question. "They need to put you to work as soon as possible, to recoup some of the money they have laid out on this additional inspector project." The sarcasm in his voice was unmistakable. We all exchanged looks of 'what on earth have we got ourselves into?' But our tutor took no notice, as if he was not really part of the Ofsted machine, just happened to be there in Liverpool by some unaccountable accident, and continued outlining the programme for the days ahead.

As well as his crib sheet, Henry always had the Handbook for Inspection beside him. If he spoke derisively about the Ofsted organisation, the handbook received nothing but praise from him and we were told to have it with us at all times, read it and refer to it at all points. Inspections must reflect the handbook was the mantra.

"You no doubt all understand the importance of early work on school documentation before an inspection is undertaken?" Henry queried, pointing at a huge pile of photocopied documents at the side of the room. "The more you know about a school before you start an inspection the better."

"But isn't that judging a school before you get there?" asked Mary. "A lot of schools, that I know, feel that inspectors come with preconceived notions and that this doesn't give them a fair chance."

"That's because they don't understand the process. Consider this. You're in school for four days, which seems a long time when you're away from home, but it's a very short time in which to gather all the information you need to make secure judgements. You're not going to see everything, and if too much comes as a surprise, then you are going to be seriously off the mark by the end of the inspection. When we review the documentation, we're raising hypotheses about a school. Inspection is about testing those hypotheses. We're often proved wrong – of course there are surprises – sometimes pretty big ones, but if you don't start with the known you are lost." Although it was Mary whose comment had triggered the explanation, it was clear that for us all this was new information; everyone was listening intently.

"Now, let's look at the material we've got to work with today and I think you will see what I mean. All these documents are from a real school – the name has been erased, of course. You'll all need a copy of each item." There ensued a busy few minutes as we passed round the mountain of photocopies. Amidst rueful comments regarding the cutting down of trees, we made sure we all had one of each.

The first document Henry asked us to look at was strangely named a pixie, or more accurately, a PICSI (Pre-inspection Context and School Indicators). This was a thirty page document full of tables and graphs to show the school's tests results, the attendance, the background of its pupils and census information about the area in which the school was situated. Although every school was sent one annually, supposedly to check their progress against that of others, it was the first time I had seen it. What had my headteacher been doing with our copy? And then I had a memory of a huge pile of documents, from various government agencies, that had gradually amassed on a shelf in her office, all staying pristine, unread and some even in their original envelopes.

"If we look at the context page," said Henry, turning to find the right page, "(it's page six), we can see that this school is probably situated in a reasonably affluent area. We can also see from this part of the table that there are an average number of children with special educational needs and hardly any pupils from ethnic minorities. We can deduce that this school is well placed in that it doesn't have to provide extra to help these groups of pupils to learn. Now, let's look at the standards this school achieves in the tests for eleven-year-olds."

Everyone was eager to check out what these told us about this school. We discovered that the results showed they were doing quite well in mathematics. They were above average. In English, however, they were below average.

"There is a very big question here don't you think?" asked Henry.

14

We all nodded and almost chorused: "What's happening with English? Why aren't they doing better at English?"

Henry then asked us to look at the other documents of which there was a hefty pile, and to organize ourselves into pairs to work together to track down specific bits of information. At this, Phil Docherty turned to me and said:

"Right ho that's you and me working together, OK Jane?" I nodded quickly because, after my poor showing with the introductions, I had quite expected to be the 'oh, I suppose I'll have to work with her' choice, like the clumsy child when football teams are picked.

Phil and I had to find out what the documents could tell us about the school's curriculum planning and their procedures for assessing the children, bearing in mind that the central question was: 'why were they not doing as well in English as mathematics?' Phil was fun and easy to work with. Pouring over the documents together, we shared our findings enthusiastically. Ofsted asked schools to fill in a series of forms which gave inspectors a lot of information about staff; what qualifications they had, what had been their main subjects, when they had trained, how long they had been a teacher and what their areas of responsibility were. We soon discovered that the co-ordinator (that's educational jargon for a teacher with a special responsibility) for English was a lady who had been at the school for 23 years.

"There," said Phil, pointing to this nugget of information, "that's probably the reason for poor English."

"What do you mean?"

"The woman's probably passed it – been in the job too long and thinks she gets her scale points for ordering new books twice a year – doesn't understand that she's supposed to be doing something about raising standards."

"Just because she's older doesn't mean she's not doing her

job properly." I said, shocked at Phil's ageist attitude.

"I bet I'm right," said Phil.

"OK, you maybe right, but I think we need to look at other things as well."

"Bet I am," said Phil again, with a mischievous twinkle in his eye.

"Who's laying bets?" asked Abby, catching the drift of our conversation. She was working with Mary, and was obviously a little uncomfortable with Mary's overpowering, motherly approach.

"Phil is damning the English co-ordinator, just because she has been a loyal staff member for twenty years."

Abby smiled at Phil. "He's probably right," she said.

"Mmm, well perhaps, but we've got a lot of other possibilities to consider," I said, turning back to the documents in front of me. Phil had started looking at a complicated grid which the school had to fill in to show the percentage of teaching time spent each week on each subject. He discovered that they were spending a reasonable amount of time on English, but then we achieved a small triumph of detection. When we looked at the teachers' timetables, we uncovered the fact that these figures did not match. The time spent on English, according to the timetables was much less. We eagerly noted this down as a potential concern. However, when we presented our findings at the end of the session, Henry found our sleuthing interesting, but advised caution as to how we would handle this on inspection.

"Evidence of this nature is not foolproof. It has to be backed up by further investigation and hopefully more evidence," he said.

"Why?" asked Phil.

"Well, the school could say that those timetables are just for one particular week and that during other weeks the time spent on English is much greater. Of course, this is probably not the case. What is happening here is a lack of monitoring by the senior staff, the headteacher in particular. Teachers are doing their own thing, which is fine in some ways but it might lead to problems."

"How would we back it up?" I asked, intrigued by the complex issues that were beginning to emerge about inspection.

"One place to look would be the children's work books. Is there enough work done in their books? If not, that would be very solid evidence."

"There might be work elsewhere, besides their books, on the walls on display, for instance," put in Abby.

"That's true, good point Abby."

"You would check their assessments," offered Mary.

"How would that help Mary?" Henry asked and Mary uncharacteristically didn't answer for a moment. "This is a time issue here – we are not trying to follow up an enquiry about the standard of work."

"Oh yes, yes I see," she said, laughing happily at herself. She was un-phased by her gaffe. We were soon to realise that for Mary, the answer to all school ills was assessment, or rather the lack of it; assessment had been her particular brief with the local education authority for which she had worked.

At the end of that first afternoon, we had to our amazement, produced a hypothetical plan of action for the inspection of a school. Henry congratulated us on the amount of work we had got through and informed us that, as it was the first evening, we could relax with just some light reading for the evening task. He added that he hoped we would all enjoy the evening meal which would be served around seven thirty. We sat back relieved, momentarily nonplussed – it had been a long day.

We took ourselves off to our rooms, freshened up, and

nearly everyone phoned home, most to a waiting spouse or partner. I had been widowed when my children were very young, so there was no one like that to whom I could recount the day's events. Every night, though I rang Kate, the last of my three daughters still at home to check she was all right. At just seventeen, she was in her first year at sixth-form college. Every night, she patiently told me that she was fine and not to worry. On the whole, I didn't worry; she was sensible and had her best friend Emily staying over for the week. It was, I told myself, no big deal but part of me did not really think that, part of me felt the guilt that lone parents always feel when they think they have not done everything they should for their children – a life-time of overcompensation.

About half an hour later, we gathered in the hotel restaurant. Because we were not paying for it, the hotel's pleasant, though unremarkable cuisine was thoroughly enjoyed; so were the two bottles of wine (which we did pay for) that we cautiously ordered to help us unwind and start to get to know each other socially.

Chapter 2

The Ofsted seven point scale was used to grade all aspects of school life including the quality of teaching in lessons:

1 excellent
2 very good
3 good
4 satisfactory
5 unsatisfactory
6 poor
7 very poor

When grading a lesson inspectors' judgements had to be based on the extent to which teachers used the following criteria effectively:

- set high expectations so as to challenge pupils and deepen their knowledge and understanding;
- planned effectively;
- employed methods and organizational strategies which matched curricular objectives and the needs of all pupils;
- managed pupils well and achieved high standards of discipline;
- used time and resources effectively;
- assessed pupils' work thoroughly and constructively and used assessments to inform teaching;
- used homework effectively to reinforce and/or extend what is learned in school.

Information found in the Handbook for Inspection Crown Copyright 1995

The days that followed were hectic, packed with tasks that had to be done before you would have thought it was possible to do them. After a full day of training, we were given further tasks to do in the evening. In order to finish, some people toiled until the early hours of the morning as all the work had to be handed in the next day to be marked by special HMI markers; any work not up to standard resulted in a warning that you may be on your way home if things did not improve. There were some who got very over-wrought and, by the end of the week, had decided enough was enough – they were not going to stay the course. But no one from our group left.

In inspection, everything has to be written down. If it isn't recorded on a form, it doesn't exist. Observation forms constitute the backbone of what is termed the inspection evidence base. Lesson observation forms are the important ones, but all the incidentals that are observed elsewhere in the school, such as assemblies or children's play times were also recorded on the ubiquitous forms.

The execution of a well-written observation form relies on a number of skills, first and foremost of which is the ability to write quickly, neatly and legibly. It is also important to be able to marshal one's thoughts into consecutive and logical sentences. Many observation forms were written on those days of training with half-finished sentences. But then, many observation forms were written on real inspections with half-finished sentences. Trying to catch the nuances of an ever-changing scene as a lesson moves from satisfactory to good, or conversely from good to not so good, tests the linguistic ability of even the most adept user of English. And all but the lucky few struggled with their handwriting.

We were given practice in grading lessons and writing observation forms by watching videos of actual teachers at work. Our first attempt at this was a tense exercise. None of us wanted to stick our necks out and grade higher than anyone else, but then again none of us wanted to grade the lesson lower than others. The lesson was PE, gymnastics in the school hall. To me the teacher, a keen young man dressed in a track suit and wearing trainers, seemed knowledgeable. He did a lively warm-up and organised the children well in getting apparatus out, so I put down '*good* knowledge of the subject'. Not all found it easy to jump on the box and so I wrote that he challenged them *well*. I also put that the children behaved *well* and the lesson proceeded at a *good* pace so that time was used *effectively*. He praised the able children and helped those struggling so I said he used assessment *well*. At the end of the lesson, I gave him a two (very good) in the lesson grade box. But, as I found out later, I had picked the wrong grade. All the descriptors I had used were those that should go towards a final grade of three (good). To me it seemed logical that lots of 'goods' made a very good, but Ofsted does not think like that. Goods, no matter how many there are of them do not get upgraded to a very good. My observation form came back from Henry with a red line through it, but I wasn't the only one. I was particularly miffed, however, because, if there was one thing I prided myself on knowing, it was my gymnastics.

The odd thing was that after the lesson, Henry gave no indication of what the correct grade might be, and here, if we had noticed, could have been a vital lesson. To some extent, the grading of lessons has never been pinned down accurately, how could it be? But here we were using a system of numbers as if it was a science. What mattered was the match of the words used in the text to the number in the box, not, in fact, whether we could actually spot the difference between a knowledgeable and a not so knowledgeable teacher, which I erroneously thought was the crucial bit.

As the week went on, the initial round-the-table thumbnail sketch for each group member began to fill out into a real person. First impressions gave way to a dawning realization of character and personality. Phil, a no more than averagely attractive man at first sight, began to seem much more so because of his quick wit and generous warmth. Mary's wide beaming smile, which seemed so attractive at first, began to pall because of her sometimes irritating, patronizing manner. Abby was the star of the group without a doubt; her beautiful features and quiet sensitivity were perfect foils to her undoubtedly large intellect. Nigel, who had upset me on the first day, was still a little stand-offish, not just with me, but with most of the group. He was a high flier who was used to being in the lead and he didn't take kindly to team playing. After a drink or two, though, he relaxed considerably and could be very amusing, if he chose to be. Trevor was the only person who made little impression. He was always smiling at others' jokes, joining in with a word or two but never really making a mark. He seemed to sit on the sidelines.

We began to socialize around an early drink at the bar before the evening meal. When the last task was finished and we were packing away our papers to take back to our rooms, the first person to leave would call out:

"See you at the bar?" Then someone else would call:

"Six thirtyish?"

"Yes fine, see you there," would be added. We would leave as quickly as we could, returning to our rooms to change or freshen up. During the day, although there was no real need, dress was slightly formal with men wearing jackets, ties and shirts and women generally in a suit or smart dress, so in the evening we dressed down into jeans and sloppy jumpers.

There came to be an unspoken rule that we spent the start of the evening talking about anything other than the work we had done that day, or the work we still had to do after dinner. We swapped notes about our families, our schools and our previous careers, getting to know the bare outlines of each others' lives.

On the second evening, I arrived down at the bar at the same time as Abby. We sat down in the comfy armchairs and started talking. I told her about my admiration for the work done by Marcus Mann and she laughed and said that he was an inspirational person but one who was driven. He couldn't stop working and the trouble was he expected the same from all his staff and that was not really fair. I agreed.

"Are you enjoying the training?" I asked.

"Yes, I am very much." There was a short pause and I wondered if she was going to ask me the same thing, but she didn't.

"I know you'll understand this Jane, because your school's like mine. But I applied to do inspections because I was so exhausted, completely drained by the demands of my school. No one realises just how much effort it is, day-in-day-out, in that sort of an environment."

"I know," I said. "It has become unfashionable to talk about the difficulties of inner-city schools."

"Exactly. Nobody says anything. They go on pretending that you can work miracles – working with abused children, children whose parents don't, can't, give their child any attention, they need so much attention themselves. Drug-taking or drink, though mostly drugs, is what my parents live for and their children just survive around the edges of their chaotic lives. Sometimes I see a parent all morning, and they are just telling me their own problems. Then, there is the violence in the neighbourhood, (someone was shot just across the road from the school last term) and the state of the buildings, the difficulty of getting and retaining staff and so many other things. I just needed a break from it."

When she finished speaking, I was unsure of what to say. Surprised at so much distress, I searched for an appropriate platitude.

"Don't blame yourself Abby – the thing is, you can't work miracles."

"I do blame myself. It was what I always wanted, to be the head of a school like mine. I worked towards it all my teaching career, and then suddenly I just want to run away." She looked at me intently, hoping to find a compatriot, someone who shared the same experiences and was in the same position. "Were you finding it too much as well Jane, is that why you applied?"

"Well, I did have the pressures you are talking about, and yes when the windows in the nursery were smashed again, so that we had to spend hours picking out fragments of glass from the toys (there are two sky-lights in the nursery that for some reason they never get round to putting grills on), I did feel like running down the road screaming. But, it wasn't really for those reasons that I applied. I like teaching, being in a classroom with kids, and I've never wanted to do all those boring admin jobs heads have to do. But I do like a challenge. I worked pretty well with my head – don't get me wrong, but there were times when I felt I was not really achieving as much as I could. When Ofsted opened up the inspection training to deputies, I just thought it was a marvellous opportunity. At one of those meetings that the authority runs to get schools up to speed on Ofsted things, a friend of mine mouthed across the table at me 'you should apply.' So I did. No one was more surprised than me when my application was accepted."

"So like Phil Docherty, you think you'll go back at the end of the year, a wiser and, what did he say, 'more effective' deputy?"

"Mmm yes, I suppose so. And I expect you'll go back as well – maybe a year inspecting will give you the break you need and help to get things into perspective. And you could always apply for a headship in an easier area."

"Yes – I suppose I could." Abby took a long drink, and we were silent for a while. "Thanks for listening Jane – I'm sorry if I've unburdened myself to you, but you're one of those people you can tell things to."

"You've listened to me as well." I said. "You know, I get the feeling from some people here that one should only admit to having worked in a wonderful school before becoming an inspector, and that everything in your life should be perfect."

Abby smiled, "Absolutely – the 'everything in my school and life is lovely brigade', as per Mary, including her wonderful delivery of the English language." We giggled together a little at this slightly catty remark. "You and I, however, are escapees. And realists. I knew there were good things at my school, but there were a whole lot of other things that needed improving as well." She lifted up her glass and said: "To our new stress-free, happy adventure into inspection."

"Do you think.....is it going to be a holiday?" I said, laughing to show that I knew that the answer to this would be 'no', and raising my glass to hers.

When the last person had arrived at the bar and ordered a drink, we would all troop into the dining room. Henry did not join us but sat on a table with the other HMI. They laughed a lot in that hearty way of people who share a high-level professional life. We, in turn, were curious and wanted to know what they were laughing about – were they sharing jokes about our ineptitude?

Chapter 3

The Team Allocation Excel form was generated by Ofsted at the start of each inspection. It was a grid of small boxes formed by horizontal lines where team members' names could be written on the left hand side and vertical lines with aspects and subjects squeezed in across the top. The lead inspector was required to mark an L in each box to indicate which team member was leading on that aspect or subject.

On Thursday night, the talk around the table began to focus on the following day which was to be spent on preparing for our first real inspection. As we speculated on what the school would be like, its whereabouts, size and context, and the grades it achieved in the end of year National Curriculum tests, no one was mentioning what was uppermost in their minds: who would be responsible for what? We knew that the eleven aspects of the framework were of unequal importance. It was, therefore, reasonable to surmise that Henry's allocation of these would surely reflect his opinion of our abilities. Henry would no doubt take the responsibility of the aspect entitled leadership and management, but who amongst us would be allocated those aspects next in importance? We drank a little more than we should have done that night, and Nigel, who was much nicer than his usual self when he had had a drink, confided in us that he really wanted to lead on the aspect of attainment and progress. He said it with such serious intent, as if it was really important to him, that I almost felt sorry for him. How could he not fail to see that such eagerness was pathetic in one of his age? Phil, who was sitting next to me, spotted my expression and nudged me, muttering under his breath "pathetic bastard."

The following morning, all was revealed. Henry circulated a copy of the team plan as soon as we sat down round the table. We stared at the little boxes, each person finding their name and tracing across to see their responsibilities. As we had thought,

Henry had given himself the responsibility of the leadership aspects. Nigel did not have attainment and progress: that honour went to Abby. Nigel was leading on teaching; Phil on curriculum and assessment; Trevor on pupils' spiritual, moral, social and cultural development; Mary on attitudes, behaviour and personal development, and I had the bottom of the pile, the rag bag of staffing, accommodation and resources, the least prestigious aspect of all.

Nigel was soon mollified as he realised that, because he had teaching as an aspect, it would mean that he would have to look at all the observation forms written by the rest of the team, and that Henry expected him to monitor the quality of these forms.

"You will have to make sure, Nigel, that what is written in the text matches the grade given in the box and also you will have to check that people are filling in all the subsidiary boxes correctly." Nigel nodded earnestly, and again I had a flash of pity for someone who took matters so seriously, like a ten-year-old boy being given the job of taking in the homework.

Mary was quite miffed that she had not been given her precious assessment aspect. She was uncharacteristically quiet. Henry noticing this said: "I really felt it was important Mary that you did not have an area you were so familiar with." She perked up a little and gave him one of her beaming smiles, although she still seemed a little subdued.

"Over the coming months," Henry said to assuage any hurt feelings, "you will all have experience of leading on the different aspects. Some aspects are, of course, more telling than others to the inspection process, but none must be ignored. All aspects of school life have a bearing on the experience of the children at that school. They may be taught well but, if they are not receiving the provision they should for personal development, then they will not be getting their entitlement to a full education."

When the subjects were given out, I was still down on the pecking order. I had history, geography and physical education while others received the important core subjects. Mary was to lead on English, Phil on mathematics and Trevor on science. Nigel, of course, was inspecting information technology. I felt a little deflated, but thought to myself of what Henry had said and of the year ahead; there was plenty of time to tackle other things and at least I would be able to learn from the mistakes of others.

We spent the rest of the day going through a huge pile of documentation and finding out everything that we could about the school. It was called Beswick Street Primary, and it was not far from the centre of Liverpool. Situated in an area that had once been solidly respectable with streets of bay-fronted terraced properties, it was now run-down in parts, with some of the larger houses converted into flats or used for multiple occupation. Some of the streets, especially those bordering on a large park were still well-looked after and housed settled families, but these were in the minority. There were a few families from ethnic groups, mainly those who originated from Pakistan or the West Indies.

Henry had gone to the school on the initial visit some weeks before our training had started. He had met the staff, governors and acting headteacher. Beswick Street Primary was in the precarious position of not having a headteacher; the incumbent had gone off on long-term sick leave, and it looked unlikely that he would be back. Henry assured us, however, that the acting head, whose name was Mrs.Jessop, was a force to be reckoned with. She had been deputy there for ten years and clearly had the confidence of the governors. We quickly consulted Form S2, which gave details about length of service, qualifications and main subjects, and discovered that Mrs. Jessop had been at the school for a total of twenty years. The now absent head had only been there for four years.

"He brought in sweeping changes both to the organization of the school and to the curriculum but things appear to have gone awry. He had a nervous break-down apparently," Henry said. We were all putting two and two together. Was he driven to it by Mrs. Jessop? The question hung in the air but was not spoken by anybody.

"Remember," said Henry, "whatever you may privately think, we are there to judge the quality of provision in all subjects, the teaching, the pupils' attainment, their progress, and the efficiency with which the school uses resources. We are not there to find out about what may or may not have happened in the past, or to surmise about the details of the personal lives of anyone." He paused while we all quickly put on virtuous expressions as if surmising about anyone's private life was unthinkable.

"I would like everyone to look at the pre-inspection commentary that I have written. I am also giving out a copy of the minutes of the parents' meeting to you all. We are being joined on this inspection by Mr. John Ainsworth. He came with me to the parents' meeting. He's our lay inspector and he's very experienced, an extremely nice chap. If you need any help, he will be very willing to give it to you."

After that, there was silent concentration in the team room as we read through the pre-inspection commentary making notes on the parts that related to our own aspects or subjects. Strangely, the data seemed to mirror what we had found in the documents of the school we had studied earlier in the week. At Beswick Street, mathematics appeared to be much stronger than English. We all turned to look at the information on Form S2 about the length of service for the teachers in the school. We couldn't help wondering, was the English co-ordinator passed it, as Phil had suggested for the school on Monday? Although I was not leading on English, I was keenly interested. The English co-ordinator, however, was new. She had only been at the school for two years and teaching for three. Surely, she was a little inexperienced to carry the important subject of English in such a situation? I checked the timetables for English lessons.

"Look Mary," I hissed. "There is a half hour slot each day for ERIC in the Juniors."

"Mmm – I introduced that into my school," she replied.

Abby gave me a meaningful look and raised her eyebrows. "Of course, ERIC can be a really good strategy," I said, " but it can also be a waste of time, with teachers just hearing one or two people read. Half an hour each day does seem an awful lot."

"Who or what is ERIC?" asked Henry.

"Everyone reading in class," we all chorused.

"I am glad I've found that out." Henry gave a slightly lop-sided smile and none of us knew whether he was being serious. "I have seen, in my time, some very time-wasting reading sessions with children looking at books and having little dozes or chats and very little learning going on. I didn't know that I could blame them on this chap Eric." We laughed, and I realized that he had subtly supported my argument.

"Well I will check these reading sessions, obviously," said Mary. "Perhaps, Jane, you would like to help with the reading, as you don't have a core subject."

"I would be pleased to," I said, ignoring the slightly waspish tone in Mary's voice.

"Ah, yes," Henry went on. "I'm glad you have reminded me there Mary; I need to emphasize the importance of working together as a team. We must all help each other out, that is how effective teams work. You've all got specific areas of responsibility, but that doesn't mean you're working in isolation. If you spot evidence that is helpful to someone else you must record it and pass it on. The whole team needs to work together. Our decisions at the end of the inspection are corporate ones." He paused a moment to check the effect of his words on us. "When you have spare time on your timetables, you might very well see a lesson that will go towards someone else's evidence base. Jane and Nigel that is likely to be you in the mornings because you are not leading on core subjects; core subject people are likely to be able to see lessons for you in the afternoon, and everyone should pick up information about IT for Nigel." He looked round at us all. We murmured our assent.

"I would like you all to go home now – have a good weekend and come back Sunday night with your timetables written. We'll have a pre-inspection team meeting then and check to see whether there are any time-table clashes." The meeting, it seemed was coming to a sudden end. We stood up like somnambulists, dimly aware that we needed to gather up the items belonging to us scattered on the tables. We were dumbfounded by the thought that the next time we would meet would be to carry out an inspection. "Until Sunday night then – around seven-thirty or so." Henry's crisps words, so plain and ordinary propelled us forward and "Good-night, and drive home safely," followed us through the door. Ready or not, we were in the game; Ofsted inspectors for at least the next week.

Chapter 4

It was exciting arriving back at the hotel Sunday evening. We exchanged greetings with each other with a real sense of comradeship. For people who had spent most of their working-lives diligently toiling in the claustrophobic, child-orientated environment of a primary school, arriving for a business meeting on Sunday evening at a business hotel was exhilarating. We sat in the lounge area in big comfy sofas. Henry grinned at us as he started the meeting, as if we were conspirators on some wild escapade.

"It's a strange life this, isn't it? You have to be something of a gypsy. One week you're in Bolton, a week later in Bournemouth and the next in Watford, living out of a suitcase. You should see the milometer on my old bus." Henry drove an extremely battered, very large hatchback Volvo, the back of which was filled with an untidy jumble of boxes. I was a bit startled by his comparison of my new life with that of a traveller. I had considered my new role to have connotations of high status and government approval, but then I had a long way to go before I achieved Henry's level of cynicism.

"Now to business – this week we are going to inspect Beswick Street Primary School," Henry said very formally, as if we did not know why we were there.

"Let me introduce John Ainsworth, our lay inspector, whom I told you about on Friday." He turned towards the new person sitting with our group. The education act that set up the process of inspection in 1994 stipulated that a person unconnected with education should accompany every inspection team as a full member of that team; the term for such an inspector was 'lay', a word which lent itself to jokes, of course. The purpose of having a lay inspector was to have an outsider's view, a representative of the parents. The irony of the matter was that, after they had been trained and carried out a number of inspections, they often became very knowledgeable about the process of inspection and education in general. In practice, they often had expertise and skills that were in short supply in the world of education, particularly as in the case of John Ainsworth, in health and safety.

John Ainsworth was a wiry individual who spoke with a very broad Yorkshire accent. He had a wicked sense of humour, a quick mind, and it was clear from the outset that he was going to be a benefit to the inspection. He smiled across at me when he realized that I was to be responsible for judging the quality of the accommodation.

"I'll be very surprised, Jane," he said, "if we don't find some health and safety issues with regard to the accommodation in this old Liverpudlian barracks. About a couple of months ago I was in a school not far from Beswick Street and they still had the most disgusting outside toilets I've ever had the misfortune to witness."

"I knew I could rely on John to lower the tone of the discussion," said Henry, and we laughed, although we all had our own unpleasant memories of school toilets.

"Why? Don't you think toilets are important?" John countered, his Yorkshire accent laid on just a little heavily. "They're a basic need. We invented the W.C., and we still send kiddies out in the yard to pee. It's a disgrace."

"I couldn't agree more," said Henry, "but right now, we haven't even got round to sorting out our timetables."

"Humm" said John, still holding centre stage. "Just a minute, I think there was a point raised by parents about the toilets." He snapped open his brief case and, in a split second, produced his copy of the parents' meeting minutes, in marked contrast to Henry and the rest of us (except Nigel, of course), who shuffled papers for almost a minute before laying hands on the relevant document.

"Here it is," said John. "Right at the end, that nice woman, who had spoken up to say she was pleased with her daughter's progress, said that she was very concerned that there were no locks on the junior girls' toilet doors. Her daughter (she was in Year 5) never used the school toilets because of this, and was very uncomfortable by the time she got home." John pointed at the appropriate entry on the minutes and we all spotted it. I felt quite abashed that I hadn't noticed it before as it clearly came into my area of responsibility. I quickly acknowledged this and said that I would check the girls' toilets. Henry agreed that that would have to be done, and then, with an almost audible sigh of relief that the matter was dealt with, hurried on to sorting out the coverage of lessons and our individual timetables.

This proved to be a very confusing business because none of us had known, when we drew up our timetables at home, what others were planning, and consequently some teachers had far too many observations on one day and others had none. Henry had a system for correcting this which worked reasonably well although it entailed much crossing-out, checking, rewriting and negotiation. Eventually, there was an even spread of lesson observations amongst the teachers and every inspector was kept busy for most of the time.

At this time, coverage was an exacting inspection obligation for everyone, but especially for the lead inspector, for the lead it could be a minefield. An inspection had to be balanced correctly. There were very specific requirements regarding the number and type of lesson observations that should fall to each teacher. Every teacher in the school had to be seen teaching English, mathematics and science, if it was on the timetable. If possible, there should be no teacher carrying a heavier burden than others. The rule was that no one should be seen for more than 50 per cent of their teaching time in any one day. Set against this was the need for each inspector to write fully about the subjects they had been allocated. This resulted in them jealously guarding their time and few bought into the team ethos that Henry had so manifestly tried to promote. Some would get very huffy if they did not see the persons they wished to see in order to gather their evidence. The lead inspector had to juggle these demands and protect the needs of the teachers.

As a group, we were only just beginning to realize the implications, but already some seismic shifts were occurring in the supposedly solid foundations of our team. For instance, when Mary had drawn up her timetable at home, as the all-important inspector of English, she had assumed that others would fill gaps that it was impossible for her to do. Consequently, when nobody was covering a Year 4 lesson for her when she was in with the other Year 4 teacher, she became strident in her demands that this was sorted out. Nobody had a vacant time slot except Nigel, who declared that he had to use it to check on computer usage, and Abby who was supposed to be looking at the records for children with special educational needs. Everyone else was seeing a necessary lesson. It seemed like stalemate but Mary was not giving up.

"I just can't fit another English lesson in anywhere," she said. "This teacher has got to be seen teaching English." We all knew that that was true, but felt Mary could get round it by shortening some of her hour-long observations. At this suggestion from Phil, she refused point blank to do so, and then Abby came to the rescue.

"I'll do my special needs records at another time – I'll do it for you," she said.

"There," said Mary brightening up and casting her beaming smile on us all, "I knew it could be sorted out." She completely overlooked the fact that now Abby had no free time during the day and therefore would have to take the records home at night to study them. Meanwhile Mary offered no recompense, or swapping of her own free time, which was quite extensive because English was hardly taught at all in the afternoon.

By the time the negotiations on timetables were sorted out, it was beginning to get late. Henry insisted on seeing everyone's finished timetable and pointing out possible pitfalls, such as the time it might take to get from an observation in a Year 6 classroom to one in Year 1. We all had a photocopied plan of the school which we studied like commandos plotting a raid. We began tracing routes from one room to another, a precaution that would seem laughable to us in three months down the line of doing the job. Henry had impressed on us earlier, the importance of good time-keeping. If you were supposed to see 40 minutes of a lesson you must arrive on time and stay for that amount of time, in this way the overall plan did not get compromised.

I had joined Ofsted at a juncture when it had been stung into action by the lackadaisical ways of some of its inspectors. Many a well-paid team had popped into school for the four days of an inspection and had had a very easy time. They used the information from the school's SAT results to make judgements, and did not bother themselves too much about seeking out corroborative evidence. They did the minimum of lesson observations, wrote the minimum of evidence forms and spent the minimum of time trawling through children's work books. Because schools were so in awe of the whole set-up, these lazy inspectors got away with it, but HMI were hopping mad. Some of these freelance registered inspectors were making much more money than they were on their set salaries and what were they doing? Chatting, drinking cups of coffee, eating biscuits in the team room and trotting off every other week to a new inspection because they had the energy to do so, clocking up five thousand pounds every two weeks of a school term. Ways had to be devised to make life more difficult for them and one of the ways was a clamp down on time. Thus, the time for each lesson observation had to be noted in a relevant box on the observation form and then recorded and tallied up: it was a burdensome task. Henry hated it. I always shared Henry's view that adding up time was in itself a poor use of time for those who had impressive letters after their name, denoting a doctorate in education or an honours degree in psychology, but many a lead inspector made a big thing of checking everyone's time.

After the timetables were sorted out, Henry went on to explain how to deal with the eventuality of one of us grading a lesson as unsatisfactory or worse. In 1996, teachers did not receive feedback, something they bitterly resented. Ofsted made no provision for teachers to understand why a lesson had been given a particular grade. Looking back, it really was the dark ages; information secreted from those who had the most right to know. The only lesson grades that inspectors told teachers about were those below four, the dreaded grades five, six or seven. With these grades, in marked contrast to the more pleasant ones, it was a requirement to tell the teacher that they had fallen from grace; If you gave the grade, you had to have the guts to tell the person to their face what was wrong.

"If you feel that a lesson is unsatisfactory, you must grade it as such. But, do be sure you are on firm ground." Henry clearly wanted to impress on us that he, of all people, did not want heavy-handed graders on his team. "Before you tell the teacher the grade, you must show your observation to me so we can go over it together. Make your exit from the lesson quickly. Still say thank you and smile, but say no more. Find me as quickly as possible and let me know what has happened. I will go through your judgements and check that they equate to unsatisfactory, poor or whatever. You will have to tell the teacher that it was unsatisfactory, but it's best to wait until after school, that way they are not going to have to go on teaching when they might be upset."

It seemed a dismal note on which to end the meeting. I closed my file, feeling bemused, so many questions still buzzing in my head. Uppermost, however, was the thought that the next day I would find myself sitting in another teacher's classroom writing down grades in four little boxes at the bottom of a form with a badge from Ofsted on my lapel to prove that I was qualified to do so.

"Before you make a dash for the bar," Henry spoke above the sounds of packing up, "I just want to remind you all of one very important thing." We all stopped what we were doing and turned to listen, expecting another task that needed to be carried out before morning, but what Henry said was: "Smile. Please smile at the teachers as often and as much as you can."

PART TWO

INSPECTION OF BESWICK STREET
PRIMARY SCHOOL, LIVERPOOL

Chapter 5

No. 26 Lacey Street, Liverpool

Susie sucked on the end of her 'Hello Kitty' pen and drew her knees up high under her pink princess duvet. After scrutinising the small notebook in her hand (part of the 'Hello Kitty' set) for several minutes, she took the pencil out of her mouth and wrote down another name. She was compiling her guest list for her Pizza Hut party for her birthday in two week's time and it was proving difficult. Mum had said ten, ten was the max, but how could she leave out Sadie if she was asking Deena? And if she didn't ask Deena there would be no one coming from Mr. Thompson's class, and she really wanted to have someone from that class. If it was just kids from her own class, it looked immature – mature people had friends in other classes – Mrs. Mitchell was so right about that. Not that she had said that exactly. What she had said was that they shouldn't cling to just a best friend or even a small group of friends. Mrs. Mitchell wanted them to be open and friendly to everyone.

Susie's best friend was Amanda, but they tried very hard to like lots of other people as well. It wasn't their fault that nobody was quite as nice as they were. Amanda and Susie never swore and they both liked reading. That was not the case for a lot of the girls and as for the boys – ugh – Susie never ever wanted to be friends with any of them, except perhaps Dillon, but only because he was so good-looking.

Susie heard her mum getting up. She put down her diary, got out of bed and went over to the mirror to peer at her face. She liked her face, but wished she was not so pale, almost white – a pinky white. She would like to be more sort of creamy, and then she would tan in the summer like Debbie Wilson.

She remembered that today was the day the government inspectors were coming to Beswick Street. She had not really forgotten at all – it had been in the back of her mind all the time because her books had been sent for. It was 'an honour' Mrs. Mitchell had said. Her books had been chosen because her work was so good.

Then Susie remembered what Mrs. Moore, one of the dinner ladies, had told her about her mum speaking up at that special meeting. The one held a few weeks ago in the evening that her mum had gone to. Apparently, at the meeting parents were supposed to say to the inspectors what they liked and what they didn't like about Beswick Street. And Mrs. Moore had said that her Mum had said she was very pleased about how well Susie had done with her work, especially her spelling – that was OK, although still embarrassing. But then her Mum had gone on to complain about there being no locks on the toilet doors.

"Your mum spoke up and said that she didn't think it was right that there were no locks on the toilet doors. It was really brave of her, I thought, really brave." Susie had been horrified. She begged Mrs. Moore not to tell anyone, and Mrs. Moore had said, "don't be silly – yous should be proud of your mum – and of course, I won't tell anyone, if you don't want me to." As far as she knew, Mrs. Moore hadn't. Mrs. Moore was very nice. Then yesterday, there had been such a surprise. When they went into the toilets they'd found that locks had been put on the doors – that had made Susie feel a little bit proud of her mum. After all, if she hadn't spoke up at the meeting, nothing would have been done. They must be important these inspectors, she thought, to have made the school do something like that.

When she had got home yesterday, she had said: "Guess what Mum?"

Mum had said, "What?"

"They've had locks put on the toilet doors – isn't that great?"

"Yes that is great, but about time too." Susie had given her mum a hug – just a little one. Then she'd told her about her books having been chosen to show to the inspectors because her work was so good. Mum had looked as if she would nearly burst with happiness at that.

Susie put her uniform on and when she looked in the mirror again she felt pleased with herself. Perhaps Mum would let her have just one more person at the Pizza Hut party – eleven was not so much different to ten – especially as she had done so well that her books had been chosen to show to the government people.

The first day of the inspection of Beswick Street Primary School started with a quick breakfast in the hotel dinning-room and people sorting themselves out into two groups. We were to travel to the school in two cars so as not to clutter up the school car park. John Ainsworth drove Henry, Nigel and Mary. I went with Abby, Phil and Trevor who was driving. It was a grey day, but at least no rain. We piled into Trevor's big comfortable Mondeo and sat back as he navigated first motorways, dual carriageways, a busy high street and then a lengthy labyrinth of back streets, all with quiet, unassuming efficiency. We arrived a few minutes before the others.

"Well done Trevor," said Phil.

"Brilliant," praised Abby. I didn't add anything as it might have looked over the top. Were we surprised that Trevor could do anything well?

We joined Henry's group so that we could all walk up to the school together. There was no indication of the way-in to the school, but Henry headed towards a stone flight of steps and entrance that said, in big letters cut into the concrete lintel above the door, 'Senior Boys': the school had, many years ago, taken children up to school leaving age. We straggled behind Henry across the black tarmac playground towards grey walls, and windows encased in ugly grills that kept vandals from smashing panes of glass. When we reached the top of the steps, there was Mrs.Jessop, the lady about whom there had been so much conjecture only a few days previously.

She stood tall at the front door to meet us. She was a good-looking person, but her appearance was oddly out-dated, bringing to mind the nineteen fifties; iron grey hair in the neat page-boy style of the period; lipstick, a bright shade of orangy-red and a black and white dog-tooth-check suit with white polo-neck jumper.

"Welcome to Beswick Street Primary School," she said formally to each one of us. To which we all replied a meek 'thank you.' Mrs. Jessop had taken the upper-hand; the message was clear – I am in charge here. She walked in front of us down the main entrance, leading the party of inspectors into her school. She stopped at the first door. "This is the office. Please sign the visitors' book." The sign-in book was already open at a fresh page, dated the 3rd October 1996.

Henry moved forward and signed, then looked up and asked Mrs. Jessop: "shall I just put the number of inspectors accompanying me after my name?"

"Oh no, Henry. I think everyone should sign individually," she said, the little power game continuing.

"Of course, Lucinda, if that is what you want," Henry conceded, with just the suspicion of a smile on his lips. I wanted to nudge someone to share my amusement at the theatrical and slightly grand name of Lucinda, which so exactly suited her. Instead, I simply signed my name after the person before me in the all-important visitors' book.

Lucinda Jessop took us on a full tour of the school, opening classroom doors as we came to them and introducing us to the teacher on the other side of the door. It soon became obvious that the cheerlessness of the exterior was matched by that of the interior. There were long daunting corridors and windows well-above child height. Bleak walls painted in a buff coloured gloss were only marginally relieved by the intermittent display boards on which items of children's work were pinned, occasionally to good effect, but often in uninspired repetition: twelve wax relief pictures of a wobbly Greek vase by Year 4; ten paintings of sun-flowers with a print of Van Gogh's original as the centre piece by Year 5; lop-sided portraits of a Tudor lady.

Only in the infant department were the displays more lively and child-friendly.

One corridor, starting from the entrance hall, took you into the infant department while in the other direction there was the large school hall and then another corridor on which the lower junior classes were sited; the upper juniors were up the stone stairways. A mid-brown linoleum was battened to the floors by decades of polish, although here and there it had come loose – a tripping hazard whispered John Ainsworth into my ear. Cleaners were still coming back to the caretaker's room with buckets, mops and brooms. Each one greeted us with a cheery 'good morning' in a strong Liverpudlian accent and Mrs. Jessop smiled benignly at this welcome from the lower orders. She did not, however, bother with introductions to these minions, or indeed to any of the support staff, some of whom were scurrying about collecting pieces of equipment from various cupboards and giving us quick shy glances.

When we had circumnavigated the whole building, Mrs. Jessop took us to a small room that was at the very end of what seemed to be the longest corridor in the school. We had passed several rooms no longer in use as classrooms, with notices on declaring them to be the 'Parents' Room', or the 'Technology Room'. Beswick Street was not short of space, owing to the inevitable inner-city falling roll.

"This is our music room but we will not be using it for the duration of the inspection. We have given it up so that you can have a base." She made it sound a significant sacrifice and pressed the point home with, "our violin players will use my office for this week."

44

"That is extremely kind and thoughtful of you, Lucinda," said Henry.

"No not at all – you had to have somewhere, besides," she said, with the first hint of any humour, "everyone thought you would be as far out of the way as possible here." We all laughed to show that we could take a joke. "Just let me know if there is anything you need. There's a kettle and some cups. Did you say you could do with some milk?"

"That would be helpful," said Henry.

"I'll get Mrs. Anderson, my secretary to bring you some up."

Henry thanked her several times. There was almost a communal sigh of relief when Lucinda Jessop went out of the door.

"Not an easy person," remarked John Ainsworth, "and no biscuits at all – not even a packet of rich tea." He shook his head.

"Well not to worry on that score John, I've brought some, custard creams actually." Henry fished into his brief case and brought out a packet of biscuits and a jar of coffee. "I thought we might be needing these."

"Not a good sign," said John, "having to bring your own tea and coffee."

"Now don't go confusing these new recruits; you know very well that there is no correlation between the provision of tea, coffee and biscuits for the inspection team and the effectiveness of the school."

"If you say so," said John laughing.

"I do" said Henry. "Our amenities may be very basic," Henry looked round at the dull room, and let out a small sigh, "but Mrs. Jessop has the respect of the teachers you know, and I think the parents and children as well."

"Is she up to scratch with new developments, though?" asked Phil.

"Probably not," said Henry, "but we must see how things go. If you gather round, we will have a very quick meeting and then you must all get yourselves ready for your first lesson observation." Everyone had been standing around in a somewhat vacant manner, unsure of the next move. Now we quickly sat ourselves down at one of the grey child-height tables that had been put together in a block. We staked a claim to a patch of desk by laying out some of the contents of our briefcases, behinds already experiencing the discomfort of sitting on small chairs.

During the meeting, Henry covered the day-to-day mechanics of organizing an inspection. There are several ways of doing this. Ofsted left it to individual lead inspectors to organize their team and administrative duties the way they wished. Henry went for a simple, streamlined system, which worked fine if all team members were reliable, knowledgeable and committed to the success of an inspection, and most importantly if you were an HMI which, of course, Henry was. It left potential for disaster, however, if none of these things, or only some of them applied. When we wrote an observation form three copies were generated and the top copy, known as the white, (for the simple reason that the other copies were yellow and pink) once written on, became almost a legal document that had to be closely guarded by the lead inspector. Henry's system for keeping track of the precious whites was very basic – they all went into a file and we entered the name and number of the teacher that it belonged to on a list on the front of the file. At the end of each day, Henry emptied the file, counted up the number of observation forms recording the different grades and then worked out the percentage of grades in each 1 to 7 category.

Inspection was driven by the percentage of lesson observations in each grade. This data was crucial for the school. The headteacher would be told the percentages each morning like a life or death shipping forecast. If the lead inspector reported a hundred per cent satisfactory or better, fine weather lay ahead; if he said a sizeable percentage was unsatisfactory, the sea and sky were going to get very stormy indeed. If 20 per cent of lessons or more was unsatisfactory, the school would automatically be placed into special measures – a failing school.

Chapter 6

Suddenly, it was five minutes to nine and I was walking down the corridor on the way to my first lesson observation. I was due to see a Year 5 English lesson. As I opened the door, thirty-two pairs of eyes swiveled to stare at me. Mrs. Mitchell had just finished the register and was passing it to a girl and boy who were waiting by her desk to take it to the office. All the children were sitting up as straight as was humanly possibly and, after their initial look in my direction, turned immediately back to face their teacher. She was a middle-aged lady with not very much to recommend her in appearance – slightly faded all round, with beige or grey being the predominant colour of clothes, hair and even face. She was talking quite quietly to the children who were almost straining to hear her – the amazing thing was though, they were all making this effort, not one was inattentive. I sat down on the one vacant chair, obviously set aside for this purpose.

I opened my file at the appropriate evidence form for this lesson and began to fill in the boxes at the top. As I sat on the all too conspicuous chair, I realized that my hands were trembling and that one or two of the straight-backed children had shot sideways glances at my direction. Why in the world was I getting nervous? The blank sheet of the evidence form seemed to have grown into a vast expanse of white – how was I ever going to fill it up? In order to get started, I wrote: 'The teacher manages the pupils very well and'…what? What should I add? My mind had gone blank – but then the next part of the sentence came to me and I wrote down... 'they are listening intently to her introduction to the lesson.' This made me relieved.

My attempts, however, at settling myself to the task were abruptly interrupted. Mrs. Mitchell for some unaccountable reason, was standing only a few feet away from me. How had she got there? The last time I had looked up she was in front of the blackboard. She was holding a piece of paper out towards me:

"I'm awfully sorry, I forgot to leave this on the chair." It was the lesson plan which I had not even noticed was missing. As I took it from her, I realized that her voice was tremulous, and her hand shaking as much as mine, and into my head spun Henry's command from the previous evening: 'Smile. Smile at the teachers as much as you can.'

I smiled – the broadest friendliest smile I could manage. "Oh you shouldn't have bothered – it would have been quite fine after the lesson."

She flushed bright red, and at that moment I knew that, however bad I had been feeling, she had been feeling ten times worse, and I took my first step towards becoming a half-way competent inspector. Breaking all rules, I said: "the lesson's going really well so far."

She headed back to the front of the class with a surer step. She turned to the children and carried on where she had left off – giving a little monologue in the role of a child evacuated during the war, describing that child's thoughts and feelings with immense empathy to her class, and I realised that the reason the children behaved so well and listened so intently was because Mrs. Mitchell was an interesting teacher.

They had over the last few weeks, been reading a book about two children evacuated during the second world war. This lesson, making use of their interest and newly acquired knowledge from the book, was to get them to write a letter in the manner of an evacuee child writing home to mum, (dad being away fighting). A real highlight was the moment when Mrs. Mitchell brought out a small suitcase. It looked like a cheap 1940s case made of pulped card with reinforced corners. It had a label tied to it. She placed it on her desk and started to take out the contents, neatly folded small vest, knickers, warm woolly cardigan and a pair of grey socks. The children's interest quickened and hands shot up to ask questions. I quickly ticked off in my head, 'good use of resources' and wrote that down on the form, filling up a little more of the whiteness.

I began to think that the grade I would be putting in the box would be a two. Surely this was a very good lesson? Then I checked the eight points on which judgements should be based according to the must-be-obeyed handbook. I had typed the list out and pasted it to the back of my file. Turning to it, I discovered that I had, in fact only commented on three out of the eight points. How could I get more of the criteria down on my form? Nothing had happened to let me know if the teacher set high expectations or challenged the pupils as much as possible. And how could what I was seeing tell me whether she gave homework? On this my first evidence form, I wanted to be scrupulously correct. I certainly didn't realise that, in many instances one had to make assumptions, nor did I realise that in a few years time a new handbook would (thankfully) do away with equating the grade given to a lesson to the number of items ticked off from these eight points.

Mrs. Mitchell began to explain how she wanted the children to set out their letter and to remind them of certain rules of grammar and punctuation. This was before the introduction of the government's National Literacy Framework in which the grammar to be taught to pupils is identified and explained year-by-year. In this case, Mrs. Mitchell had presumably picked those aspects of grammar she felt her class needed to work on, mostly it seemed to be punctuation and, in particular the use of inverted commas for speech. Here, I began to feel a little less secure about the quality of the lesson. Why focus on inverted commas when the children were going to write a letter? There was a general deterioration in the children's attention now. They still kept quiet, but there was no pizzazz in the room. Over the years, the teaching profession in primary schools had abdicated the responsibility of teaching anything about constructing a sentence other than the basic knowledge of noun, verb and full stop. There was a general feeling that children could not remember complicated things such as the correct names for parts of speech and that explanations about verb endings, clauses and the like would cause confusion. So adjectives were called 'describing' words, and verbs 'doing' words. There was a real need for the Literacy Framework.

Another disincentive for the children at this point was that Mrs. Mitchell's exhortations were full of 'don'ts': 'Don't forget a full-stop at the end of each sentence'; 'Don't forget to check your spellings'; 'Don't cross out messily'. Without realizing it, she was stifling the very confidence to write that she wished the children to have.

When work started, there was almost complete silence, with only the sound of rulers and pencils being picked up and put down. I waited for a while on my chair. I was supposed to be going round talking to the children as they worked. But how could I do that if it was so quiet? Eventually, I got up to see how the children were getting on. There had been great attention to writing the date very neatly and underlining it. Most had started 'Dear Mum,' and some had got down a few sentences saying how much they were missing home, that they had cried, that the train journey had been long, that they were scared and wanted to go home. One girl seemed to have written much more than most of the others. When I got to her table she had written almost a full page. She was working on a piece of paper and so I knew she must be one of the children whose books we had to sample. I guessed that she must be one of the higher attaining pupils. Her name was neatly printed at the top of the page.

"Well Susie, You have done a lot of work. I think you have understood a great deal about how it must have been for evacuees, and you have written a super letter." I said. She smiled up at me in response. "Do you like reading and writing?"

"Oh yes, I love school. I want to be a teacher when I grow up, like Mrs. Mitchell."

I looked at her pretty, shining face, so unlike that of her hard-worked teacher and thought what a good job Mrs. Mitchell was doing to inspire this pupil. I'm sure you will be able to be whatever you want to be when you grow up." I said before moving on to the next child.

A few children had got no further than 'Dear Mum'. They were the prevaricators to whom writing was a painful activity – they tried to find other little things to do that would put off the actual moment of having to get on with the job; pencil sharpening was a favourite. A few made great use of the rubber, writing one or two words and then rubbing them out. For one or two of these children, Mrs. Mitchell had written a sentence for them to copy. I looked back in their books and saw that work was often unfinished or very short. It had been marked, but comments often went: 'This is not enough' or, 'Try to finish next time'. Mrs. Mitchell, in common with many other teachers, was good at inspiring interest in a subject matter for writing, but fell short in understanding how to develop pupils' confidence in their own efforts as writers. I looked at my watch. It was time for me to leave and I had only written down about half of what I had observed.

I forced another bout of much smiling, managed to say 'thank you' and left the room. When I got outside I scanned what I had written. It was messy, my writing had deteriorated to a scrawl and I hadn't put a single grade in any of the boxes. I also had a nagging feeling of doubt. How would I reconcile all the different elements of that lesson into a single grade? Parts had been good, even very good but then, what about the parts that were weak? And most worryingly, what about those five or six children who just did not like writing? By now I was almost five minutes late for my next lesson. I closed the file thinking, 'I'll sort it out at lunchtime but no way am I letting anyone else see this mess.' I would have to re-write it. With this thought in mind,I hurried off down to the infant department.

The infant classroom was very different to the one in the juniors. The room was festooned with bright, colourful displays. Pictures hung like banners from the ceiling, a row of model houses made from painted cereal boxes created a little street down a central divider, and everywhere there were neatly stacked resources with labels to tell the children what they were. There were words, words and more words everywhere. These lists, together with the few words the children knew themselves, enabled them to compose their own short pieces, which the teacher had then used to create large, imaginative class story books. I picked one up entitled 'Our adventures at the Seaside'. Children had written 'stories' such as: 'I went to the beech and mad a masssif sandcastle and the sea wshd it way'. This was good work for those not yet turned six, especially for those coming from a background of inner-city deprivation.

When I entered the room, it was quite hard to see the teacher at first because she was sitting at a table with a group of children writing, her head only marginally higher than that of her small charges. Earlier that morning, she had read them the story of the Little Red Hen from something teachers call a 'Big Book'. This is a book with much enlarged pages, as much as three feet high, the words of which are large enough to see half way across the classroom. The book was still on the stand, and three children were reading it themselves – one playing at being the teacher pointing slowly and carefully at each word while the other two read aloud, quite loudly in fact, no lack of confidence there. The six children with the teacher barely registered my presence as I approached the table, so intent were they on writing the 'Not I said the pig,' 'Not I said the cat'. They could all write 'Not I' and only needed a small amount of help to spell the different animals correctly. The teacher reminded them of the letter sounds when they got stuck with a word.

"G-g-g-g," she encouraged a small boy who was unsure of the last letter ending the word 'pig'. I smiled, this time with real enthusiasm. This was very good teaching without a doubt. All around the room children were busy on a variety of tasks. Some quite simple, that were not much different to play, some more challenging such as the one where the children had to place sentence strips one underneath the other to match the sequence of the story. The teacher expertly kept an eye on this group, as well as the writing group, popping over every now and again to check that they were on the right track.

"I'm going to take mine home tonight to read to my Ma," one little boy informed me as I watched him carefully sticking down his strips. I smiled. That's the 'uses homework effectively' bit ticked off. All the children were occupied and almost tangibly happy. Whoever thinks learning is a trial has never been in this kind of an infant classroom.

After about fifteen minutes, the teacher stopped the class and asked the children to tidy up. She was an attractive, soft-faced girl in her late twenties and she seemed just as happy as the children to be in the classroom.

"Hello," I said feeling very relaxed. "There is so much going on in this room, I will just have to sit down and start writing it all down now."

"I don't envy you."

"Is it OK for me to sit at one of the children's tables?" I asked as there was no 'inspector chair' in this room.

"Oops – I forgot to put a chair out." She clamped a hand to her mouth in mock dismay. "Please sit anywhere, we are going to have our phonic session now."

Right, I thought, there is no way I can start on my form now, I will have to witness this session, whatever it is. It turned out to be an amazing session of phonic teaching using a system called THRASS which stands for Teaching Handwriting Reading and Spelling Skills. I had, to my detriment, only dimly heard of it before but then that was the same for the others on the team. THRASS teaches the forty-four phonemes (speech sounds) of spoken English and the graphemes of written English together. Children learn to read and spell and form the letters at the same time. It has charts, pictures and a range of resources. Very well-thought out and researched, it uses something that in 1996 no one paid much attention to – a multi-sensory approach. I sat and watched the session, captivated. The children knew exactly what to expect and followed the teacher's commands to a child – not an eye wandered, not a head turned. I came out, (after giving a smiling and genuine thank-you to the teacher), wondering how I was going to make the small comments I had been able to get down on my form into a legible and reasoned argument for what surely could only be an excellent lesson.

It was lunch-time, 12 o'clock. I had ordered a school lunch, if only because Henry had said that it was a good way to socialise with the children and so get the feel of the school. I knew I couldn't go to lunch with the rubbish that was currently filling my file, so I hurried down the corridor to the team base, remembering a door that said 'Technology Room'. Perhaps that would be empty? Sure enough it was. I settled down at a bench and rewrote the first observation form so that sentences were finished and crossings out eliminated. The messiest bit was about the slow writers, so in my re–write, I just left this out. When it came to the four boxes at the bottom, requiring a judgement on each of the following:

- The standard of pupils' work;
- The progress they make;
- Pupils' attitudes and behaviour;
- The quality of teaching.

I put 4 – 4 – 2 (for the pupils' very good behaviour) and, after much debating and soul-searching 3 for the teaching. With this grading, I had set-up my own dissection by Nigel, but fortunately I was not going to be aware of this until later in the day.

The observation for the excellent lesson in Year 1 was very easy to write; my enthusiasm for the lesson, the quality of the teacher's work just poured out on to the page and I filled the boxes in quickly, ending up with a triumphant one for the quality of teaching.

By the time I had finished, lunch-time was nearly over. I wondered if there would still be anything to eat, and hurried off to the dining hall, feeling incredibly hungry. Sure enough, there were still a few tables left out by the dinner ladies for the slow-eating children who were pushing bits of their dinner around their plate, as they always do, before putting a very small piece into their mouths. I went to the hatch and made myself known to the cook. She spoke with such a broad Liverpudlian accent, I had a job to understand her. First chiding me for not making time to eat, she finished off her admonishment with:

"Well it has paid off for you – such a slim figure! Though you'll have to be careful not to fall through any cracks in the floor boards," – a joke and a compliment at the same time, as befitted a sparky cook from Liverpool!

My lunch, consisting of a sausage of indeterminate origin, a spoonful of extremely orange carrots, bullet-hard peas, and quite the opposite in the way of limp chips, would thankfully not take many minutes to eat. I sat next to Sharon who did not want to finish her dinner because, or so I thought, she had fallen out with Kylie over a matter she was not disclosing. I asked her if this happened often and didn't she have any other friends, hoping against hope that I was not sitting next to a child who was being bullied. After quite a period of sullen silence, in which I became more and more concerned about Sharon's social life, she suddenly offered:

"I'm wearing Kylie's new shoes and I don't want to get them dirty out on that playground. We'll swap back when she comes to mine for tea tonight." With that she picked up her plate and skipped off in Kylie's shoes to put her plate on the pile near the hatch. Just before she left the hall, she turned and gave me a cheeky little wave and a dazzling smile. By this time, the dinner ladies had nearly packed away all the tables and I too carried my plate to the pile near the hatch.

In the afternoon, I saw two history lessons, both of which were workmanlike affairs, verging on boring. In both, the teacher competently imparted facts about an historical period. Unlike Mrs. Mitchell in the English lesson, neither teacher brought the period to life, nor was there a sense of discovery about the lessons.

The first lesson in Year 4, was about Henry the Eighth and had the potential to be a good lesson, but the teacher was so methodical. He went over each point meticulously and finally managed to send almost everyone, including me to sleep. In the second lesson, the children in a Year 6 class were doing an exercise from a history text book which consisted of comparing the life of a poor child with that of a rich child in Victorian times. This, most were managing easily because they could find out what they needed from their text book; it did not present much challenge to the higher attaining pupils (Ofsted language for brighter kids). For these children the differences, between rich and poor such as 'ragged clothes' and 'smart clothes' were reduced to two workaday lists, correct but in no way reflecting the heart-breaking disparity of the period. I graded both lessons as satisfactory. I really wanted to jump up and down and say to both of them: 'this subject deserves so much more – it's our past – it's the incredible lives of people only separated from us by the smallest of time spans in the reality of the great stretch of time that is the history of the world'. Of course, I could not do that and if I had said the lessons were unsatisfactory the teachers would have been totally mystified as to why their very carefully planned lessons, that certainly reflected the requirements of the National Curriculum, were so treated.

I managed to write both observation forms reasonably well as the lessons proceeded and felt pleased that I would not have to write them out again. At the end of the Year 6 lesson, I heard the bell for the end of school. I closed my file and watched the children stream out of the room until there was only me and the teacher left. It felt strange, knowing so well what thoughts she would be having now at the end of school, what she was going to do next – look at the children's work, think about how they had done, pack up the day and then go and have a cup of tea and a natter in the staffroom. It was all so familiar to me. And then she spoke:

"Was it OK? I know you are not supposed to say what grade it was – but was it OK?" She was a small, very active woman and from the displays in her room I imagined she was a good teacher – it was just that history was not very important to her. Now she was looking at me as if my approval or disapproval would alter the course of her life.

"It was fine," I said, "absolutely fine. Thank you very much." I ducked out of the responsibility of saying how much better it could have been – this was not what she wanted to hear, (nor was it my brief). She only wanted to know whether or not she had fallen into the chasm that divided a satisfactory lesson from an unsatisfactory one, with professional acceptability on one side and calumny on the other.

I felt an unbridgeable gulf between us, and with it a sense of loss. All my past experience made me feel as if I was a colleague of this lady – BUT I didn't work at this school. I worked for … who was it I worked for? I left quickly and went to find that small part of the school that had been temporarily annexed by Ofsted, the inspection base.

Chapter 7

When I got back to the team room, it was to find Abby, Mary and Nigel talking about the fact that Nigel had given an unsatisfactory for IT. His was the only 5 of the day and he was looking smugly pleased with himself for this fact, as if he had been the only one really getting down to the job.

"IT is definitely an issue in this school," he said. "The standards are low and I don't think the teachers have had any training at all worth speaking of." Nigel's tone was doom-laden as if the school should go into special measures straight away because of this state of affairs.

"But, it's only the first day Nigel," I said. "Perhaps tomorrow will be better."

"I doubt it, I doubt it very much, Jane." He was just about to expound further when Mary's crystal cut–glass voice broke in with:

"But the English in the infant department is wonderful." She positively bubbled with excitement at these unexpected findings. "They have introduced a simply splendid system of teaching phonics – it's remarkable. I would have used it in my own school if I had known about it." This was praise indeed. Mary's school, it went without saying, was a model of excellence. She went on to expand on the virtues of the THRASS system. She had been given the teachers' instruction manual for this relatively new innovation by the English co-ordinator, who it appeared also met with Mary's approval. "She's a lively lass, go-ahead and knows just what needs to be done to move the school forward. I'm really expecting great things from her lesson tomorrow."

Abby contributed to the conversation about THRASS with equal enthusiasm, her usual irritation with Mary completely forgotten in their combined cause, and it only took me giving Mary my lesson observation from Year 1, with its shinning 'ones', to make Nigel give up any attempt at trying to regain the conversation back on to the parlous state of IT.

Abby had gasped when I said that I had given an excellent for teaching, and immediately wanted to read the observation form. I handed her the white copy and she read it quickly and intently. "Absolutely right Jane – You have been brave to give an excellent, instead of settling for a very good. It shows that you're secure in your judgement. Well done." The thought that it was brave to give a one startled me a little, but I felt really pleased at Abby's praise and interest. She handed the form back, and I passed it to Mary, who should, after all, be the person most interested. Our conversation was interrupted as Phil, followed closely by Trevor, entered the team room. They had been chatting together, clearly in agreement on something. It turned out to be an issue for me – the boys' toilets.

"The smell is shocking," said Phil.

"Thanks for that," I said. "I am going to make a full check of accommodation on Wednesday." I was not feeling at all inclined to rush out and inspect the boys' toilets. There ensued much jocular pushing and shoving as we all tried to put the white top copies of our observation forms into Henry's file. Trevor and Phil were both quite up-beat about their day's work. Phil saying that the maths was looking better than he thought it might – still work to be done but nothing too untoward and Trevor, as usual saying little but seemingly in a good mood.

"Science looking OK, Trevor?" I asked.

"Not too bad, not too bad at all," was the non-committal and brief reply.

Henry came in and the banter subsided. He sat down and asked if anyone had made a cup of tea. Mary who was by the kettle immediately sorted this out and, after a bit of the usual paper shuffling that always preceeded Henry's announcements, he smiled broadly and told us we had done very well. Mrs. Jessop was pleased that no one had upset the teachers and that they appeared to like us. Even the teacher who had been told by Nigel that her IT lesson was not up to scratch, had been placated because Nigel had focused his feedback on the need for the staff to have some training.

"Well done for that Nigel," said Henry. Nigel immediately perked up, re-assuming his slight air of superiority that had been somewhat dented by our refusal to listen to him earlier on. Abby, Mary and I sent each other colluding glances that silently read 'what a pompous prig'.

Henry looked at his watch. "Four o'clock," he mused. "Your next task is to look at the work the school has put out for you on tables in the hall – there is one table for each year group. You must get all the work sampling done tonight, as the books will have to go back to the children tomorrow. You have until 5.45 to finish." Something about the way Henry spoke made me think that this was not going to be an enjoyable task, and besides which I was struggling to remember what it was I was supposed to do when tackling the work sample. I looked round at the others. Nobody seemed particularly eager to get started. It was pretty obvious that they too were struggling to remember the instructions we had been given on the matter.

"We covered what is expected from the work sampling on Thursday last week didn't we?" Henry added, wondering no doubt why nobody was making a move, even Nigel looked stumped.

"Well," said Phil, filling in the now awkward silence. "We did cover it, but very briefly. As I understand it, the school has been asked to provide a set of books from each year group to reflect the work of three groups of pupils, the higher ability, the average and the lower ability. From what we see in these books, we need to make a judgement on the standard of work at the end of both key stages, the progress children make, the quality of teaching as shown by the marking and, in some respects, infer the children's attitude." We all looked at Phil with gratitude, and renewed respect, which made him smile. "All I did was make a few brief notes, and I've stuck them in the back of m' file."

"Thank you, Phil. It seems everyone else needed some reminding," said Henry. "Work sampling is not easy" – and then with more honesty –"Nobody likes it. It's very hard not to get bogged down, but do try to write something about each of those things Phil has pointed out." As soon as we entered the hall, we realised why Henry had used the term 'bogged down'. A long row of tables was groaning under the weight of the books that the teachers had put out for us to look through in one and three-quarter hours. There were inspections to come when I would willingly have swapped with Hercules the sweeping out of the Aegean stables with the job of work sampling. As if the books weren't enough, around the room were portfolios of children's artwork, a collection of models in various states of soundness, or more accurately unsoundness, and volumes of photographic evidence of such delights as trips to country parks, the theatre, the carol service and the annual sports day.

On top of each pile of books, a small label indicated that the child was either an AA, an A or a BA which equated to above average, average and below average. Where to start? Everyone was rooting out their subject and gathering piles of books to examine; taking them to one of the chairs placed strategically around the room. The only trouble was that in so doing labels were misplaced. We weren't, at this juncture, aware that this would cause a problem when, some time later, another inspector would approach a pile only to find the label had disappeared.

The searcher would cry out in exasperation: 'someone's knocked the label off this pile. Is Joseph Slater in Year 4 an above average child?' Of course, no one would know and a guess would have to be made on the grounds that the work looked a great deal better than that of the child in the next-door pile. It was one of my triumphs about a year later to come up with a fool-proof system for doing away with these wretched labels. What also changed, after a while, was this system of setting out the books in the hall on a Monday night, but for the time being, it was sacrosanct, and schools were especially fond of it, no doubt because they had an inkling as to the pain it could cause their tormentors.

I set to work on the history books first. I discovered a lot of pictures and writing about Viking settlements in Year 3; about Egyptians and their tiresome gods in Year 4 and about Roman villas, centurions and another inevitable set of gods in Year 6. I tracked down the fact that last summer on a visit to Chester (with photographic evidence in the bulging albums to prove it) even the lower ability pupil had made a stab at empathising with a centurion patrolling the thick Roman walls around the town. An hour later, I must have written two full pages, but had made no decisions on the standard of work or the progress the children made. Time was pressing, just ten minutes before leaving time. I decided to go for satisfactory on both counts but I felt my reasons for doing so were fairly flimsy. I felt on safer ground, however, in judging that what I had seen in books backed up my earlier thoughts about the school not teaching the skills of historical enquiry. Did this make it unsatisfactory? No, surely not – how did you reconcile all this work on learning the significant features of a period and the number of wives of Henry the Eighth, not to mention the name of the Egyptian god with a head like an eagle with children understanding the whole point of history; to throw light upon one's present life, after all few adults understood that, else why would we have wars?

Geography was much of the same, facts and figures about the number of shops, roads, railways, hills and rivers in the locality compared to the same facts and figures relating to Chombakili, a small village in India, which at this time was described in detail in a popular geography scheme. There was, however, some good map work which started in Year 1 and grew progressively more difficult as the books went up to Year 6. Hurrah! – a skill being taught progressively. I felt as if I had found a nugget of gold and, eager to share my good fortune, I told the person next to me, who happened to be Phil.

"Look," I said – "Look at how good they get with mapping skills. They improve in their drawing and understanding of maps as they move up the school." I said, waving a book in his face. Although deep in his math's scrutiny, Phil turned to look and agreed that the map work was good.

"Hey," he said, "thanks for that – that links in with mathematics – they are using measurements and calculations well in Geography," and he wrote that down in the corner of his observation form. "It's certainly worth mentioning that – good cross curricular stuff. You and me working pretty well together – eh what Jane? "

"Absolutely – team work, as Henry requested," I said.

"If only everyone else was so helpful. Look at Abby. She hasn't shared a thing about her models. I am sure there must have been some mathematical skills needed in the making of those."

Abby, who was responsible for design and technology, had been attempting to start the motorised Year 5 model cars, a few of which made whirring sounds when switched on, but failed to move across the floor because of disengaged axles and the like. She came over to us. "I have some first-class evidence for you – calculations by Year 6 when they did a topic on building a shelter last year." Sure enough, written in the top corner of her evidence form were the words 'copy to Phil'. "I just hadn't given it to you yet." Trust Abby to do things properly.

"So kind, so thoughtful," said Phil obviously teasing, and getting a little flick from the observation form in question for his troubles.

At 5.45 promptly, we trooped out of the hall in a near state of exhaustion. I was very glad that someone else was going to drive us home. Home? Yes a hotel with all its anonymity feels strangely like a home when you have been all day in the hostile environment of a school you are inspecting. I sat in the car thinking, surely we must have done enough work for one day? But the team meeting lay ahead; there would be a post mortem on our day's work – would my lesson observations be good enough? I started to fret about having graded the Year 1 lesson as excellent – perhaps it was too extravagant?

Henry had suggested that we ate first and then gathered in one of the side rooms that had been booked especially for our team meetings. The meal was a very subdued affair with Henry and John being the only two who talked. They gossiped and chatted about events on other inspections and people we had never met.

Shortly after the meal, we assembled for our meeting. Henry started off with numerous pleasantries about how hard we had worked and said that we had made a very good start. Then he began on the criticisms, all of which related to our writing of the lesson observations and these seemed so multitudinous mortification set in. We had brought notepads with us to write down Henry's comments, remembering how well this had served Phil with the work sampling. The list went something like this:

- Too much description and too few judgements, called the 'so what' pitfall.

- None of us had included enough about the children with special educational needs – a really bad error.

- Too many generic statements lifted straight out of the framework making the writing formulaic – no life in it.

After Henry's comments it was Nigel's turn. Nigel had picked out specific errors on people's observation forms and embarrassingly proceeded to read them out. He made a great deal about the number of boxes that were short of data at the top of the observation forms. Everyone was guilty of that on at least one occasion, and Mary had even managed to leave out what subject she was watching on one of hers. He gave grudging praise to both Abby's and Phil's forms and then became serious as he spoke of where the grade given did not match the text. He held up one of Trevor's forms as an example. "You've not written many positive statements, Trevor and yet you grade it with a three. I can't see why it's good – it looks no more than satisfactory to me."

"Well, it was a good lesson," said Trevor and for once he seemed to be sticking to his guns. His expression was almost belligerent. He took the form from Nigel and started to read it through. As he read, his face began to change; he did not exactly blush but you could tell he was not happy with what he was reading. "I've not really written it how it was," he said, shaking, his head in a perplexed manner.

Before Nigel could speak, Henry took over: "You know this is easy to do – you are trying to cover so many angles when you sit there in the class, and sometimes what you are thinking is just not conveyed on the paper. It happens to all of us. How about you have a go at re-writing that one, Trevor? If it was a good lesson say what was good about it." Then Henry turned to Nigel who still had one more form in front of him for dissection – mine. "Let's hear about Jane's crime, but better be fairly quick we still have some important matters to get done about the school. This feedback is for your benefit as trainees. We mustn't let it distract us from our real purpose, the inspection of a school." Nigel picked up from Henry's tone that he had perhaps been over-zealous in his role as monitor, so he started somewhat cautiously. I was expecting my excellent to be the cause of Nigel's complaint but it was not.

"Jane's given a three for teaching for a lesson on English in Year 5." Nigel paused.

Margaret took the opportunity to butt in: "And I agree with this grade. Jane has made it quite clear why the lesson was good."

"Yes that's true," said Nigel, "but she's only given a four for the progress made by the pupils – that is where there is a mismatch. When teaching is good, pupils should make good progress." There was silence and puzzled looks from everyone.

"Well," said Henry, "in some respects, Nigel is correct here. Good teaching should result in good progress overall, that is taken over a period of a time, such as a term but, in an individual lesson, it need not be the case. For instance, if a topic or skill is being introduced, the teaching may be good, or even very good, but the children will not be up to speed and so the progress they make in that particular lesson might be less than they will make in the ensuing weeks when they really get to grips with the new ideas."

"I had not really thought through this issue before," said Phil, "and I can see what Nigel is saying but it is quite complex – in this case, Jane why did you think the children's progress was satisfactory rather than good? Was it for the reason that Henry's just given?"

How I wished I could truthfully say 'yes' in answer to that question. As I tried to gather together a defense for my judgements, I knew that Nigel had spotted the trouble I had had with this lesson, and without me realizing it, I was in the position that would constantly face me for the next eight years – trying to be fair to a teacher but knowing in my heart of hearts that not all the children were making as much progress as they should. I was not, however, prepared to go down without a fight. I felt an unreasonable affection for the quiet little teacher who had so inspired a young pupil and I thought her efforts in the first part of the lesson should be acknowledged by a good, and in any case, I did not want to be made to look as ineffectual as Trevor by owning up to a fudge on this my first lesson observation.

"The teacher was linking history and literacy in a thought-provoking way," I waffled, "but the children needed time to empathise with the problems faced by the evacuee children. It was a new idea for them. That was why they started slowly – I am sure when they pick up the lesson tomorrow, they will build on today's experience." I felt really pleased with my answer. I knew it was important not to say anything about the slower writers, whose struggles I had documented on my first form, but which I had air-brushed out of my re-write, without my realizing it.

"That sounds a pretty good explanation to me," said Henry. "Nigel, I think Jane has fully explained the mis-match, but thank you for drawing our attention to this issue of compatibility between grades – not an easy one. Jane, in future, please try to observe more of what the slower learners are doing and get it down on your form. It's something everyone will have to improve on in the next few weeks." At these words, I hoped that the guilt I was feeling was not written on my face.

"Why so serious?" asked Abby as we made our way back to our rooms.

"I don't know – I just feel as if whatever we think we have observed, is probably never the real truth – I wonder if I will ever find this easy."

"Of course you will, don't take things to heart… you can

69

only ever make an approximation you know – do what you think is right at the time."

Chapter 8

O n Wednesday morning, I arrived back in the team room just before lunch, now a seasoned trouper into my third day of an inspection having completed ten lesson observations in total. John Ainsworth was making himself a cup of coffee.

"One for you?" he asked,

"Oh yes please."

"I've just walked along the top corridor and the downstairs one and there is a pretty long list of problems. I expect you've noticed them all but, in any case, I've written them all down on this observation form." He ripped the top white copy off from the two coloured sheets and handed the yellow one to me.

"John, I have to tell you that health and safety are not my strong points – I'm really grateful for any help."

"I never mind helping anyone out," he paused, stirring the tea absent-mindedly. "It's those that know it all I can't stand."

"Well," I laughed, "you certainly don't mince your words."

"Absolutely no mincing – say it how it is, is my motto. And on this inspection there are one or two who pretty well do know it all. But it would be surprising if there wasn't, I suppose – give it a year or two though and then they'll be like the rest of us, bewildered by life's imponderables." He accompanied this with a cheery wink and I smiled back, acknowledging the fact that he was probably talking about Nigel, although heartily doubting that Nigel would ever be bewildered.

John's form was neat and easy to read. There were obstructions to fire doors, an electric cable that was not secured properly, a patch of lino that was sufficiently frayed to cause concern about an accident, and no yellow lines painted on the edge of stairs to ensure safety for ascent or descent for those who were partially sighted or for full sighted persons should there be, for instance, smoke clouding vision. My mouth nearly fell open at the comprehensive and damming list.

"I would never have noticed all of these, John," I said.

"It's not satisfactory," said John.

I nodded in agreement. "I am grateful for you help."

"Course, some can be quickly put right but the fact that they are there on the week of an inspection just shows that the school is not up to scratch with these things."

"I am going to do a tour of the building now," I said, "and, of course, the toilets, playground and outside toilets as well. I've got to be ready for the team discussion on my aspect at tonight's meeting, so this will be very helpful. Thanks John."

I was not looking forward to presenting my evidence at the team meeting that evening. Each night from Monday onwards, people had to lead the discussion relating to their aspect, so that judgements could be reached and formalised by a grade from the Ofsted one to seven scale. These grades were recorded in the relevant box of an Ofsted document known as the Record of Corporate Judgement (RoCJ). In team parlance, this was called 'putting the scores on the doors'.

On Tuesday night, John, Mary and Phil had told us their findings. John had spoken with regard to the school's relationship with parents. He had been well prepared and concise, listing the plus points and then any minuses. Because none of us had any other information to add, we all agreed with his judgement of a satisfactory relationship. In comparison to John, Mary's delivery had been rambling. She spent a great deal of time telling us about her visit to the playground, and about one little boy who said he was being bullied, but she didn't have any evidence from other children to make this a solid judgement. She carried on about the general problem of bullying in schools until Henry had got exasperated and said that we all needed to ask children about bullying and we would get back to the matter tomorrow. Phil had been much more decisive about the quality of the curriculum. He gave convincing arguments as to why the school's curriculum planning was satisfactory but no better. Of course, I was keen to emulate Phil and John.

I was going to start my evidence gathering out on the playground, while covering the bullying aspect as Henry had requested. I gulped my coffee down and was on my way out as some others were coming in. When I got down to the end of the corridor, I spotted Abby and Phil. They were deep in conversation so much so, that as I went past saying a quick 'Hi there', they didn't look up. Abby was sitting on one of the small chairs with a table that dotted the corridors. Phil was leaning towards her, his hand on the back of her chair. I didn't doubt that they were talking about inspection matters, but I couldn't help noticing that there was a touch too much intimacy about the position of their bodies. This was not the first time I had thought this when I had seen them together.

Out on the playground, there was a strong wind blowing, although it was mild, with a warm, late September sun dodging out every now and then from behind thick white billowing clouds – a true Liverpool day. I enjoyed the unmistakable sound of numbers of children playing out; cries, laughter, shouts, whoops and screams, buffeting in the wind, as the children played tag, the inevitable football and make–believe games, turning their coats into Batman capes flapping behind them or twirling them round their heads to fly though the air as a Spiderman net.

The Beswick Street playground was mostly tarmac. At the rear of the building, where the tarmac ended, there was a piece of field that was already out of use because recent rain had made it muddy. This small bit of greenery was bounded by a tall unsightly chain fence held up by rusting metal spikes. All-in-all a fairly typical inner city school playground with nature suppressed by man's disregard, and only represented by scrubby grass, the occasional weed sprouting between a crack somewhere or other and, of course, the birds. The full gusty wind had brought seagulls in that swooped occasionally on any remains of a packed lunch. From a distance, you could imagine them swooping down and flying off with the small figure of a child. There were a lot of pigeons. They strutted around pecking here and there and perching on the boundary wall and on window ledges. I wondered about their droppings, which were quite apparent near to the side of the building. Surely a health and safety hazard? I would need to ask John.

As I walked purposefully across the tarmac to find those I could tactfully question on the bullying issue, I learnt a very simple inspection lesson – that it is not possible to record evidence when you are outside on a flimsy paper form, unless you first secure it firmly with clips at both ends. Only clips at the top secured mine, so it kept blowing up every time I tried to write on it. This, however, was not the most important lesson I learnt on that playground. This was to come from Carly. It was a lesson which has stood me in good stead for all my time as an inspector. I met Carly after I had asked several children of differing ages, if they enjoyed playtime, had friends, could tell an adult if they were upset and lastly, the big question, had they ever been bullied. Every child seemed happy with their play and no one knew any bullies. I was about to go back inside when Carly approached me and asked me in her strong Liverpool accent what my name was. As she was about nine years old, I showed her my badge on which my name was printed. She squinted hard at it and then made a good attempt at reading 'Schaffer'.

"What's your name?" I asked.

"Carly."

"That's a very pretty name."

"My sister's called Shelley, I like that better."

"That is a nice name," I agreed, "but I think Carly is just as nice."

Now we were friends, Carly linked her arm through mine as we strolled along. We chatted for a bit about her favourite lessons and the fact that she had a dog called Bounce. Then suddenly, she stopped me and crouched down to look closely at my picture on the Ofsted badge, which swung from the bottom pocket of my jacket. She teetered a little as she did this, hampered by the thick, high wedges at the bottom of her shoes. With a very serious face she asked, "Is that really you?"

"Yes," I replied puzzled. "Doesn't it look like me?" Carly looked at the picture and then back at me and then delivered the killer blow.

"You know you must take the trouble to put lipstick on every day." She emphasised the 'every day' very particularly. "You look tons better with lipstick on like in the photo." I smiled through my discomfort, and was quite thankful to hear the whistle blow for the children to go in for the second lunchtime sitting. Carly, like all the children responded immediately to the whistle, disengaging herself to join the quickly forming lines of children. When she was a few feet away, she turned to admonish:

"Don't forget, put the lippy on." I have never forgotten. On days when I have felt under the weather or just too tired to bother, I have still made an effort to look smart – to look the part, if adults don't expect it children do, and when I got home from Liverpool, I went out and bought myself two new lipsticks.

I made my way over to the dreaded boys' toilet block. This was adjacent to the building but still outside. Just as Phil and Trevor said, it was very smelly. The old porcelain was cracked in places and the tiles were too porous to allow proper cleaning. I spent no more than a few seconds looking inside before beating a hasty retreat – definitely unsatisfactory.

After my outside visit, I decided to check the facilities in classrooms. When I entered a Reception class, the teacher was busily preparing the afternoon activities. I smiled at her and told her my purpose for being there.

"You have some really lovely displays." I remarked not just to put her at her ease but because they were truly eye-catching. She smiled back pleased and then began a tirade about the problems in the room – there was only one small sink, no real wet play area, there was no immediate access to outdoor play so this had to be a timetabled activity, which did not allow the children any free choice, as highly recommended for this age group.

"We have to take everything out on to the playground from the storeroom and then bring it back in again at night. It's such a drag."

" It must be," I sympathised. "Where do you set up?"

"We have to use this end of the playground because the juniors often have games on the open end."

"I noticed a lot of pigeon droppings this end," I said.

"Oh I know – it's disgusting. We should really have our own secure play area that we could access from the classroom, but it would cost a fortune to do."

I wrote everything that she had said down, assuring her that somehow I would try to see that some of these problems were in the report so that the school could begin to rectify them.

"Well, I know there is no money," she said. "There never is."

"Yes, but if we ignore it, it's as if it doesn't matter," I said, thanking her for her information before leaving.

I was satisfied that I had enough information on accommodation – now I only needed to gather evidence about the school's resources, and I was not looking forward to this very much. One of the things teachers most resented about Ofsted inspectors and, about which there were many a would-you-believe-what-they-did story going the rounds in schools, was the fact that inspectors looked into cupboards. It smacked of nosiness.

"Imagine, they poked around in my stock-cupboard," a teacher might say, rightly incensed that their private space had been invaded. I wasn't going to look in the classroom stock cupboards, but I did need to check out whether there were enough resources for lessons such as PE, music, art and the like.

I started in the hall with the PE equipment. It was all old and mostly in need of replacement but there were enough benches, boxes and other items for vaulting or climbing. The music trolley, however, appeared to have been upgraded. Along with ancient triangles and tambourines, there were some shiny new items for scraping or tinkling all of African, Asian or Caribbean origin, acquired to indicate a good approach to the music of other cultures. I rifled through the cupboards in the bleak technology room where most things were very old and boring, except for a woodwork bench which was shiny and new. (Untouched by human hand?) After an hour of delving into cupboards, that was how a lot of the resources seemed – lots of old stuff that nobody really wanted, but nobody got rid of, and some new items, which the school had hastily bought on finding that Ofsted was on its way. I smiled ruefully to myself to think that at least our visit brought some benefits – some poor co-ordinator, who had probably been requesting a few pounds to spend for years, suddenly got a windfall.

I tried to ponder whether the resources I had seen were satisfactory or unsatisfactory. I thought I would go for satisfactory but then I remembered Nigel had not been happy about the amount of computers. The day before, he had given me a form, with something to that effect written on it. I trawled through my file but couldn't find it. Typical, I thought, I go and loose evidence provided by Nigel, but then I was losing a lot of things. I was becoming overwhelmed by the organisational needs of inspection – I just did not have enough sections, pouches and other sorting devices, and if I did I would probably not use them correctly – organisation was not a strength of mine. Surely, I asked myself for the umpteenth time, I should not be doing this job?

Towards the end of the afternoon, I spent a few minutes making notes so that I could give a clear and concise feedback at the meeting. I decided that with the state of the toilets and all the hazards noted by John that the accommodation should be graded with a five for unsatisfactory; staffing was satisfactory, but what about resources? What I had seen was more or less satisfactory. I had a further search for the Nigel's form but then decided I would stop worrying about it. It probably said unsatisfactory but with all other areas being mainly satisfactory, Nigel would just have to put up with an overall grade of four.

Feeling quite satisfied that my preparation would meet with Henry's approval, I found that there was just ten minutes to spare before the end of school. I decided I would walk back down the infant corridor. I was struck, yet again, by how hard the teachers worked to make the forbidding old building appealing to very young children. Displays hung from every wall and much use was made of cushions, soft hangings and book displays. Children were coming out of classrooms and getting their coats on before going back inside. I looked up at the high windows that no small child could see out of, and realised, as I did so, that the big white clouds of earlier in the day had changed to an ominous grey. The sky had darkened, and then there was a loud clap of thunder. At this, the children in the cloakroom who were laughing and chattering a moment before went absolutely quiet and motionless, eyes wide and frightened.

"Come on come on," said the teachers. "It was only thunder." They began marshalling their classes towards the wide outside door. Here parents stepped forward to collect their child. It was not really raining yet – just big drops bouncing intermittently off the tarmac.

"It's really going to chuck it down," I heard one mum say to a teacher as she grabbed her child's hand and hurried away. She was absolutely right. We all got soaked as we dashed from the school to the car park that evening.

When we met up in the team room at the hotel, John told me that he had been on the upstairs corridor when the rain had started. There was, he reported, a leaking roof at the far end of the corridor. Someone had placed a bucket strategically under the drips – it was obviously a well-established leak. This, I thought, was further good evidence that the accommodation was unsatisfactory. I asked John about the pigeon droppings and he agreed that it was unpleasant and should be dealt with.

Chapter 9

Henry's guidance on inspection procedures might have fallen short in providing us with workable systems for organising inspections, but these were things a reasonably intelligent person could easily pick up or adapt for themselves. His tutelage, however, provided us with something much more important – a sane and sensible view of how to survive in the inspection world. One of the most important principles he imparted to us was the need to keep team meetings to a manageable length. At this time, some lead inspectors seemed to think that their worth was measured by the lateness of the hour at which they concluded their meetings.

The whole point of team meetings was to arrive at corporate judgements about all the aspects in the framework and to record these in the Record of Corporate Judgement (RoCJ), an extremely important document. It was sent, at the end of the inspection, to Ofsted where it was kept for all eternity, and in secrecy, as the Freedom of Information Act had not yet shone it's light upon the world. Team discussions on grades were often heated. Disagreements, however, were not always about what was happening in school. Inspectors frequently argued over interpretations of the framework, which would result in much consulting of well-thumbed copies and the reading out of sections to others in a hectoring manner. Sometimes this would happen when someone, as I was about to do, confused the criteria from one part of the schedule with that in another.

Once all judgements had been arrived at, and grades agreed, then the team had to identify the 'Key Issues for Action'. These were the nub of it all. They came from any grading in the RoCJ which was less than satisfactory. Schools had to draw up an action plan to address the key issues and to send this plan to Ofsted. Their resentment would be huge, and would often rankle for years, if they did not agree that the thing needed doing in the first place, that is if they did not agree that what we said was unsatisfactory really was. This was the battleground.

The team meeting, on the final evening, was always longer than meetings on other nights. The lead inspector needed to have a clear view of what the team agreed were the main issues for the school, in order to discuss them with the headteacher the following morning.

That Wednesday night, we started by revisiting Mary's aspect about attitudes and behaviour. Mary made a much better go of it this time. She had summarised the grades on the lesson observations and came up with very good behaviour with which we all agreed. What we were not so sure about was the children's attitudes to learning. Of course, they were very willing and biddable, but there were few instances of them using their own initiative or thinking independently. We were seeing, the old school of child management, done very well, it had to be said, but not allowing for personal development. Then there was the question of bullying. What had we discovered that day? It seemed that my experience of finding generally happy children was similar for Trevor, Nigel and Phil, but Abby and John had both met with kiddies whose experience of school life was not so happy. There was no serious issue on bullying but there was an occasional undercurrent of spitefulness.

"This is what you would expect in a very authoritarian regime," said Henry. "It is a really difficult one to unravel, but I think it would be useful to point out to the school that children do not take enough responsibility for their own actions – there is no school council, no system of children supporting others on the playground; everything is adult controlled."

Boxes were filled in and we moved on to the aspect of Attainment and Progress, with me getting a faint anxious feeling that the time was drawing closer to when the spotlight would be on me. Abby took charge of the discussion with confidence. She spoke quietly and could give a clear picture of standards in the core subjects. Standards in English and mathematics were both below average, but because children started well below others when they began their schooling, progress was satisfactory. In science, standards were better. The children were reaching an average standard by the end of Year 6, but Trevor was concerned that there was not enough investigative work. Despite this, we would be able to say that science was a strength. Then Abby handed over to Nigel who explained the position in IT, standards and progress being unsatisfactory. He had nothing good to say. He seemed to relish pointing out all the negative aspects, poor machines, insufficient software, weak assessment and badly trained staff. He spoke for nearly fifteen minutes and Henry had to interrupt his flow.

"I think we can say that IT is an issue, Nigel but we must move on to the other subjects." Henry turned to me to report on the standards in history, geography and PE I said that standards were satisfactory for all three but, in history and geography, I was concerned about the lack of opportunities for children to do research.

"Does that not make the standards unsatisfactory then?" asked Nigel.

How did Nigel do it? How did he put his finger on every weakness? My mouth opened and closed, as all I felt like saying was 'I don't bloody well know,' and then Trevor came to my rescue.

"If you remember, I said that investigation in science was weak. I think this is a similar picture, and it ties in with what we are saying in Attitudes and Behaviour – too much adult control, not enough opportunities for independence either in personal development or learning."

"Absolutely spot on, there Trevor," said Henry. "I think we have a key issue here, and what a nice one – ' help pupils develop an independent attitude to their learning by more investigative work in science, history and geography and, (he paused here to emphasize the comma) to their own personal development.' What do you think everyone?"

There were murmurs of assent. Nigel's confrontational comment forgotten, and all of us amazed at how quickly Henry had drawn together disparate strands and constructed a meaningful sentence that would sit perfectly in a list of key issues. "I think," Henry went on, "it might be useful if tomorrow, Trevor and Jane, you took a group of pupils from Years 5 and 6, perhaps the two of you together, and asked them about what research they have done." Trevor and I nodded our agreement.

Henry thanked Abby for a clear picture on Attainment and Progress, then turned to John and asked him to give his judgements for the aspect of Support, Guidance and Pupils' Welfare. John was as prepared, concise and clear on this aspect, as he had been the evening before on Parents. As he spoke, I was aware of the general drift of his delivery but I was not listening too well. I was too conscious of the fact that I would be the next person asked to speak. My notes lay open on my lap and I kept glancing down at them. I gathered that John covered some of the safety aspects to do with the premises and that these were judged to be unsatisfactory. All too soon the grades had been recorded, and Henry was turning towards me.

"Jane, can you run through Staffing, Accommodation and Resources?" The trouble was, he seemed to be talking down an echoing tunnel so that the words bounced back in my brain. I could feel myself making an effort to speak but nothing was coming out of my mouth. For a few awkward moments there was silence but then, miraculously, I was speaking as if operated by some outside force.

"There's an adequate number of staff with appropriate qualifications." That all sounded fine, I thought to myself in amazement and set off again after a quick look down at my notes. "Staff have the qualifications, and, in most subjects, the training to deliver the National Curriculum. Of course, as Nigel has made clear there is a shortfall in the training for IT, but this is just one subject amongst nine and the good knowledge in the infant department that has brought in the THRASS initiative must be taken into account." I looked across at Mary and she beamed me one of her megawatt smiles. "So, with plusses and minuses on both sides, I think overall this aspect is satisfactory."

Henry said, "right, so we put a four in that box – agreed?" There were a lot of nods. What I failed to see was that these were mostly bored nods; there is generally nothing of interest in Staffing, Accommodation and Resources.

I decided to cover the matter of the school's learning resources next, leaving accommodation to the end. I reported that, although the school had recently acquired some new resources in music, and design and technology, there were some very antiquated resources in cupboards but overall the position was satisfactory. I remembered to say that, however, in IT were resources were unsatisfactory.

"Yes," said Henry rather quickly, "we've had that information already – so resources a four then Jane?"

"Yes," I said, and pencils quickly recorded the ubiquitous four on everyone's copy of the RoCJ. I now only had accommodation to get through. "As John has covered many of the points to do with the unsatisfactory elements of health and safety with regard to the accommodation, I don't need to go over them, but he did not include the risk to health caused by the many roosting pigeons – there is quite a build up of pigeon droppings along the side of the building in the playground." There was no indication from any of the team as to what they were thinking at this point, but somehow, I began to feel uneasy. I carried on. "There are a good number of rooms, and classrooms are of an adequate size, although the windows are too high and the rooms gloomy. The hall is of a reasonable size, but taking into account the health and safety issue, I would suggest that accommodation is…" I paused a moment, "unsatisfactory."

There was an immediate reaction, in fact a sort of snort of derision from Nigel, followed by a strange silence, and then he let forth with: "how can it be unsatisfactory?– they have a hall, a technology room, a parents' room, a library and there is even a field outside. It is perfectly adequate to teach the National Curriculum. Look at the guidance, page 110." Nigel picked up his handbook and waved it at me and then thumped it down, open at the inspection schedule for Staffing, Accommodation and Learning Resources. His finger scrolled down from the top of the page to the section right at the bottom.

"Accommodation should be inspected in terms of its *adequacy* for the numbers on roll and ages of pupils," he read out aloud, "as well as the range of curriculum activities." He said the word adequacy very slowly and loudly as if speaking to someone with a brain shortfall.

"Hmm, yes," said Henry. "The accommodation is certainly adequate, Jane. I think you have confused the judgements that need to be made in your section with those that rightly belong in John's." Then Henry kindly added, "you may be right about some aspects not being 'stimulating and well-maintained', as it describes in the next paragraph to the one Nigel has just read out, but it is adequate and so can be no less than a four."

"I would think, better than a four, said Nigel. I think, in some respects it is good."

"Oh, no Nigel, said Mary. "The accommodation for the under fives is a weakness."

Very grateful to Mary for reminding me of my chat with the Reception teacher at lunch time, I took up this argument; "yes, when I talked to the Reception teacher at lunch-time, she listed a number of unsatisfactory aspects to the accommodation for the under fives. They have a long way to go to the toilet, which is upsetting for timid children, there is no access for safe outdoor play – they have to go out for a special session and all the play things have to be taken out and then brought back in again. And she was concerned about the pigeon droppings where the children played – it was not just me."

"Accommodation a four then," said Henry, looking round for agreement. Everyone murmured their acquiescence, except Nigel who kept quiet. Henry looked at me and said. "You've been too enthusiastic Jane, I know just what you mean – children should not receive their schooling in a shabby old building like Beswick Street, but as Nigel says we are to judge the adequacy – we are going to criticize them on grounds of health and safety in John's paragraph so it does not do to take them to task twice, even if the pigeon droppings do offend." He said the last comment with a benign smile and there was a general chuckle from everyone.

"Pigeon dirt never stopped a child from learning," said Nigel, also smiling, magnanimous now and patronising at the same time. I felt so mortified, I could not wait for the meeting to be over. After what seemed an unbearably long time, we were packing up our things and leaving the team room. I just wanted to get away. I could see that Trevor wanted to speak to me about the arrangements for talking to a group of children but I pretended that I hadn't noticed him and I was out of the door as soon as possible.

I opened my hotel room and stepped inside, not switching the light on – my bruised ego needed the soft anonymity of darkness. Why had I made such a stupid mistake? Surely I could see what it was saying in the handbook? Nigel's right, I'm not up to the job – that's what he has thought from the start. Henry will tell me to pack up and go home. I moved forward a few steps and collided with the edge of my suitcase, painfully catching my ankle and knocking my file out of my hand. It hit the floor with a whack. I groped about to the left of me for the light switch. I couldn't find it. Suddenly, I was as upset about not being able to locate a switch on the wall as I was with my dismal showing at the team meeting. I could feel tears pricking my eyes. My fingers came in contact with the switch and light flooded the room. As I looked down, I saw that when my file had hit the floor it had burst open and all the pages had come out, which should have made me more upset, but instead it checked the floods of self-pity. I sat on the floor and patiently sorted the papers back into their correct sections.

There is something very soothing about the standard interior of a Travel Inn room, each one so exactly like another. I went into the bathroom and switched the light on so that a faint hum came from the extractor fan. It sounded a friendly noise, the sort of noise that tells you that you are being looked after, taken care of, like the hum in the bowels of a ferry boat when the captain and crew are navigating through stormy seas and you, the passenger, can leave everything in their capable hands. As ever in my life, when things were not going too well, I comforted myself with thoughts of how much worse things could be. I was not, after all homeless, tramping the streets, looking for somewhere to shelter for the night, no I was tucked up in a comfortable hotel room and should thank my lucky stars. The curtains were closed across the wide window, but I went and looked out at the darkness. It was still raining – hard, heavy driving rain, hitting the window and leaving streaks across the glass. The patch of grass at the bottom of the school's playground came to mind – it would be a quagmire by now.

I sat down at the long work surface and started to draw up my timetable for the following day. I should have spoken to Trevor about our plans for talking to a group of children. Perhaps I should go and find his room and ask him now? It had been very childish of me to dash out the way I had done. As I leafed through my file, the missing form given to me by Nigel popped up. Typical, pieces of paper eluded you when you needed them, but were there in front of you when they no longer mattered. I was just about to stir and go to find Trevor's room when I heard a knock on the door. I went to open it, and there was Abby. She had a bottle of red wine in one hand and two glasses in the other.

"I would really like some company tonight and I don't want to go down to the bar." She held up the bottle for my inspection.

"You mean, you thought I might need some company and you would be perfectly right in thinking I don't want to go down in the bar." I smiled at her.

"Well, yes, that as well." Abby came in and put the two glasses and bottle down in a space that was unoccupied by my papers. "Do you want to work – I can come back later?"

"I've finished really. I was just paper shuffling, and trying to be busy so I didn't think about my disastrous presentation."

"I knew you would be stressing – but don't. You don't need to – everyone makes mistakes."

"Oh I don't think so. I have the easiest section in the framework and I can't even get that right…..Henry's going to get rid of me. (You know, Gill Ashmore's axed someone already.) And in any case, I think Nigel's right – I am not the right sort of person for the job, which is why I will go and tell Henry, first thing tomorrow, that I will leave after this inspection."

"That's just nonsense. We are all learning, and we have all made mistakes, that's why we've got Henry with us on this inspection, and as for what Nigel thinks – he is far more unsuitable for the job than you. He is much too superior and jumps to conclusions about people and that's why he underestimates you. He is the sort of person who has got on in life by making others around him appear less than him. I would hate to have him inspecting my school. You work with the school's best interests at heart and you get on well with the teachers – look at the way that lady in the Reception class poured out her frustrations to you. She wouldn't have told Nigel. You mustn't go and say anything so stupid to Henry." I didn't reply, embarrassed a little by her fulsome support.

Abby picked up the bottle and poured two large glasses of red wine. She passed one to me.

"Thank you." I said, meaning both for the wine and the words. We drank one or two long mouthfuls in companionable silence. I could feel the red stuff warming me in lots of places, but mostly the heart.

"Oh that feels so much better," I said.

"Of course, it does. No more talk of quitting?" Abby stared at me.

"You're right, of course, I don't want to leave. I don't know what it is but inspection has me hooked. It's just so fascinating working out why things are as they are in a different school – you could never get to see so much about a place in any other way."

"Exactly – you like the job – so why leave it?"

"Well because I'm not good enough, I suppose, and after tonight, everyone will think I'm a nincompoop." The old-fashioned word sounded ludicrous and I laughed at myself.

"Yes, yes nincompoop," mimicked Abby.

"An idiot." I corrected myself.

"Yes, yes, idiot, nincompoop and forever, they will laugh about pigeon poo – they can tell that story to team members, and make them laugh and they'll always be grateful to you for that."

"I thought you were supposed to be making me feel better." I giggled, the wine truly doing its job.

"Well stop feeling sorry for yourself."

"I've stopped, honestly and I won't say anything to Henry about leaving. I suppose I was a bit silly about the pigeon droppings but the Reception teacher was quite vehement about it."

"She's probably right – you're probably right. Mmm, yes if it was my school, I would sort it out. You can get things to stop pigeons roosting on buildings – it needs to be done at this school. I think Henry should mention it to the governors, or John should when they go to the feedback meeting – not put it in the report, of course, but not ignore it completely."

We both nodded.

"Health and safety is a bit of a minefield." I said

"Yes, but let's have no more talk about Beswick Street – talking about schools should be banned after," Abby looked down at her watch, "ten past nine."

There was silence again for a little while and then I knew that I would have to say the sentence that kept forming and re-forming in my mind:

"You've got very friendly with Phil."

The statement landed between us with a dull thud.

"I knew you were going to say that," was Abby's response.

"I shouldn't have said it."

"No you should have said it – I am glad you've said it. I want to talk about Phil because you're right. I have got very friendly with him. I do like him, a lot.

"He's married." I said.

"Yes, he is." She raised her glass which was empty now and turned to fill it up, then poured some more into mine. "And it is not fair – not fair at all because I've not liked anyone so much as I like Phil for such a long time."

I felt awkward, but asked, "is he happily married?"

Abby shook her head as though bemused by the question. "He is married with two teenage children, one of seventeen and one fourteen, and a dog called Chippy – probably a hamster or two and a cat, though I don't know for sure about the cat, but certainly mothers and fathers-in-law, aunts and uncles, cousins, brothers, sisters who all visit on birthdays and Christmases and go away together on holidays, and whether or not that is happily married, I don't know." She stopped and drank another mouthful. "So isn't it silly to like him?"

"Yes, it is."

"I shall stop liking him."

"Good. And the next inspection is in the Manchester area: I think it's going to be Stockport, and you and I and Trevor will be able to travel from home. We won't need to stay in a hotel, so you won't see so much of him."

"You're right, and if I don't see so much of him, I am bound to forget how much I like him."

I stared at Abby, wondering whether I could ask her another question.

"How did you come to like him this much in so short a time?"

"I don't know, I really do not know. But I liked him from the first moment I saw him, almost as if I had known him before."

After Abby had gone, I knew the evening, and the bottle of wine that now stood empty on my desk, had made a friendship. Friends come in all sorts of guises and for all sorts of reasons but they are most potent when they take you down a new road in your own life, or invite you to accompany them along a road in theirs. Both happened that night. I wouldn't resign. I would, unless Henry chucked me out, be a team member with Abby and all the others, on our next inspection. This turned out to be not in Stockport, as I had thought, but in Scarborough – a very significant difference in locality. But before this, the Beswick Street inspection had an unforeseeable outcome.

Chapter 10

I went down to breakfast the next morning, having slept surprising well, to find that all the rest of the team were already tucking into bacon and eggs. Trevor was sitting on his own. As I slipped into the place opposite him, he was just mopping up the last of his egg with a hunk of toast.

"Good morning. How are you?" I asked him.

"I'm fine and you?"

"Oh well I've recovered from yesterday's debacle – I'm sorry I didn't catch you at the end of the meeting to arrange our session with the children."

"Oh that's all right. I've sorted out a time I think will be fine for both of us. You had better get some breakfast."

"Oh yes, I had. I'm late aren't I? Don't leave will you, till I get back? I won't be a tick."

I hurried over to the breakfast bar and got orange juice, toast and a plate of cooked breakfast items – best to stock up while the going was good but I didn't spend any time deliberating on my choices. I needed to ask Trevor for help to get to the school. Because we would be driving straight home at the end of the day, we were all taking our own cars to the school that morning; the trouble was, I only had a sketchy idea of the route that Trevor had navigated so obligingly each day. Although he had clearly finished, Trevor was still sitting at the table when I got back.

"I'm so glad you're still here – you see I need to ask you about the route to the school." I confessed.

"I thought that might be what was on your mind. Don't worry. You can follow me. Calm down and enjoy your breakfast. I've still got to pack my things into the car and anyway, I've no reason to hurry to school. I've got all the evidence I need." He got up to leave. "I'll wait for you in the entrance hall – twenty minutes

OK?"

I was eating as quickly as possible, gulping coffee in between bites.

I nodded my agreement, flapping my hand to indicate that I couldn't talk because of my full mouth.

"You'll get indigestion if you eat so quickly. Don't worry – I won't leave without you. See you at…" he looked down at his watch, "ten to eight."

Trevor was as good as his word. We both set off from the car park together with me tailing his big Mondeo. He drove slowly and carefully, signaling well in advance of any change of lane or direction so I had no trouble following. Once, when he had no option but to go through the lights without me, he pulled over to the side of the road as soon as it was safe for him to do so, enabling me to catch up and slot in comfortably behind him.

After we had parked the cars at the school, we crossed the playground together. There were big shallow puddles lying on the playground tarmac and the whole place looked washed out by the deluge of the night before. We chatted about the different teachers we had seen. There were one or two strugglers; teachers too set in their ways and unimaginative in their approach, and we agreed on who these were but we also agreed that there were some talented staff who were enthusiastic and lively. We had both been involved in checking out the usefulness of the reading sessions known as ERIC for Mary. Beswick Street had surprised us with how well they organized and used these sessions.

"I was quite anti ERIC, because I had often found it to be a waste of time," I confessed. "But they have some really good ideas here, like those reading games they play and using all the support staff and dinner ladies."

"I agree," said Trevor. "It just goes to show that you must never have pre-conceived ideas about anything when it comes to methodology."

"Mmm you're right. No sign of pigeons this morning." I smiled wryly at my own mistake of placing any importance on the pigeon population whatsoever.

"They'll all be still sheltering under eaves," Trevor said.

Inside the building, the entrance hall was deserted, which was strange. There seemed to be a great deal of activity in the hall, and when we got on to our corridor staff were scurrying about all over the place, carrying boxes and piles of books into, of all places, my haven, the design and technology room. When we opened the team room, Mary Abby, Phil and Nigel all looked up and said simultaneously:

"There's been a flood."

"What?"

"Three classes in the infants are under water apparently," said Phil.

"How did it happen?" I asked.

"Henry's talking to Mrs. Jessop about it – he said to stay out of the way as much as possible for the time being and he will fill us in as soon as he has a clear picture of the situation himself."

"Well I'm blowed," said Trevor and then he turned to me and said with a real twinkle in his eye, "looks like you were right about that five for accommodation, Jane." There was general laughter at this and Mary and Phil kept the joke up by suggesting psychic powers on my part or possible witchery to have created the situation in the first place.

"Well if you did summons up the storm clouds Jane, it was a good ploy for getting us away from the inspection early. They may have to close the school," said Abby.

"If it's just the infant classes, perhaps they will still carry on as usual with the juniors." Mary suggested. "And I think some of the infant teachers are trying to set up classrooms in other parts of the building."

"Yes, there was a lot of activity on this corridor. Trevor and I passed staff taking books and boxes into the design technology room."

"I don't think they will be able to carry on because there must be issues around the electrics and the heating," said Abby. "I'm sure the health and safety people will want the building closed."

This turned out to be an accurate assessment of the situation. Henry came in with a very serious expression on his face and indicated that we should all sit down around the table to hear the results of his talk with Mrs. Jessop.

"They were most anxious to carry on as normal this morning because of the inspection," he said, "but the building works from Liverpool have been in and there is no way they can function as normal. The school has got to close. There's to be an announcement on local radio and staff will have to go to the school gate to tell parents that the school is closed. Any children who come unaccompanied will, of course, be let on to the premises and looked after until such time as they can be collected."

"Does this mean that the inspection findings are negated?" asked Nigel.

"Well here's the lucky thing," Henry replied. "Because we are well over and above the number of team members that should be on an inspection for a school the size of Beswick Street, we have, in fact, covered the requisite number of days. Beswick Street should have a 22 day inspection and there are eight of us who have been in for three days each, making a total of 24 days, so we are still over and above the number of days required." We were all suddenly aware that Henry was smiling. "We will be able to go home early." As he said this we saw that now Henry was not just smiling, he was grinning from ear to ear – a great big happy grin.

"Go home early?" Nigel queried, in marked contrast slightly crestfallen, as if such an idea was foreign to his nature. "I'm not sure if I have got all the evidence I need."

"Well Nigel, I'll check over what you have got and I am sure it'll be more than adequate." Henry's tone of voice was placatory, almost as if giving Nigel a comforting pat. There was no doubt in all of our minds that Henry was extremely happy about slipping away before the due time and most of us were quite happy about it as well, already thinking about how the evening we had planned to spend at home might be a little more pleasant with an extra few hours at our disposal.

John Ainsworth, who had not been present during this interchange, came in. He drew up a chair and sat down a trifle noisily. He crossed his legs and looked around at us with the cocksure air of someone with some information everyone would want to know.

"Well – I don't think I've ever come across anything so...." slight dramatic pause, followed by a splutter of laughter, "funny in all my time inspecting, and believe me I've come across some strange do's."

"What is it John?" asked Phil. "Don't keep us in suspense."

"I've just been talking to the site manager and some of you are seriously going to have to eat your words. What was it - 'pigeon shit never stopped a child from learning?' Well it has done just that at Beswick Street this morning!"

There were general gasps and everyone looked at me.

"Well, yes," said Henry. I'd not got round to telling you what caused the flood. Apparently there is a central gulley in the roof between the two sections of the building. Rain water is led away down the gulley to two down pipes at the side. The pigeons roosting on the roof over a long period of time have filled the gulley with their" – Henry paused, deciding which word to use and finally settled on a polite term – "their droppings. With the exceptionally heavy rain that fell last night, this residue was washed down the gulley and blocked the down pipes. The water backed up under the roof on the south side of the building and escaped through the ventilation shafts that come out high up on the wall in the ground floor classrooms on that south side, the infant classes. It was still spurting out from the ventilation bricks when the caretaker arrived in school this morning."

"Well I never!"

"Who would ever have thought such a thing could happen!"

"How disgusting!"

"It's unbelievable that it should happen on inspection!"

"Gosh!" Everyone uttered a phrase of bewildered amazement at the turn of events – no one more dumbstruck than me.

Henry suddenly went serious. "The really awful thing is that it has happened before, about fifteen years ago, apparently. Mrs. Cartwright, who has been at the school for twenty odd years, can quite clearly remember it happening."

"Well that's the judgement on the governors down the tubes," said John. "How could they be so dilatory in their guardianship of kiddies' education?"

"And," said Henry, "of course, we need to alter that four in accommodation Jane." Henry turned to me while pulling his copy of the Record of Corporate Judgement out of his brief case. "What grade do you think should go in the box?"

"Under the circumstances, and even taking into account all the plus points we identified yesterday," I said trying not to sound too smug, "I think it should be worse than a five."

"Oh definitely" said Henry. Shall we put it down as poor – a six?" There were murmurs of agreement all round.

No 26 Lacey Street: Six months after the inspection of Beswick Street Primary School

"Mum. Guess what?" Susie said to her mum.

"What Luv?"

"Our classes are going to be mixed up – our class with Mr. Thompson's for when we go into year six."

"Why's that?"

"I don't know really, but Amanda's going to be in my class and so are Sadie and Deena."

"Oh good. I thought they were both nice girls when they came to your party."

"But Cheryl's not and Clare's not."

"Oh."

"And a man and lady came today to explain about the new buddy system."

"What's that then?"

"Well, children in Year 6 are going to act as playground buddies. It means you sort of patrol the playground and look out for any trouble or anyone who is on their own and you try to find a friend for them to play with."

"That sounds like a very good idea."

"Everyone in Year 6 will have a go at it, but us in Year 5 get to try it out as well. Just so we know what we're doing next term. And you know what? They're making the playground much better. There's going to be some nice new benches, and a proper little garden area. A bit of the playground is going to be fenced off so that the kids in Reception are going to have a safe place to play. We were asked to do designs for the garden area in art today. I made mine with a little winding path into the centre with a fountain."

"Goodness, Susie – a fountain – I think that's a bit ambitious," laughed her mum."

"That's what Mrs. Mitchell said, but I said, there was no harm in being ambitious."

"You did, did you? And what did she say to that?"

"She said I was right and that I must never stop being ambitious." Susie went quiet for a moment. "I will miss being in Mrs. Mitchell's class."

Chapter 11

After the Beswick Street inspection, we were no longer based in the hotel in Liverpool. Our group and another one, tutored by an HMI called Matthew Longton, were now based at Ofsted's Manchester Office, four stories up in an unremarkable office block in Old Trafford. This was convenient for those of us living around Manchester, but of course, not so for those from further a field, most especially Nigel. He had to come all the way from Blackpool and he voiced loud complaints about the injustice of this. Because it was Nigel, I found myself smiling a little at his inconvenience, which I knew was unfair of me.

We didn't see much of the other group of trainees, but Henry and Matthew Longton were obviously good colleagues and spent some time together organising their work load. We were told that, in November and December, the groups were likely to be mixed for the next two inspections, so we eyed the others curiously and a little reluctantly, feeling as we did that we were quite all right as we were.

We began our long apprenticeship in writing the dreaded Ofsted Report, starting with the writing up of our various sections for the report for the Beswick Street inspection. These had to be handed to Henry on the Tuesday of the first week back. Everyone was anxious about getting this right. Were we using the correct terminology? Had we followed the framework accurately? Were we being fair to the school? Abby and I phoned each other several times, comparing notes and reading out bits we were not sure about over the phone. Phil and Trevor were in constant communication and I even had a phone call from Mary, worried that she had not written enough for her English.

Henry put all our pieces of writing (called paragraphs, even though each paragraph contained several actual paragraphs) together to make a thirty page document. He wrote a four page summary which was called the Main Findings and, of course, the list of things the school had to do to improve, the Key Issues for Action. The full report, with several other items such as the RoCJ was then sent off to the quality control reader. During the inspection, Henry and John had muttered lots of comments about 'the reader' such as; 'I'm not sure the reader is going to go for that;' and 'we must make that quite clear for the reader'. So we had cottoned on to the fact that a reader was an essential, if somewhat feared person, breathing down the necks of inspectors, but about whom schools were blissfully ignorant.

When the report came back from the reader who, in this instance, was a chap called Geoffrey Bobbington, we had a meeting to go over the edited report. We were stunned when we saw the amount of red ink. The report was covered with a rash of comments, heavy underlining and vivid slashes that crossed out things we had thought essential. We couldn't help but feel a spurt of indignation when we saw our own contributions treated in this way. Indignation, however, changed to chagrin when we realised that several corrections referred to weak grammar, or worse, sloppy sentence structures such as a failure to make the verb and subject agree. Geoffrey Bobbington was particularly vicious when he spotted the use of the passive tense, and for some reason we had all lapsed into this mode of writing, perhaps because we felt we needed the distance from our subject (the teacher) that this tense seemed to offer.

Henry was not in the least put out by the reader's work, in fact he seemed quite happy with the outcome. "Actually this is not too bad," he said. "Geoffrey hasn't queried any of our main judgements and he is quite happy about my explanations regarding Mrs. Jessop's leadership of the school which was what was worrying me most. He's a pretty good reader is Geoffrey Bobbington, very thorough." We all agreed silently about his thoroughness. Then Henry, surmising that we were reluctant to accept some of Mr. Bobbington's comments, gave us a lecture on the importance of the reader.

"Although, the pain they inflict is often severe," he said with a touch of sarcasm, "they are invaluable and can save you from making some dreadful mistakes. They are almost always right because they are looking at the whole thing as an outsider. We get very closely involved with people in school, and so cannot always see that what we're doing is making excuses for them, and this can result in serious errors. Also, it is unbelievable how you can stray from the requirements of the framework and leave something out which you know perfectly well should be in." We listened, but rather sullenly. "Look here at Abby's paragraph," went on Henry. We clustered round. "Even though Abby's writing was probably the strongest out of you all, and don't forget, I checked over all of your pieces before assembling them in the final report, her paragraph on attainment and progress doesn't include a statement on the standards in RE. That's a serious omission. We both missed it, but the reader has picked it up."

"I can't think how I did that," said Abby quite taken aback.

"It's just very easy to do," replied Henry, "and that is what readers are for – to pick up mistakes, to check that the balance of the report is right and to see that there is nothing left out that should be in. Of course, they also pick up the mistakes people make with style, grammar and so on. People often write much too much about something and not enough about something else. Often too much use is made of the wording from the handbook. Mary you've done that in your paragraph on the children's behaviour and attitudes – its almost word for word from the handbook in places. What is needed here, Mary, is a well-chosen example. In fact that is what is needed in almost everyone's writing."

After having felt very pleased with ourselves for getting through our first inspection and producing our written pieces, we were now humbled by our own errors, finding it difficult to swallow the unpleasant pill that we were not infallible. I looked across at Nigel, surely he would be finding this difficult, but Nigel's expression, for once, was impossible to read. Henry told us not to worry, we were no worse than many a working inspector. We nodded as if we understood, but we had all spotted that there was much less red ink on the pieces done by Henry and John. John's paragraph about health and safety even had the comment: 'Well done, you've tackled the difficulties in this aspect well'.

While my writing for the subjects was as full of red ink as everyone else's, I was pleased to see that my paragraph on Staffing, Accommodation and Resources was relatively lightly marked, and my sentences about the flood and subsequent closure of the school given a small tick, although a caution was added about not over-doing it with regard to the pigeon droppings being the cause: 'Is it necessary to identify this?' Mr. Bobbington asked.

Henry gave a sigh and told us that it was his job as lead inspector to edit the report. We would have to do it when we were leading. It looked a ponderous task, but he assured us that in time you got used to it and that it wouldn't take him much more than a day to get this one straight.

"Believe me," he said, there are often much worse problems than we have here. When the reader doesn't agree with your judgements – then you're in trouble."

It was time to move on. The great thing about inspection is that, provided you don't trip up on any of the Ofsted snares, when one inspection is finished, it's a clean slate a new start, fresh fields and pastures new. We were booked to inspect a school in Scarborough in just over a week's time. We had to forget about Beswick Street, the teachers, the children, the report, everything and get to know the next school.

This time we had no time to conjecture about who was doing what as Henry launched into the matter before we had time to realize that we'd finished with Beswick Street. He explained that although he was, of course, coming on this inspection and had set it up with the school, now he was going to hand over the role of leading the inspection to one of us. There was immediate attention from everyone as the implication of this sunk in. Someone had to be picked to lead for the first time. Joy of joys it was Nigel. Nigel nearly burst with elation, or so I thought. In actual fact, he just pursed his lips and straightened his back, but any Nigel watcher, which is what I had become, would know that this was a sign of extreme pleasure for him. Then Henry gave out the team plan. There was a switch about of responsibilities for the aspects and subjects. I was to be responsible for attitudes and behaviour, and (joy of joys for me) English! I was quite happy that Nigel was given the prestigious role of leading, I had my beloved English. I had cracked it, given the responsibility of the main core subject! Mary was also pleased because Henry had acknowledged her expertise (or so she thought) and given her the aspect of Curriculum and Assessment. I thought it was probably done under the heading of anything for a quiet life on Henry's part.

We had to write the initial pre-inspection commentary as Henry had done for Beswick Street. Everyone's efforts were to be sent off to another HMI for monitoring, as part of the on-going evaluation of our work as inspectors. We were asked to work on this at the offices so as to reduce the amount of photocopying to be done. Henry said it should take us no more than a full day. He suggested we all came as early as possible the following morning.

We arrived by nine o'clock and slogged through the day, managing to finish by four-thirty or thereabouts. As we handed in our work, someone suggested we went for an evening meal in Manchester and everyone except Nigel agreed. He cited his long drive back to Blackpool. We all knew he just wanted to make a point so there were cries of: "Oh come on Nigel, you must come," and "we can't go off without our leader," so, of course, he was persuaded, gratified by our seeming eagerness for his company.

We started off the evening in a smart bar, had a drink and then all agreed that the best place to eat would be in China Town. We made our way to this colourful quarter in the city centre with its own square and grand pagoda style arch. Ambling down the small streets of the long established quarter, peering at the unintelligible menus outside each restaurant, we swapped notes about what we had written in the pre-inspection commentary about the school in Scarborough. The resolution of the group was dissipating in indecision about which restaurant to pick, until Phil took the initiative.

"Come on, we'll go in here," he said. "The Golden River, I'm sure I've been before – it's pretty decent." With the confidence of someone who expects to be followed, he bounced his way up a short flight of stairs to an upper floor entrance, everyone straggling behind in a long tail.

"I don't think he has you know," Abby whispered to me, "been before. He's just saying that because he can't stand the dithering." The Golden River was quite sumptuous inside, with little trickling waterfalls and gold and red chandeliers. Smiling waiters appeared instantly and seated us at a large round table covered expansively with a white cloth. Miraculously it wasn't too expensive and we all decided to make things simple by ordering a banquet for seven.

The evening was beginning to feel very jolly, and the

thought came to me how different it all was to working in school. We were getting to feel very comfortable with each other, despite the undercurrent of competitiveness engendered mostly by Nigel. Trevor was still an enigma and slightly ignored, although people were always making a conscious effort not to do so. As the food began arriving, and the waiters poured out glasses of wine, we were full of high spirits. There was plenty to talk about and the food was good. Then Mary lent across the table to Trevor. Loudly above the chatter, we could hear her say what a mystery man he was, that no one knew anything about his private life, even if he was married or not. In the sudden hush that ensued, Trevor went almost pale. He stared straight in front of him a strange dull look on his face.

"My wife died last year. It was cancer – she had been ill for eighteen months, and when I knew she wasn't going to get better, I didn't know what to do with myself. After she died, I decided to do inspections, just to get me out of the house. I couldn't stand being in the house on my own." All of us heard every word that he said and there was a discomfited silence.

"Oh Trevor, I am so sorry – I shouldn't have asked." For once Mary looked really embarrassed, not able to laugh this one off.

"No, I'm glad you did ask," said Trevor. I think he really meant it, which went some way to forgiving Mary for being so intrusive. He managed a weak smile across the table at her. "It's been hard not telling you all, not speaking about it. I am really glad you asked Mary." People murmured condolences and said that they understood, but, of course, no one did. I realised then, that what had been noticeable about Trevor was a blanket of dull impenetrable sadness wrapped tightly around him. Up until that moment, he had not let anyone prise it from him. For all her tactlessness, Mary had probably done the right thing.

The conversation was difficult to start up after that and, because we wanted to get back on to a safe topic, we started talking about Scarborough again. We mulled over the context and the data from the school's test results. At this school, the data looked as if the school might be doing well. Contrary to what you might have conjectured about a charming seaside town, parts of Scarborough were very poor. The school was situated on a large local authority estate, just north of the main town. The free school meals figure was high and many of the parents worked in seasonal, low paid jobs or were unemployed. This meant that the children were probably starting school with some disadvantage, but the end of year test results showed them to be in line with the national average. Henry said that, as far as he could see from a quick look, we had all made a good job of the pre-inspection work and he hoped that things would go much smoother than they had for Beswick Street.

Phil suddenly stood up and with a grin and mock solemnity proposed a toast:

"To an inspection with no fire, theft or flood," he said in a loud voice and we all raised our glasses. Then we laughed, and the lingering tension ebbed away. I looked admiringly at Phil. He was quite a special person – I bet he's a very good head, I thought and then looked across at Abby and saw she was smiling at Phil and he was smiling back at her almost, it seemed, as if there was no one else round the table. Just then Trevor, who was sitting across from me on the other side of the table, caught my attention. He was saying something I couldn't quite catch, so I got up and went round to where he was sitting.

"I was just wondering," he said, "if you and Abby would like to come in my car to Scarborough – save you driving, as we all live fairly close."

"Oh Trevor, that would be absolutely great. You know I

was just dreading the thought of driving all that way. I'm sure Abby will want to come as well. I'll ask her." I slipped back to my place, which was next to Abby and told her what Trevor had said. She smiled her agreement and mouthed, "yes please" to Trevor across the now noisy chatter and laughter.

PART THREE

INSPECTION OF HIGHAM PRIMARY SCHOOL, SCARBOROUGH

Chapter 12

Trevor turned the car sharply off Marine Parade away from the sea. Snaking up the steep cliff in low gear, we passed overhanging rocks and patches of seashore flora, large clumps of rustling sea holly and the coarse sea grasses that cling precariously to such terrain. Momentarily we were in the wilderness, a no-man's land between sea front and the civilisation of hotel habitation. This came into view again suddenly, as we crested the top of the slope. Facing us was a classic sweep of Edwardian seaside frontage. Trevor stopped the car in front of the Sheridan where we would be staying for the next four nights. It was one of several medium sized, reasonably priced hotels strung out along the cliff top parade of the North Shore, never as fashionable or as pricey as South Shore, the two divided by the Castle headland.

"Henry said we could stop at the front and unpack the cases, and then to go round the back where there's parking," said Trevor. Abby and I bestirred ourselves after the lassitude of the journey. As we opened the doors and got out, we felt the sharp buffet of wind tug at hair and clothes, and the smell and sound of the sea tingle the mind.

"I feel as if I'm on holiday." I laughed.

"I know it's strange, isn't it?" said Abby. "Listen to the gulls."

We lifted the lid of the boot and dragged out our cases and bags, including Trevor's. He came round to help but we shooed him back into the car, telling him that we could see to his stuff and he deserved to have something done for him. When we had everything on the pavement, Trevor drove off to park the car and we took the luggage up the short flight of stone steps and in through the revolving doors, a swanky start to the Sheridan. As I followed Abby up the stairs I still couldn't quite get out of my mind the thought that I was on some strange and exciting holiday.

We rang for reception, and a pleasant lady came out to help us register and to tell us that other members of our party had already arrived, and did we want to book an evening meal at eight thirty like the others. The Scarborough week had been organised slightly differently to that of Beswick Street. We had been asked by Henry to arrive around five o'clock on this Monday evening in order to go with him to the parents' meeting, to start at six thirty, so we could see how this was done. Legally, the parents' meeting had to take place before an inspection, but there was no specific ruling on how long before, although general practice was for the meeting to be done a week or so beforehand. In this instance, it was convenient to have it on the Monday. Because of this, the inspection was going to start on Tuesday and finish Friday night. We told the receptionist, who turned out to be Mrs.Henderson, the owner of the hotel, that we would definitely be having the evening meal and that this would be the case for Trevor. We indicated that Trevor was the third member of our party and that he would be in to register as soon as he had parked the car.

"His luggage will be perfectly safe here, you can go on up to your rooms and I will sort out Mr. Barnes when he arrives," she suggested helpfully. "Mr. Calderbank asked me to tell you that he would like you to meet in the lounge, at five thirty. Our lounge is situated on the first floor." We both checked our watches – there was less than twenty minutes before the meeting so we decided it was best to find our rooms and settle in as quickly as possible and leave Trevor to Mrs. Henderson's capable care. There was no lift and there did not appear to be a porter or such like, so we struggled up the stairs with our suitcases first, leaving the boxes and bags with files in the hall for a second ascent. The Sheridan appeared clean and pleasant, but more suited to a holiday stay than accommodating those needing to work.

The large key with an owl fob that Mrs. Henderson had handed to me informed me that I was in room number 29. This was situated up the first wide flight of stairs, a turn to the left, then up two steps and along another short corridor, to take the second very narrow flight of steps to the third floor. By the time I reached No 29 my arm carrying the suitcase felt as if it had been wrenched out of its socket. The painful thought occurred that I would have to do the stairs again carrying the rest of my belongings.

The key stuck in the lock and needed several jiggles to open it. The opened door revealed a room, decorated in a style best described as eighties boudoir. My senses swirled with the dark pink swirls on the carpet and the plump bed with flower bedecked bedspread and little satin cushions, small lampshades with twirly tassels, and a busy flowered wallpaper, with an even busier border. Several pictures of bucolic scenes hung in any space that could conceivably be thought of as empty. Besides a wardrobe and a very small chair, a spindly-legged dressing table was the only other piece of furniture in the room. It must have been a squeeze to get even these meagre items of furniture into the room. The obligatory hotel tray with kettle and tea making paraphernalia took up most of the surface space of the small dressing table. Where was I going to work?

I was about to be introduced to the writing-on-the-bed technique that would, over the next few years, become a finely honed inspection skill. Foreign correspondents on national daily papers learn to write up reports, under fire and in tight corners, sleeping in every type of hotel in outlandish spots all over the globe. In our own modest way, British Ofsted inspectors broke boundaries regarding working in tight corners. We learnt to balance files, and later laptops, on knees while sandwiched between bed and wardrobe, entering data, compiling reports and even holding meetings in whatever version of Fawlty Towers we found ourselves. There were many categories of B&B, hotel and guest-house. The Sheridan fell into the category of overpoweringly twee (I was to meet with worse).

The en-suite was not much more than a cupboard without a door. It had a toilet with a plastic seat that managed to deliver a sharp nip if you sat on it hastily, a tiny wash hand basin and a plastic coated shower cubicle. There was no more than half a hand span between each facility.

After I had got all my things up to the room, I made use of the miniscule en-suite, had a quick wash and issued forth to find the others in the lounge.

"Rooms OK?" asked Henry as we sat round in the comfortable chintz covered armchairs.

"Oh absolutely fine," we all murmured.

"I'm not sure which bunch of flowers will smother me first, though," said Nigel, more truthful than the rest of us.

Pink not your colour then?" asked John.

"Absolutely, my favourite. Can't you tell?" Nigel lisped, and did one of those limp wrist gestures.

Although Nigel was not married, we had no suspicions that he might be gay, although Mary had floated this idea during the first week. Since we had been working in Manchester, we had all met the undeniably gorgeous girl he lived with because she sometimes took the opportunity to come with him from Blackpool to do some shopping in Manchester. She would appear at the end of the afternoon, looking enviably like a footballer's wife, happily smiling, with a clutch of store carrier bags, just as we were rumpled and creased from a day's work. Nigel had told Phil about his whirlwind romance. It was the classic headteacher, or in this case deputy headteacher, liaison with the newly appointed nursery nurse. Of course, it was not the scandal it sometimes is because Nigel wasn't married. Inevitably though, it had caused raised eyebrows because of the age difference. Because of this the young lady had left the school and was currently not working.

"She does a lot of my admin work," Nigel had said which seemed a bit over the top to us, but then Nigel had a number of other interests besides doing inspections. One of these was buying and selling property – canny Nigel was in there at the beginning of the property boom.

"Hmm well, you'll soon be too busy to notice wallpaper." Henry laughed, "and besides don't knock flowers – it could have been a herd of elephants charging across your walls, now that really does get to you."

"Oh Lincoln you mean," John said. " And that huge stuffed bear on the landing!" They both chortled. We were getting used to previous inspection reminiscences between John and Henry.

Henry had called the meeting mainly to tell us how to get to the school. We learnt that it was not more than a ten minute drive from the hotel. He then went on to explain that he was going to lead the meeting. He would introduce Nigel as the lead inspector to the parents; he, Nigel and John would sit at the front, with John's main job being to take the minutes. We would all sit with the parents and have nothing to do but observe.

"Do butt in John if you see me getting side-tracked too much or if I leave anything out."

"How can you doubt it?" John replied.

"Do you think there will be many parents?" asked Abby.

"The head seemed to think so," Nigel replied. Nigel had arrived in Scarborough at mid-day, and had already been to the school and met the headteacher.

"You can never tell, but it is a friendly school and I think they have a good relationship with the parents," said Henry.

We arrived at the school with plenty of time to spare. The headteacher, Mr. Roberts was a large, good-looking man with a warm, open manner and friendly smile. He showed us to the school hall which was already filling up with parents. There was a buzz of voices and some joking going on about not sitting in the front seats. Mr. Roberts went over and cajoled some parents into moving forward so that there wouldn't be a barrier of empty chairs. We sat in a row to one side. I looked round at the audience. They had mostly come in pairs but there were also slightly larger groups with what must have been grandparents. You could tell that there was not much money to spare; jackets, shoes and other clothing well-worn for some and most originating from the lower end chain stores or from market stalls. One or two individuals could be described as scruffy. They all looked a little long-suffering, as if giving up an hour or two of television was a sacrifice. Had they been persuaded to come by the charismatic personality of the head or were they curious about these 'government people'?

Henry started the meeting on the dot of six thirty. Nearly all the chairs were taken – there must have been at least fifty people in the audience. (We learnt later that this was a good attendance.) Henry spoke in his perfectly modulated BBC tones, not appearing to make any concessions for his mostly working class audience. The surprising thing was that, by some mysterious means, he immediately connected with these parents. Within a few minutes of him starting to speak, there were ripples of laughter and expressions changing on men's faces from 'I've only come 'cos the missus nagged me', to 'eh this bloke's all right'. The women all looked very pleased as if they were personally responsible that the front of house act was turning out as good as they had said it would.

There were several reasons Henry went down so well. Firstly he used simple, easily understood expressions, translating the wording of the agenda into plain English so that no one should be in any doubt as to what he was talking about. For example, instead of asking them if they thought their child was making enough progress in say English, which is what it said on the agenda. He said:

"Now what about reading and writing? Do you think your child's getting on OK? Do they like reading? Are they keen to read to you?"

Then he quickly got the audience laughing by making John, Nigel, the headteacher and even the staff of the school the butt of jokes or humorous remarks. There was whiff of conspiracy when he told them how the headteacher was not allowed to attend the meeting.

"He's probably pacing up and down now worrying that you are going to tell me about him siphoning off school funds to pay for that trip of his to Barbados." Of course, no one thought he meant it, but it was nice to laugh at the thought and to think that a gentleman from London could make jokes with them about someone as important as the headteacher.

John's fondness for checking out toilets, was used to good advantage and raised guffaws of laughter. Nigel was described as a raw recruit, and a throw-away comment about how he could not imagine why any one should want to do the thankless, badly paid task of leading an inspection, made inspection seem less prestigious, similar almost in drudgery to the jobs that many of them did. Most importantly, though, Henry made himself the subject of jokes or anecdotes. He referred to his mis-deeds as a parent; dodging the job of hearing his child read, sending his daughter off to school with nothing in her lunch box because of absent mindedness, not wanting to miss a football match on tele in order to attend parents' evening – all designed to make them think – 'He understands. He's just like us'

When he got to serious questions, such as whether there was any bullying in the school, he completely changed the tone of the meeting. He went quiet for a few moments and then he asked the question very simply and directly. "Has your child been bullied in school?" By this time, he had everyone's confidence and those with concerns were not afraid to speak up. He obviously cared about the real worries that parents had. In case there was a danger of anyone not wanting to give their opinion, because of shyness in front of others, he said "Why don't you tell me about that after the meeting? I will stay for a while and anyone can tell me whatever in complete confidence."

None of us had been expecting Henry to be quite as good as he was, or to find the parents' meeting as interesting as it was. We felt as if we were getting a very privileged in-sight into the school already. These parents were obviously mostly very happy with their school. The teachers were liked, and the headteacher seemed very popular, a big improvement on the chap before was what one parent said. At the start of the meeting, as part of the introduction Henry had asked parents not to identify individual teachers. But, despite this exhortation, it was pretty obvious that there was one, possibly two teachers, in the Juniors that parents did not like as much as the others. One man even went so far as to refer to one of the staff as a 'bully,' and was going to say more, but Henry had stopped him, politely reminding him that individuals should not be identified.

I had made a lot of notes about English as the parents had explained how reading books were sent home, how the library was organised and how often spellings were given out for children to learn. As the raw recruits Henry had spoken about, we began to see how much the parents' meeting could tell you about a school. Throughout the meeting Abby, Mary and myself, had shared whispered comments, mostly to the effect that we hoped that we would be able to lead a meeting as well as Henry. Now, as we joined the parents making our way out into the night, we heard snatches of conversation: "Who'd a thought that a chap like that could crack 'em jokes – I think this inspection is a right good thing – they seem all right this lot from London." I smiled wryly at the automatic placing of anyone who spoke like Henry as being from London.

As we mingled with the parents of Higham, we couldn't help feeling a sudden and renewed sense of responsibility as inspectors – not to let these people down who had faith that we would check up on the things it was impossible for them to check, on behalf of their children.

Chapter 13

Steven clicked the tele on and threw the remote up in a curling arc as he crash landed on to the settee, all in one unbroken movement. Crash landing was one of his specialties; it was falling backwards without bending your legs – and it was his favourite way of sitting down. The black fake leather of the settee felt really cold, but he didn't bother, he didn't mind cold. It didn't register much. He got up a minute or two later and plummeted into the armchair where the remote had landed, wriggling around until his hand came in contact with it. He switched channels, nothing on there. Oh well might as well watch Super Heroes, little kids stuff but anyway. He flicked back to the original channel. There was a huge lizard writhing about on the screen thrashing its tail at the diminutive 'Hero'. Megan's sleepy figure stood in front of him.

"I want some breakfast Steve."

"Git it yerself."

"I can't."

"Yer can."

"I can't"

"Yer can."

They did this ten, maybe twenty times, just like they did every morning and then Steven got up and went into the kitchen and poured rice crispies into a bowl for his six-year-old sister, just like he did every morning. A steady stream of crispies missed the bowl and sprayed on to the table. He went to the fridge and picked up the only thing in there, a half carton of milk. This time, he poured it carefully. He needed to watch it or there wouldn't be enough for him.

At six Megan knew a lot of things. For instance, she knew, unlike probably anyone else in the world, that Steven would do anything for her. She loved him unconditionally the way that Prince loved him. At the moment, Prince was snuffling at the back door and she knew Steve was going to let him in.

"Don't let him in." begged Megan. Steven grinned and let

the dog in. He was wagging his tail nearly off his trim thick-set bull terrier behind, snuffling and licking Megan's bare legs. She squealed and got up on to the table where she sat down with her legs safely crossed out of the reach of Prince, crunching on the scattered crispies. She picked up her bowl and started munching. Steven got his own bowl of cereal, the rice crispie spillage hitting the floor this time. Prince snuffled it up in seconds. Steven poured in the milk until the carton was empty. Serve them right he thought. His Mum and her current boyfriend would get up at lunch-time and grumble about there being no milk for a cup of tea. Serve 'em right – lazy bastards. Ever since this Jason bloke had moved in, his Mam had gone right off. She used to get up and make them breakfast but Jason had said that she didn't need to do that, that Steven was old enough to do it. True he gave him a few quid at the end of the week – 'Yer wages son, you've earned it' is what he said when he gave him a fiver perhaps, but sometimes he forgot and he didn't like being reminded. Anyway, it wasn't right. His Mam should do it. It wasn't fair on Megan. And he did plenty of other jobs for that measly fiver.

Megan said, "Please Steven put Prince out –Yer know I can't get ready for school wi' 'im licking me." Steven opened the back door and booted Prince out into the back yard again. There wasn't much time to spare – they couldn't be late. He hated school but he was never late – never away and never late. Ever since he was six, he'd won attendance awards at the end of the year and his Gran always took him into Leeds for a day out – shopping for new trainers, taking him to MacDonalds, and making a fuss of him. It was the best day of the year, almost better than Christmas. His Gran did it, she told him, because his Mum never went to school and Gran had nearly got sent to prison over it. Anyway he liked to make his Gran proud of him. She was the best person in his family. Grandad came second, way behind Gran. But he wasn't bad, granddad, he could drive a car and sometimes took them places, when he wasn't in the bookies that is.

Megan went upstairs and tiptoed into her mother's room looking at the two mounds in Mam's bed. She rooted around for the hairbrush, panicking because she couldn't find it until her bare foot came in contact with it, mercifully with the bristles downwards. Just the same it made her wince. She picked it up and went to the bathroom mirror to brush her hair. It always got a lot of tangles in the night. It was thin hair and it looked ratty when it wasn't brushed. When her Mam had first stopped getting up, she used to go to school without brushing it and a couple of the kids had teased her. "Can't yer Mam afford a hairbrush, Megan?" they had jeered. She scrambled into her school shirt, skirt and cardigan that she had left on her bed the night before. Her socks were on the floor. Steven came out of his room and they both went downstairs quietly although there was probably not much danger of disturbing the sleeping mounds.

"Ready?" he asked.

"I've not got me shoes."

"Well get 'em." Then Steven saw them sticking out from under the armchair. He kicked them across the room to her and she squeezed her feet in without undoing the straps. Megan really, really wanted a new pair of shoes and she had been hoping to persuade Gran to buy her some, but Gran hadn't been around for a while; it had been since Jason had moved in. Megan put two and two together – it wasn't hard. She went into the kitchen and picked up her reading book where she had left it the night before. She always put it in something called the veg rack. It was four wire trays joined at the side by thin metal strips – potatoes were sometimes put in the bottom tray, but ever since she could remember Megan had never seen vegetables in it. Mam put anything she thought vaguely important in there like letters from the council. Megan put her reading book in there every night. She was a good reader.

On the way to school Megan said. "Steve, why don't yer like school ?"

"I 'ate school."

"Why?"

"Because Mrs. Mason thinks I'm stupid, that's why. I'm not stupid. I just have trouble with words." Steven glanced down at the reading book in Megan's hand. Reading made him feel bad as if something was really strange about him.

Even so, he was pleased, even a bit proud, that Megan could read so well. At least they couldn't say the whole family was thick, like the Dawson's. The Dawson's really were thick, like Mandy Dawson who sat on his table and thought Mrs. Mason was nice, even though she never said a kind word to her.

"I hate 'er. I wish she'd die."

Steven had said this about Mrs. Mason before and Megan was not fazed. She just sighed and thought to herself that she hated Mrs. Mason as well, but she wished Steven wouldn't say the bit about her dying.

Tuesday dawned chilly and damp. There was an unpleasant mizzle of rain. Even on such a dull day, Higham Junior and Infant School appeared much more inviting than Beswick Street. A one-story building circa 1960, it was surrounded by fields and gardens. The car park was roomy and set among a few graceful ash trees, which still had most of their golden yellow leaves hanging from branches like limp washing. There were well-maintained flower borders, paths were swept and sensible notices told you the name of the school and where to find the main entrance.

The entrance hall opened out from a small vestibule into a large rectangular communal space. As soon as you entered, your attention was attracted by the display, a celebration of sea and shore, in pictures of many different genres. There were hugely enlarged photographs of sandcastles built by the Reception class on a summer visit to the beach; pencil studies of sea birds by Year 4 with much better shading and texture than children usually manage; fabric designs by Year 6 using shell motifs for block prints; and chunky collage pictures of black fishing boats tossing on wavy seas by Year 1. I felt a twinge of envy that Mary was inspecting art. If this display was anything to go by, art must be a strength.

While we were waiting in the hall, Nigel went to find the headteacher. When Mr. Roberts appeared with Nigel a few minutes later, he apologised for not being there to welcome us but he had had to help with a crisis with computers in Year 3. Nigel commiserated and said how often he had had to do a similar job. It was easy to see that these two were going to get along. Mr. Roberts showed us to the inspection base, a pleasant room that was generally used for interviews. We found that we had been made very comfortable; there were plenty of chairs and tables and a well-stocked trolley with coffee, tea, juice, a pile of tempting biscuits and a home-made cake from one of the parents. We all secretly thought that perhaps John's theory about judging the quality of a school by the quality of its hospitality might just hold true.

Nigel was in a very good mood: his talents had been recognized! Not only was he the first in our group to be leading an inspection, but everything was looking as if we were in a good school. Strangely, he seemed to be appropriating the success of the school as his own. He said that he wanted to remind us that the school had done well in the tests last year, especially in English. This would probably be backed up by what we saw in lessons and in the children's books. We all nodded, though not quite sure of what he was meaning. Was he trying to tell us to let the school's success in their tests affect the way we looked at their teaching?

"Jane, I think you'll agree it was a very commendable effort, their results in English last year."

"Yes Nigel," I agreed dutifully, "very commendable," though I thought it a strange expression to use. I wasn't sure we should be commending them prior to an inspection – surely you did that afterwards when, or if, everything had turned out well?

Next he told us of a little innovation he was introducing.

Instead of trailing round the school and meeting with teachers in their classrooms in an ad hoc way, as we had done at Beswick Street, he had organised with the headteacher that there should be a short meeting with the staff on the first day of the inspection. This would be more civilised – we could all introduce ourselves and staff would know who we were. There were murmurs of approval for this idea and Nigel looked pleased.The meeting was due to start in a couple of minutes, so accordingly we set off to find the staff-room. When we got there, we filed in through the door and stood about trying to look friendly and not out of place. Although Nigel had said we would introduce ourselves, in practice he did it for us. His high-pitched squeaky voice informed the assembled teachers our names, our backgrounds and our inspection responsibilities. As a consequence, he left us with very little to say but we all somehow managed a bland, fatuous remark about the weather, the pleasantness of the building or the beauties of Scarborough. Despite this, we were impressed with Nigel's innovation and could see that the teachers liked him. He had made quite a hit, and he rounded it all off with a few jokes at our expense, mentioning my forgetfulness, 'would they return anything I left in their classroom?' and not to confuse Phil with Terry Wogan, referring, of course to his Irish brogue.

The morning started well for me with a good lesson in Year 2 and I was pleased that the observation form I produced was readable. By play time, the rain had stopped so I decided to walk round the playground to gather evidence for my aspect on behaviour and attitudes. The children all seemed to play well with each other and I couldn't spot any lost or lonely ones. The headteacher had introduced a 'friendship bench', a place where anyone could go if they had no one to play with. It was looked after by two prefects, a boy and a girl from Year 6 who took it in turns with others in their class. On the ground in front of the bench there was a large, yellow smiley face and the two prefects wore badges with the same smiley face. I asked them if they thought it was a good idea and if they had any children come to the bench.

"Oh yes, it's used a lot especially at the beginning of the term," said the girl.

"It's definitely a good idea," said the boy.

"Do you begrudge the time you spend here – wouldn't you rather be playing with your friends?"

"No, we like it," they both said, and I was sure they meant it.

The rest of the day went well. The only grade I gave was three and at the end of the day it appeared that that had been the case for most people. There had been one or two fours and Nigel had given an excellent, a one. It was for an IT lesson, which amazed us.

After school, we were to meet with the subject co-ordinators. These meetings were an important part of the inspection process. Co-ordinators worried about them and, as this was my first with a co-ordinator as important as English, I worried too. I had drawn up a list of questions, using the framework as guidance, but I was anxious that I would get sidetracked, or forget to ask something important. My English co-ordinator was a pleasant, capable young girl in her late twenties called Hillary. I had watched her lesson earlier in the day – it had been very competent if a little uninspiring.

Hilary had brought with her a large, fat file, labeled, segmented and covering every aspect of the curriculum for English. She asked me if I wished to see the file and, of course, I said that I did. It was far too lengthy to read through there and then so I said I would take it away and look through it in the evening. She looked gratified, and I knew she had probably spent hours getting it immaculate for just such an occasion as this.

I went through my list of questions, answers to which would help me understand how effectively she managed the subject. The questions covered such things such as the length of her tenure as English co–ordinator, what assessment procedures the school used, staff training and so on. She answered confidently on all questions until I asked the question about monitoring.

"What do you mean by monitoring?" She looked genuinely puzzled.

"Well do you monitor the quality of teaching, for example," I said. Now she looked horrified.

"Do you mean going in to other peoples' classrooms and watching them?" She made it sound as if I was suggesting some sexual perversion.

"Well, yes – you could do that, but there are other ways of monitoring the quality of teaching – you could, for instance, look at teachers' planning. As I spoke, I could feel the atmosphere of the meeting change from bonhomie to cool antagonism. Hilary became defensive: our very short-lived friendship summarily terminated.

"Mr. Roberts takes in everyone's planning at the beginning of term. It's his responsibility to look at planning." There was an awkward pause. "We don't need to check up on each other in this school. We work as a team. We share ideas and anyone who wants any help only has to ask." Hilary was putting the case for accountability by consensus. I was to hear it many times in the coming years. I wanted to say, 'I know what you mean' – to agree that everything to do with checking up on others (given the grand name of monitoring) was a pain. But how could I say that? Where would it leave my job? And in truth, such cosy arrangements only work in small schools, very small schools, as events at Higham were soon to prove.

I threw her a life-line. "Perhaps you look at children's work sometimes?"

"From other classes?"

"Yes."

"No, I don't, but… perhaps it is something we could do." The defensiveness was beginning to veer towards curiosity, and I could almost hear her thinking – 'Is this what other schools do?'

I accepted the small concession and followed up with: "it's a good way to start and nobody need feel that you are being pushy." I decided to introduce the idea of greater authority: "you are after all responsible for ensuring that the National Curriculum is fully delivered."

"Yes, I can see that." Hilary was clever. She knew that one day she would move on with her career and a good account of her subject management in an Ofsted report would do her no harm. We ended up on friendly enough terms, although I could still sense some coolness – was it fear? I picked up the weighty file, and jocularly praised its immensity, although my heart sank at the thought of wading through it later that evening.

When I got back to the inspection base, Abby, Phil and Trevor were all fussing round the tea and coffee. Mary and Nigel were still in their meetings.

"How did yours go?" asked Phil.

"It went very well – a really nice girl, very well organised," I replied, " but…

"Doesn't do any monitoring," supplied Phil.

"That's right – no monitoring," I agreed.

"Same for all of us," said Trevor.

"Nigel is going to have to admit that something in his lovely school needs improving, and I don't think he is going to like that," Abby said, a small smile quivering round the edges of her mouth.

"Oh you don't say?" said Phil. "Why he's acting like we've

landed in Utopia. IT absolutely blooming marvelous!" Phil accompanied his remark with a 'pssh' noise.

"Isn't it as good as he says?" I asked.

"Oh Jane you are such an innocent – I don't know how you are going to survive in this game," said Abby. "Have you seen anyone using IT in their lesson?"

"Well, no, but surely Nigel wouldn't make it up, about it being good I mean?"

"No not make it up – just look at it through rose-coloured glasses," said Phil. "Our laddo, Nigel has quickly sussed out that if everything in the garden is lovely, then, for hisself as lead inspector, there's quite a bit less work, and certainly less harassment from that 'nice' headmaster, Mr. Roberts." Phil stopped talking just as there were sounds of someone entering the room. It was John, very shortly followed by Mary, then Arthur and Nigel, and we all settled ourselves down round the table, files open ready for the evening meeting.

Nigel opened the meeting by thanking us all for the hard work that day, which was patronising, but there was nothing to do but smile and acknowledge his kind remarks. He went on to sum up as he termed it 'a very successful first day for the school.' Despite our scepticism, it was true that everything seemed to be going well, and what did it matter if Nigel was over-egging it a little?

We were not going to discuss leadership and management that evening so the lack of monitoring did not come up and the only person who found anything to detract from Nigel's eulogies about the school turned out to be John who said that there were some issues with care. Nigel did not look at all happy at this. John looked down at his notes and then efficiently reeled off his list of concerns.

"There's been no training for the lunch-time staff; there is no record of any playtime falls or other accidents; the staff are very lackadaisical with the registers, sometimes they come back by ten o'clock and sometimes they don't," he said, "and I've still a few things to check out."

"Well, are you saying that care might be unsatisfactory?" There was heavy sarcasm in Nigel's voice, and he went on angrily, not giving John a chance to reply, "because, I don't see how that can be when children are clearly very happy in the school and parents are happy with the care their children receive. According to the framework, these are the most important criteria."

John sighed and shook his head as if not really believing what he had just heard. "You've jumped the gun entirely lad." He spoke very quietly, the ultimate professional. "I'm not suggesting for a minute care is unsatisfactory. I am just saying that I have some concerns about one or two matters that come under care, and rather leaving them to the last day of the inspection, maybe you had better just broach them with the head tomorrow."

"That would be the best course of action, Nigel," Henry said.

At this, Nigel looked a bit sheepish and backtracked. "Oh I see – I see John what you mean, just some minor matters, perhaps you would let me have a list."

"It's all on the observation form."

Nigel hastily closed the meeting after that and we all thankfully piled into the cars to go back to the hotel. I was amazed at how Nigel was handling the inspection. It seemed so simple and straightforward and yet his over-eagerness to please the school, which was so transparent, was leading him to make mistakes.

Chapter 14

On Wednesday the weather had changed; the sky was clear in places and every now and again the sun broke through. A healthy sea breeze tugged at our clothing. "Lovely day," we remarked to staff as we made our way down the corridor to the inspection base.

I was in the Reception class in the morning. It was a happy experience with children fully engaged in their activities. A huge 'beanstalk' wound its way up to the ceiling in the centre of the room and children tied messages to the leaves to tell Jack to take care and to watch out for the giant. There were lots of activities to develop talk, independent writing and a love of stories. I gave the lesson a two (very good), and then wondered whether I was being stingy, not giving a one, but the nursery nurse had not been as good as the teacher at encouraging the children to write, so I kept at a two. I had a coffee at break time and chatted to Abby who had done an English lesson for me in Year 4. She said that it was good and that the teacher, who was newly qualified, was doing very well for someone so inexperienced. Once again, everything in the school was looking rosy and Nigel was getting happier with every good grade that came in.

After play, I set off to a Mrs. Mason's class. It was a mixed age group with 20 Year 5 children and 12 Year 4's. The headteacher had told Nigel that there were some of the less able Year 5's in this class who needed to go a little more slowly than the others in their year group; they would benefit from doing some Year 4 work again. I arrived at the classroom just as the children were lining up outside the door. They still had that after-play-on-a-windy-day, fresh air look about them with tousled hair, bright smiles and red cheeks from running strenuously. In the line, one or two whispered a fleeting word to a friend, while some pulled up socks, or wriggled with their jumpers and girls flicked their hair or pulled hair fasteners tighter.

"Come along you can do better than this," exhorted Mrs. Mason, her voice so loud and booming it seemed to bounce off the corridor walls. It took me completely by surprise and I almost jumped to attention like the children. Surely she didn't need to use quite such loud tones?

"Some of you don't look ready for work at all. I want the very best from you today. Are you listening..." a prolonged pause, mid-way through the question and then in an even louder voice, "Steven?" A boy lifted his head to look at her, but otherwise gave no response – no doubt the naughtiest boy in the class, reminded straightaway that this was his status. There was a general straightening of backs and, (did I imagine it?) dulling of eyes. When satisfied that the line was 'ready for work', Mrs. Mason opened the class door and they all filed in to take their seats.

The teacher walked over to the board and wrote on it, 'Off on holiday'. The children stared at these words in complete silence. I was expecting an explanation of what they were going to learn, or at least what they were going to do in the coming lesson, but the next thing the teacher said was, "Marianne and Adam, give out 'Looking at Texts' to everyone."

Marianne and Adam got up quickly and went over to a pile of books on a shelf. They split them into two halves, and set about placing one on each desk in front of a child, whereupon the recipient said 'thank you'. While this was in progress, Mrs. Mason stared across the class not speaking, her hands tightly folded in front of her. She was a woman of around forty or so with a pleasant face and attractive, red-brown hair. A very noticeable thing about her was her rather ruddy complexion which made her look as if she was a country person, which I later found out she was – never happier than striding out across the moors, but as the lesson was soon to show, not really happy in a room full of nine-year-olds

So far, her management of children appeared a well-oiled machine and there was no waste of time, but somehow I began to feel uneasy. My mind flicked back to the Year 5 class at Beswick Street where behaviour had been very good, but not this sterile straightjacket. I wrote down a sentence to the effect that the lesson started promptly and all children were behaving very well. As Marianne came passed me, she offered me a book which I took with a 'thank you' like the children. I looked across the room to see where Steven was sitting. He was on a table right in front of Mrs. Mason. Besides him sat a slightly plump little girl with her hair done in an old-fashioned style of shiny fringe and bunches. She had a soft, angelic face. She stared up at Mrs. Mason as if she was about to hear the words of a prophet.

There was no welcome back to the class or other similar pleasantries from the teacher. Instead she started briskly with; "Open your books at page 73." When the children had all accomplished this, she continued: "as you can see, the piece we are going to read today is called 'Off on Holiday'. I want you *all* to follow carefully." There was heavy emphasis on the word 'all', and a pause while she scanned the room so that the children were quite clear that she meant all of them. When she was quite satisfied that this simple commandment had been understood, she said, "Charlotte would you start us off?"

The inspector chair had been placed near the back of the room so I was not very far away from Charlotte who was obviously seated on a table of able pupils. The teacher's system of seating was less able at the front, grading to most able at the back. Charlotte started to read in a clear, loud and confident voice. She was definitely a good reader. I could see that all those on her table were following the text with their eyes, and I guessed that they could no doubt read as competently as Charlotte, though not necessarily with her very clear diction. I got up very quietly; conscious that I was the only person besides Charlotte making any noise whatsoever. I moved cautiously down to the middle of the room in order to see how the children on the three tables there were keeping to Mrs. Mason's request to follow the text. Not that I thought there was any great intrinsic worth in this exercise, but simply because it was part of her very minimal planning for the lesson. Marianne and Adam sat at one of these tables. I could see that most of the children appeared to be following reasonably well, although some used a finger to keep them on track. A few were not being quite so diligent, occupied with thoughts of their own, their eyes strayed to the windows or down at some small object in their lap.

Suddenly, I noticed that Mrs. M. had left her post at the front and was also moving round the room checking on children. She was working her way up the opposite side to myself, and I wondered if she had taken her cue from me. I was glad she had left the front as now I could make my way to these tables (the last thing I wanted to do was collide with her on my way round the classroom). After checking all the children on the table near me, I headed towards Steven's table, but before I could get there a loud; "Stop right there Charlotte," boomed out across the room. "I would like you all to put your finger on the word Charlotte has just read."

The word Charlotte had finished on before the blast was 'Montgomery', the name of the dog belonging to the family who, the text had informed us, were in the throes of packing up to go on holiday. Montgomery, named after a famous British General (again information available in the text), was very fond of socks and he had just pinched a pair from the dad's suitcase and run off out into the garden pursued by Mum and children. Mrs. M.'s class had clearly enjoyed this episode and quite a few had stopped the exercise of following to enjoy more fully Charlotte's lively rendition. However, most of those on the back tables quickly spotted where they were supposed to be, and fastened a forefinger to the appropriate word as if it had been glued there.

Those on the middle tables took a bit longer to get it right, and some needed the help of a friendly neighbour, while one or two plonked it down without a great deal of concern as to whether they were right or wrong, gambling on not being the one picked by Mrs.M to call out the word. They were probably right in their gamble as it was pretty obvious that Mrs. M. was heading back towards the Steven table. She arrived there just after I did, and I realized with consternation that it was propably my decision to head in that direction that had prompted her checking up procedure. It only took a quick glance to show that the children on this table were all at sixes and sevens with the matter of identifying the right word. They hadn't a clue, but they made a stab at it nonetheless; all but Steven and the dreamy girl were pointing to a word of some sort. Steven was clearly panicking, and the more he panicked, the more he found it almost impossible to put his finger on a word and keep it there.

"You don't know do you Steven?" said Mrs. M. triumphantly, as if catching him out was equivalent to getting the answer right on Mastermind. Steven didn't say anything, but kept his eyes fixed on the page in front of him. For a while Mrs. M. also said nothing and so there was silence in the room. Then she let out a sigh as if greatly troubled and said, "Well I suppose that is no surprise. Adrian, what was the word Charlotte finished on?"

"Montgomery," replied Adrian, one of the boys who sat on Charlotte's table.

"And who, or what is Montgomery, Adrian?" asked Mrs. M.

"The family dog, Mrs. Mason."

"Thank you Adrian." There was another long silence while Mrs. M. seemed to be dwelling on the great imponderables of life, and then she let out a sigh, shook her head and said, "Steven, how many times have I told you to follow the text while we are reading?" Steven did not answer. By this time I was sitting back in the inspector chair. Mrs. M. repeated the question and continued to look meaningfully at Steven.

One of the boys on the 'clever clogs' table whispered under his breath, "Go for it Steven, pick a number – anything over fifty will do, say 53 – *she* doesn't know."

"Nah more like 153," said the wit sitting next to him.

They were both rewarded by a fleeting smile from Charlotte who, besides being a good reader, was a pretty girl with long golden brown hair. The teacher gave up on the question, cleared her throat and then said, "Danielle, will you continue please." Danielle read well, though not as well as Charlotte. At times her voice became too quiet and there were exhortations to 'read up' and another rhetorical question. "How often have I told you to speak up Danielle? You are not making the most of the passage."

I did not move from my chair, and was glad when, 24 minutes after the start of the lesson, Mrs. Mason gave the instruction for reading to stop and for the children to start on their written work.

"Remember, I want your best handwriting at all times. Put the date and the number of the exercise. You are answering questions about the text we have just read. Those of you who have been listening will find it easy. BUT, I DO NOT WANT YOU TO COPY OUT THE QUESTION." All of Mrs. Mason's commands were delivered at full throttle, but this last one came out so loudly, I thought that it must have been meant for the entire school.

Just then, there was a timid knock on the door and Mrs. M. pointed to a child who got up to open the door.

"Mrs. Mason, it's time for your readers." The woman, who was a member of the support staff, looked almost as in awe of Mrs. Mason as the children.

"Right, Mrs. Watson – who do you want?"

"I would like David Jones and Steven Parker, Mandy read to me yesterday and so did Carl."

"Well, I don't need to know that, Mrs. Watson – it's up to you to keep track."

The anger that I had begun to feel in this lesson was given sudden impetus at this quite uncalled for rudeness to another staff member. Mrs. Mason clearly thought of classroom assistants as lower orders. I had, by this time, only filled half of the form, intending to fill the rest with comments about how the children carried out their tasks, but now I wrote: 'Lesson very badly planned, and support staff not used well.' And then I put a 6 (poor) in the quality of teaching box. It gave me an undeniable feeling of satisfaction, as if I had righted wrongs.

Mrs. Mason told David and Steven to get their reading books and go with Mrs. Watson. Then she told the class who were waiting in suspended animation to get on with their work. The tasks, in fact, turned out to be marginally better than the first part of the lesson. Those in the top and middle groups answered questions from the exercise book; the bottom group, which comprised the six remaining children on Steven's table, had cards, which presumably Mrs. Mason had made. These asked similar questions to those in the book but were simplified to just a few words per question. Most of this lower group coped with them, slowly and laboriously writing out their answers. The exception was Mandy, the girl with the angelic face and bunches who sat next to Steven. She wrote the date from the blackboard and then copied out the question but obviously did not know what the words said.

"Hello, Mandy," I said. "Do you mind if I look at your

work?" She smiled at me happily and nodded. After looking quickly through her book, I could see that most of her work was copied. When I asked her to read what some of the sentences said, she struggled to read more than one or two of the words that she had written only a few days before.

I went to ask Mrs. Mason if I could see Mandy's individual education plan, something a child with such marked needs should have. Mrs. Mason had it all right. As she passed it to me, she whispered behind the sheets of paper that made up the plan: "She shouldn't be in this class at all – she's not even up to Year 3 work. I have told Mr. Roberts."

Although Mrs. Mason was quick to produce the plan for me to read, unfortunately she had not taken a scrap of notice of it when planning work for Mandy, which meant that the plan was more or less useless. Mandy was indeed very behind for her age. She needed to be doing work at the level of a six-year-old. What had she been doing trying to follow a piece of reading suitable for a child in Year 4 or 5, a child of Charlotte's obvious level of intelligence?

After spending about ten minutes watching the children work, I noted down that they all worked diligently, and gave Mrs. Mason credit for this industriousness, even though it might be said to lack eagerness. I wrote several sentences about the lack of progress Mandy was making because the work was much too difficult for her, and I had just decided to leave when I spotted the two wits up on the clever clogs table surreptitiously swapping collectable cards of some sort. I quickly backtracked up to their table and saw that they had finished. Their work was accurate and very neat; you didn't need to be a genius to work out that they had not been challenged by it at all.

As soon as I left the room, I felt a sinking feeling at having to tell Nigel that I had seen, not just an unsatisfactory lesson, but one that I had graded with a six, in other words a poor lesson.

"A six, Jane, a SIX !" Nigel had changed from his usual pallor to a bright red. "You've given a six! Who to, who to?"

"Mrs. Mason in the Year 4 and 5 class," I said.

Before showing the offending form to Nigel, I had spent a little while in a quiet corner, going through what I had written. I had been surprised how tidy it was. I had begun to think that it was much easier to write up a good lesson observation than one that was not so good, but this one had been straight forward. I surmised that it must have been because it was awful right from the start and there had been little agonising over my choice of words. I had not doubted for a minute that I was right to grade it 'poor'. But now that I was showing it to Nigel doubts were creeping in. I had had some trouble finding Nigel. I had finally tracked him down during the lunch-time Year 6 computer club, talking to the IT co-ordinator in a small bay that had a bank of computers. I had quietly approached the two men, and waited for some minutes before Nigel had turned to me so that I could tell him that I needed to speak to him urgently. He had looked a little aggrieved and then seeing the serious expression on my face, raised his eyes upwards as if to say, 'oh my goodness, there are so many important matters for me to attend to' and said that he would be in the base in about ten minutes and he would 'catch up with me' then

Waiting for Nigel to come, had given me a few minutes to show the form to Abby who was writing at the table and Mary who was already tucking into a sandwich from the generous pile the kitchen sent up every lunchtime. Mary always made sure she got a good lunch, keeping her energy levels high was a priority for her. They had both read it through, expressing their surprise that there was a teacher of this sort in the school but neither suggesting a wrong grade.

Now Nigel was shaking his head in disbelief. "We have got to be absolutely sure about this Jane," he said. "I mean I really don't believe it. I can't believe there is a teacher in this school who could warrant a grade of six." He said this last statement very forcibly. He plonked the offending form down on the table as if not wanting to have anything more to do with it.

"Well, she did, " I said, feeling a strange sense of impotence.

"She was seen yesterday. I'm sure of that. Surely if she is such a bad teacher that would have been obvious in the lesson that was seen yesterday – what was it?" Nigel had bent down to his tidy box of inspection files and selected the one in which the copies of the previous day's observations were kept. He was flicking through looking for the observation with Mrs. Mason's number on it.

"Here it is." He turned to look at me accusingly. "Mrs. Mason was seen yesterday by Mary and the grade was good."

"Oh yes," Mary spoke up, her mouth full of sandwich. "It was music. She's the music co-ordinator, and she is a very competent musician. She played an excellent accompaniment on the piano and the children sang beautifully. She does all sorts of things with the children after school, taking them to concerts – there's a thriving choir and lots of children learn an instrument."

"Yes, but you don't need piano playing in English," said Abby, the small voice of reason. "Nigel have you checked the teaching points that Jane is making? Perhaps if Jane gave you a bit more of any explanation about some of those it would make matters clearer for you." I looked at Abby gratefully, but I was already beginning to feel my resolve falter. I felt as if I wanted to screw the form up into a little ball and throw it in the bin. The room was beginning to fill up with the others. John and Trevor were now making themselves a drink and turning to listen, aware that there was an altercation going on.

Nigel snatched up the offending form, and was quiet for a moment as he read it through again, his lips drawn together tightly. While he was reading it Henry and John came in. Then Nigel turned to me and said, "you've written that the lesson was very badly planned. What was very bad about the planning?" He emphasised the very bad as if it was hard to believe.

"There was none."

"What none?"

"Not that I could see."

"Perhaps she had just forgotten to put it out for you – did you ask to see it?"

"No, but even if there was anything written down, it was still very badly planned." By now Henry was standing besides us listening to the arguments, obviously checking the situation.

"How can you say it was *very bad* if you didn't see it? I would think to make such a harsh judgement you should at least have given the teacher the benefit of explaining why it was not out for you to see."

"It was bad planning because the lesson was bad." I could feel my frustration rising.

"I thought Jane had written that there was no objective for the lesson shared with the children?" Abby queried, again coming out in my support.

"Well?" asked Nigel

"If there is no objective to the lesson, then planning must be weak."

"She's only said that it wasn't shared with the children."

"She couldn't share it with them because there wasn't one," I said. At this point Henry stepped in. He took both mine and Mary's observation forms and went to sit at the top end of the room to read them as he ate his sandwiches. Then he came back and said that he would like to have a word with Nigel and myself separately. The room we were in was large and L-shaped so that there was a part at one end that was quite private. Nigel and Henry's voices could be heard but not what they were actually saying. Nigel came back to get the school timetables and I waited feeling anxious and annoyed with myself. Had I not made the lesson clear on the form? Everyone else busied themselves or talked about other things. John, Phil and Trevor were having a heated discussion about Rugby that was quite unintelligible to the rest of us. Abby went on with her work and Mary looked across at me and said, "don't worry, you can only do your best," as if it was a forgone conclusion that I was wrong. Then she got up and bustled out, leaning over towards me before she left and sharing another platitude, "we can all make mistakes," and bestowing on me one of her brilliant smiles. Abby looked across and just shook her head. Then Nigel came back and I went to speak to Henry.

"Jane, I've read through your form and it does read like a six but I am a bit concerned, especially comparing it with Mary's view of this teacher yesterday. There's a couple of points that I would like you to consider. First, Nigel is right. Without having seen the planning, it is unfair to condemn it as bad, don't you agree?"

"I suppose it must seem like that, but the lesson was so" – I struggled for the right words, "lacking in interest."

"Yes I can see that," said Henry, but that doesn't equate with bad planning. Reading between the lines, Jane," he said in his kindly manner, "I think this lady's style and some of her methods are not to your liking. But you have said here that the children got on with their work industriously and even those of lower attainment were given work matched to their abilities, with the exception of this one very needy pupil, and that, of course, is a weakness in the lesson."

"And the pupils of higher attainment," I said.

"Well you have said that they finished their work quickly and that they were not given any more to do but you haven't said that they weren't challenged."

"But, that is what I meant," I said miserably.

"But you haven't put it. What I am not sure about is whether you have looked at the overall picture in this lesson. A lot of children seem to have made progress, got on with their work and behaviour is very good. What I have suggested to Nigel is that I go into one of this teacher's lessons this afternoon and see how I find her work. She is taking history this afternoon which equates well with English, doesn't it? Not like the music which doesn't really have a bearing on the matter. If I find a different picture to yourself, perhaps we can discuss changing this grade, before you speak to the woman, at least to a five, and possibly you might consider a four. In any case, I will ask for her planning if it is not left out, and I will check what was planned for the English."

By the time my talk with Henry had finished, the others had all left the inspection room to go to their afternoon lessons. I felt completely deflated by what Henry had just said to me. I picked up my things and set off to find the hall where I was due to see a Year 3 PE lesson. I was glad it was PE, I felt as if I would have a struggle concentrating, and PE is very easy to watch. Something inside me was churning and I felt an almost irrational hatred of the teacher in Year 5.

I was lucky, the Year 3 lesson was good, the teacher giving clear and quick commands, the children leaping, jumping and climbing over apparatus or balancing with faces tight with concentration on a low bar. Everyone enjoyed themselves, including me and by the end of the lesson, I was amazed at how I had cheered up. Then I was off to the Reception class for the end of day story. It was a lovely re-telling. The teacher used hand signals and pictures of scenes from the book, painted by the children themselves of the popular 'We're going on a Bear Hunt'. I found myself almost joining in as the children chanted the bits they knew by heart. By half past three when it was time to go back to the inspection base, I had almost recovered, and thought to myself, 'what the hell – so what if I change the grade on Mrs. M's lesson to a four to please Nigel, what does it matter?'

As I opened the inspection door, I saw Henry talking to Nigel. Henry appeared to be agitated – you could say smoke was coming out of his ears, and then I heard: "that woman shouldn't be allowed anywhere near children. She's not got a sympathetic bone in her body. She eats children and spits them out like pips. A six Nigel, a six! Never mind a six, I'm putting a seven on this – and as for planning, she doesn't have any, not a scrap, and what's more she doesn't think she needs any!" Henry's normally quiet, subdued manner was nowhere in evidence.

I stood with my mouth open. Phil came over and said with a mischievous twinkle in his eye, "looks like you've been a bit too generous Jane with your grading. Tut tut now. How did you do that?"

Chapter 15

On the last evening of the inspection, I managed by some miracle, to finish the day's paper work and tedious checking of data at around eight o'clock – an early finish. Now that my judgement about the Year 5 teacher had been ratified by Henry, there was nothing really contentious in any of my subjects. The aspect of behaviour and attitudes was going to be good, so no problems there. I was, however, missing one lesson observation sheet, and after a great deal of checking, counting and re-counting, I realised that I had not got the copy of the English lesson Abby had seen for me on the Wednesday. I searched for the owl key fob in the small claustrophobia inducing room and found it on the floor, it having ended up there after vying for space on the tiny dressing table. I went and knocked lightly on Abby's door, just across the landing from mine. After a few moments, the door opened.

"Jane! I was just about to come across and see you."

"Were you? What about?"

"I was going to ask if you wanted to come for a walk down to the seafront. I suggested it at dinner, you remember?"

"Yes... well I suppose I could. It's not raining or anything is it?"

"No it's lovely out – really mild for the time of the year. Please come."

"I am feeling a bit stuffy – the décor does get to you after a while."

"It certainly does."

"Is anyone else coming?"

"Phil is."

"What you and Phil? I'm not sure Abby – I don't want to be..." I searched for the right words not wanting to say 'a gooseberry' but meaning that. I settled on,"de trop."

"Plea…ease." Abby pulled a face. "That's nonsense. What are you thinking? Do come." Just then there was a sound on the landing and I turned round to see Phil already in his coat and smiling broadly.

"I've finished m' work – everything neat and tidy, know what I'm going to say to the co-ordinator tomorrow and it's only," he looked at his watch, "eight fifteen. Are you two ready to get some fresh air – to let the sea breezes blow the whole bloody lot out of your head?" Phil looked ridiculously pleased with himself.

"I'm just persuading Jane to come," said Abby. Oh by the way what did you want me for, Jane?" I explained about the observation form for the lesson on Wednesday, and Abby being Abby turned to a file and pulled it out straight away, apologising and blushing over her forgetfulness. She handed it to me while gently pushing me out of the door.

"Just get your coat."

"Oh all right," I acquiesced.

We tumbled down the stairs in a jolly group with Phil singing an Irish shanty quite loudly, and Abby and I shushing him to be quiet so that he didn't disturb the other hotel patrons.

When we got outside, I realized that Abby was right; it was a lovely night. It was clear enough to see stars and the wind that was blowing was no more than a light breeze. An occasional buffet of cold air whipped up from the cliffs. The roar from the sea below meant the tide was high. It sounded as if it was right up, high against the sea wall that ran along the coast road. The cliff path down to the coast road was almost directly across from the hotel. We were quiet to start with as we made our way down, concentrating on the path's snaking turns. It had a concrete surface and in places it was cracked or reduced to stony patches. It was lit by low street lamps, but they were quite some distance apart so that there were pools of darkness in between. Phil broke the silence first, shouting a little above the sound of the sea and the cry of gulls.

"This reminds me of when me and m' brothers used to go down on the dunes near Kerry at night, slipping out of the house with cans of beer to sit drinking on the sand – looking out over the Atlantic and imagining we were going to set sail for America."

"Did you live near Kerry?" I asked.

"Oh no, we were on holiday. I was brought up in Dublin, but my ma's sister had a cottage near Kerry and we rented it from her every year. Sure it was champion, champion it was. What about you Jane? Have you got childhood memories of the seaside?"

"Oh definitely. I loved the sea. We only lived about twelve miles from the coast so I used to go a lot as a child, although my family being farmers didn't always have much time to relax in the summer months. The best was when we used to go as a big group with another family we knew and sit on blankets on the sand, all the kids playing together. Of course, it was Essex, not Yorkshire, so no cliffs."

"And you Abby?" Phil asked casually as if he wasn't really interested.

"We went to the South of France for a month every year," Abby said.

"That sounds very grand – how lucky you were; places like Cannes, Nice – the Cote d'Azure?" he asked.

"Yes, places like that," said Abby flatly, not offering any more information.

"That must have been wonderful," I said a little amazed at anyone having such sophistication when they were young. "You had a very privileged childhood Abby."

"It might seem that way," Abby said. "But I think I would

have much preferred to have been taken to Scarborough where my mother would have had a job to get a perfect tan, which was the whole point of our holiday, and I could have built sandcastles. I had to learn how to do that when Sam was little because no one had done it with me as a child, and somehow it wasn't the same."

"Abby that sounds quite sad." I was a bit shocked.

"It was. You see, in a way, I was the spoilt child that had everything, except the one thing a child really wants." In the darkness, I could see Phil's hand come out and grasp Abby's. He was in the front, leading now as the path had become quite steep and narrow. Then, Abby reached out and got my hand so that we were going down in a chain together, picking up speed as the incline increased. We finished with a breathless run at the end. Suddenly, we were at the bottom, on the flat paving of the coast road, and Phil tucked first Abby's arm under his, and then mine, so that we were either side of him, walking along three abreast. It was much windier and nosier down here. We walked on the side of the road by the sea and a few feet below us dark waves pounded against the protecting wall. The smell of the sea and the feeling of marching together like one were intoxicating, and for a reason I could not explain I felt happier than I had done for a long time. I started singing, 'I Do like to be Beside the Seaside' and the other two joined in and then we sang, 'Knees Up Mother Brown' loudly and lustily. There were quite a few people about and they smiled at us benignly when they passed, almost as if we were youngsters enjoying ourselves.

We saw the little pub a few yards up the road, its yellow lights welcoming us in from the dark. Inside, we ran our hands through our tousled hair and laughed at each other. But in the bright lights, we were grown-ups again, inspection colleagues. Phil was the only one who had brought any money so he went to the bar to get the drinks while Abby and I sat down. We all had halves of lager. We sipped them slowly, chatting about the week, sharing notes about Nigel taking himself too seriously and changing his attitude so insidiously. When I had finished my half, I knew Phil was going to get some more drinks, but I thought I would get back. I could feel their wanting to be on their own.

"I'm going back now," I said. "I've just remembered something I haven't finished." I lied. They protested saying I mustn't walk back all that way on my own, but I said that was silly. "There's plenty of people about still. I'll be fine." I got up and walked towards the door before they could protest any more. As I turned to look back at them and wave, I had the strange imagining that their two figures had blended into one, a modern sculpture of moulded figures that mirror one another, occupying a single space.

I walked briskly along the seafront, not minding my own company at all. The words Abby had used to describe her childhood re–played in my mind: 'I had everything, except the one thing a child really wants.' I stopped at the rail for a while and gazed out at the blackness that was the surging sea. There were one or two small pricks of light from vessels on their way up or down the coast. There were still plenty of people about. But when I started up the cliff path, I passed fewer and fewer strollers. I began to speed up, feeling the stirrings of disquiet. It was much too steep to run but I kept up a good pace, almost colliding with a couple coming down with a spaniel. Then I passed a street lamp that was out. I thought it odd that I had not noticed it on the way down. I was almost walking in darkness and could not spot the next lamp because of a turn in the path. I was much more aware of the scrubby sea grasses and boulders at the side of the path than I had been on the way down.

Then suddenly, in front of me, the man appeared; a strange figure in a long over coat. He looked unreal, a cartoon character with a bowler hat, which should have blown off in the now blustering wind. He was walking very slowly, with a very strange rolling gait. I steeled myself to pass him on the narrow path, but as I drew almost level, he threw open his coat. He was completely naked from the waist down with his trousers round his ankles, which accounted for the strange rolling. His penis was sticking straight out like a stick. I screamed a full-throated scream. It took me completely by surprise, as if it was some automated response. I carried on screaming even as I shot forward, swerving off the path and passing him in a few seconds. I kept running for several yards before the sheer effort of uphill flight slowed me. As I slowed and turned my head to look back, he was out of sight round a bend, but I could hear a strange whooping sound, and I imagined him jumping up and down. The insane fear that had gripped me subsided. I strode forward as fast as I could but didn't try to run. I realised that there was no way he was going to catch me with the handicap of his trousers, and in any case, I was nearly at the top. A few more strides and I saw a car's headlights, and then I was up, running now on the flat road towards the hotel entrance.

Of course, when I got to the hotel door, I couldn't manage the key. Never very good at unlocking doors, I put the key in but it didn't turn. There were several locks – which one had the landlady told us was for guests? As I fumbled at the outside door, irrational fear set my heart thumping again. I gave up trying to use the key and rang the bell. Mrs. Henderson came to the door.

"Did you forget your key?" she asked. "Why goodness you look shaken up."

I walked through into the warm, wonderfully safe hall and sank into one of the armchairs besides the visitors' signing in book.

"Are you all right?" she asked. "Can I get you something?"

she was slightly irritated at being disturbed, dragged away from the telly by a forgetful guest.

"I've just seen… a man on the cliff path – I've just seen a man…" I seemed to have forgotten the words to describe what I had seen, the words 'flasher' and 'exposing himself' escaping from my vocabulary.

"Oh no!" she exclaimed. "Don't tell me you saw the bowler hatted flasher."

"Yes, that's right. He was on the cliff path."

Mrs. Henderson was suddenly all consternation and care. "You poor thing. What a dreadful thing to happen. I must tell Geoff. Just you sit there and calm down. I'll get you a drink." Geoff came out and phoned the police, and he must have rung up to Henry's room because the next minute Henry was sitting in the chair opposite me and asking me if I was all right.

The sight of Henry looking extremely embarrassed, for once lost for words, together with the double whisky handed to me by Mrs.Henderson, began to restore my equilibrium as a modern woman who would find the antics of that poor little man amusing, rather than terrifying. How we kid ourselves. Yes, I was much recovered, and quickly resuming the life of urbanity, but I knew I had brushed against fear, all consuming and uncontrollable. I was almost ashamed to say to the others that I had screamed aloud.

We soon learnt from Geoff that the bowler hatted flasher was well-known in the area.

"The police have been trying to catch him for years, but he's very crafty. He appears one time and then isn't seen again for months, and never in the same place twice. He has been seen on the cliff path before, but it was – well, how long ago would you say Maureen, that we last heard about him on the cliff path?"

"Must be at least eighteen months ago," said Mrs. Henderson. "It was that time when Alison, the barmaid at the Golden Cock was involved. Don't you remember? She took time off work, and Stan said she was making the most of it, but she was a nervy sort of girl."

"I don't think she ever went back behind the bar, actually after that."

Henry smiled then and looked at me and asked, half joking, half worried. "Will you need time of work then? Do you think you'll be able to come into school tomorrow?"

"Of course, I will. Goodness me, I'm only sitting here now because I think I'll have to tell the police about it. Geoff has rung them. But I think perhaps I could go upstairs until they come." I got up and Henry stood up with me. "I'm going upstairs now, Mrs. Henderson. Can you ring me when the police get here?"

About half an hour later Geoff rang up to let me know that two police officers were downstairs. It was a man and a woman, both young. I sat with the policewoman and described the whole incident. It was quite a slow business because she took notes and read them back to me. How similar her job was to mine, having to record everything in writing. She was a very fast writer but held her pencil in that strange crablike grip that left-handers often use. I couldn't help asking her if her teachers had tried to make her change the way she held a pencil.

"Oh all the time at school," she laughed.

They asked me if the bowler hatted flasher was caught, would I appear as a witness. Of course, I agreed, thinking how strange it would be to go back to Scarborough for such a thing – or would it be in York or maybe Leeds?

I got to bed about half past eleven in the end, exhausted. I supposed that Abby and Phil must have come in during the time I had gone back upstairs. I wondered if they knew what had happened.

Chapter 16

Despite my untoward experience of the night before, I slept soundly. When I woke up I realised that I had forgotten to set the alarm early enough to give me time to finish packing my suitcase and take it downstairs. On the last day of an inspection, the team has to check out of the hotel and take their luggage with them to the school. I showered in three minutes, shoved arms and legs into garments and applied a smattering of foundation; then peered anxiously in the mirror to make sure that there were no smudges or nasty streaks. A knock made me jump. It was Abby. She had just heard about the flasher at breakfast and had come racing up to speak to me, blaming herself for letting me go back on my own the night before.

"Look, stop worrying, these things happen – I'm none the worse for the incident, and now I know to be more careful. Sometimes these things are warnings – something much worse could've happened." I said.

We went down to breakfast together and Henry said I shouldn't worry about getting to the school a bit late and that it wouldn't matter if Trevor was late as well because he was bringing me. Everyone was very solicitous. I felt as if I was recuperating from a serious illness.

The day in school went well, and the afternoon saw the close of the inspection. At four o'clock, we all met with the co-ordinators of our subjects to tell them our main judgements, and what they could expect to see in the report. Hilary, my English co-ordinator, seemed pleased with what I told her. I explained to her that her work as a subject co-ordinator was good, but because there was no monitoring going on in the school, which was no fault of hers, leadership and management were satisfactory. She accepted this happily, a clever girl who learnt quickly and would soon move up the ladder of school management, of that I had no doubt. She nodded when I told her about the unsatisfactory teaching in Year 5. The school grapevine had been working well. At the outset, when Ofsted first arrives, everyone closes ranks, even if it means protecting a colleague that you know perfectly well is not up to scratch. Most of the staff at Higham had probably been aware that Mrs. Mason's lack of planning and and her weak teaching would get her into difficulties. Generally, once the bad teaching, or whatever else is the problem, has been dragged out into the open by Ofsted, everyone is relieved. Bad teachers in a school are bad news for everyone as they have to be carried by the good ones. Nothing is more galling than teaching children well, only to see them slip back when they go into their next class with a not so good teacher. Hilary and I had had quite a few chats since our first meeting, and I knew that her original defensive stance had been through fear that one bad egg might ruin it for them all.

Dislodging bad teachers is never easy, but in 1996 it could seem impossible; at that time the unions had a lot of power and always fought the case for any teaching member. Once Mr. Roberts had been told by Nigel of the two poor lessons, he said that he knew all along that Mrs. Mason was a liability. He tried to excuse himself by saying that the budget was very precarious, meaning that, if Mrs. Mason took the usual route of going off sick, the school would be in financial difficulties. We knew that Mr. Roberts had something of a case, but wondered if Mrs. Mason had survived so long because she was the only piano playing member of staff. Headteachers' priorities could sometimes be very strange.

Nigel had scheduled the final meeting to start at half past four. We had the main findings and key issues to agree. We didn't have as many identified weaknesses as we did at Beswick Street, but even so, Nigel nit-picked as much as possible. He tried to get us to up the grades at every opportunity. At one point, it looked as if it would to come to blows between him and Mary. She would not budge on her grading of satisfactory for assessment and Nigel kept demanding a recount: satisfactory for English, good for maths, satisfactory for science, good for IT, art and physical education and satisfactory for the other subjects. He reeled them off with an enquiring expression on his face that seemed to say 'that adds up to good' but it didn't.

"Jane, I thought you said that assessment in reading was good?" Nigel tried to put pressure on me to change the English judgement, but there was no way I would change, not now. Now I knew Nigel to be the man of straw he had proved to be over the Mrs. Mason debacle, there was no way I would let him push me around.

"Yes it is Nigel, but assessment of writing is no more than satisfactory, as I have already told you, and the quality of marking overall is only satisfactory. I can't change to good. Assessment in English is satisfactory, and that is what I have fed-back to the co-ordinator."

"They have a very good policy and the assessment co-ordinator is very effective." Nigel wasn't giving up.

"Nigel, she has only been in place two terms. Accept it – it's satisfactory," said Phil. Henry didn't say a word, but very pointedly looked at his watch. Nigel, spotted it and knew what it meant. Meetings were supposed to be concise, constructive and purposeful, and judgements were corporate. He begrudgingly conceded to Mary.

There was much to praise, most importantly the overall good progress the children made from Reception to Year 6, despite the dip in progress in Year 5, caused by Mrs. Mason. There were also quite a few subjects which were doing well, one being music, so Mrs. Mason had a consolation prize. As we had thought when we had stood in the entrance hall on the first day, art was a particular strength. We all agreed that it would probably be a long time before we saw such good art work again.

The teaching came out as good, even with Mrs. Mason's two sixes and we were all pleased with that. "They're a good bunch of teachers, with one exception," said Phil. "They deserve some recognition."

The Key Issues for Action were quickly agreed and at about a quarter to seven, we all breathed a sigh of relief when Henry took over from Nigel. He said that he knew Mr. Roberts would be happy with our judgements and thanked us all for having carried out a fair but rigorous inspection. He then said Nigel had done a good job, and slightly reluctantly we all chorused – "Hear, hear. Well done Nigel." Then Phil very quickly got up and started packing up his brief case with John and Abby hot on his heels.

After leaving the meeting, we went to say goodbye to the head and we discovered that nearly all of the staff had stayed on to wait with him. They were gathered in the staffroom. Despite it being so late, they wanted to support their headteacher. Nigel would take about twenty minutes to give Mr. Roberts the final feedback of the inspection judgements and explain the key issues, and then Mr. Roberts would tell his waiting staff the judgements. As we poked our heads round the staffroom door, the teachers all looked up from their seats, some having kicked their shoes off, others with a glass in their hand, relaxed and laughing at last.

"You were not nearly as bad as we thought you would be," said a bouncy Year 3 teacher and we laughed and waved and said; "See you soon," which got the expected response of cries of; "Oh no! We hope not." And we said; "Only joking."

When I got to the car park, I suddenly realised I had left one of my files behind. Trevor was just opening up the boot.

"Trevor, I'm awfully sorry, I've left a file behind. I think it must be under the chair I was sitting on. I'm so sorry to hold you and Abby up. By the way, where is she?"

"Oh she's going back with Phil. She didn't put her case in my car this morning. Didn't she tell you?"

"No, she didn't."

"They've set off already."

"Goodness that was quick."

"Mmmm, I think they wanted to get away before the others spotted them."

Trevor and I were speaking in code. What we were really saying was. 'Abby and Phil are driving home together because they are starting an affair but we are not going to put it into words.'

As we left the outskirts of Scarborough behind, I found myself thinking about the boy in Mrs. Mason's class that she picked on so much.

"You know," I said, "we think we've done a good job, but we only scratch the surface."

"You can't put right all the wrongs in the world and you can't even do it in one school."

"I know, but when it's children you want to."

"Some kids just get a bum deal."

"It shouldn't be like that."

"No you're right, it shouldn't be like that – but it is."

We drove on for quite a way in silence, and then Trevor said, "I wouldn't mind getting a bite to eat on the way back, what do you think?"

"Good idea, it's a long way to drive on an empty stomach." We discussed the evils of this and what it did to your digestive system, while I kept a look out for somewhere to eat. Just before leaving the pleasant Yorkshire countryside and meeting the Leeds network of motorways, I spotted a pub with a sign outside for food and Trevor managed to pull up in time. We both got out of the car and stretched, feeling a strange sense of freedom.

"You know, the best thing about inspection," I said, "is leaving it all behind on the last day."

"I know it's great," said Trevor.

The pub was, as Trevor put it, 'not bad' inside, and we were soon enjoying an evening meal. We both ordered the fish and chips. "Always a safe bet," said Trevor, and something in my head said, 'Yes Trevor would always be a safe bet.'

"I never thought inspection would be so eventful." I said.

"Well, everything seems to happen to you." Trevor said.

"Not just me."

"Oh yes – floods, flashings and dire teaching, to name but a few."

"They were not my fault."

"No, but I am wondering if you are a kind of catalyst. Like those teenage girls that cause poltergeist to manifest themselves – the Carrie of the inspection world."

"Oh thanks." I grinned. "Anyway, things happened on this inspection to other people besides me – with much more potential complications than my random events.

"Such as?"

"Two people," I paused a minute and then I said: "fell in love."

"Oh I think that happened long before this inspection – and love? Do you think it's love?"

"Yes I do, don't you?" As I spoke, our night walk along the seafront flickered in my mind; the three of us walking arm-in-arm, our steps orchestrated by the surge of the sea, our feet slipping on the eddies of sand deposited by the wind and the last high tide that had swept up on to the road.

"Yes, I suppose I do – but I don't understand it." Trevor sounded surly.

"No I don't either Trevor, but…"

"It's happening before our very eyes. Like you said, Jane, who would have thought inspection would be so eventful?" There was a flippancy in Trevor's comments, which, I surmised, masked his real feelings about the matter.

"I take it you don't approve."

"No I don't. I don't approve at all. The man's got kiddies and a wife sat at home. It's wrong and it will end in a lot of people getting hurt."

"Maybe its just one of those things that happens to people for no accountable reason," I said, and even as I spoke, I knew I sounded feeble, as if making excuses for something that was in-excusable.

"What do you mean happens to people?"

"Sometimes relationships are about finding out about yourself – things that you are, that you can't find out with anyone else."

Trevor looked up from his fish and chips. "Jane you've completely lost me. I don't know what the fuck you are talking about."

"Trevor!" I exclaimed. I would never have thought Trevor would use such language. He apologised immediately for swearing. I tried to explain that I meant that their relationship was something they both needed in order to grow and change and that it wouldn't mean anything like breaking up the marriage – Phil and his wife splitting up. Trevor snorted at such an airy fairy view of things.

"Oh Phil won't leave his wife. You can be sure of that. He's a catholic."

"Yes, but not a devout catholic."

"Even if his religion means nothing to him, he'll never leave his wife. It's ingrained in his mental processes to protect hearth and home. He may not love his wife, not in that sloppy passionate way, but that's what she is, his wife and he'll never change that. He'll never leave his wife."

"I am sure Abby wouldn't want him to." I said this with certainty, but where did this certainty come from? I had only known Abby for a short while, since the beginning of September. Why did I think I understood so much about her? I suddenly felt very awkward talking to Trevor in this way. He had started eating with determination. Looking down at his plate, he speared chips forcefully. We both wanted to close the subject of Phil and Abby. We sat and ate in silence for a while.

Then Trevor said, "well, another lot of writing up to do when we get back – that's the worst of it."

"What is it you don't like about the writing?"

"It should be easy enough but it's just the fact that they want it done in a certain way, but then complain that it's formulaic. We mustn't use phrases from the handbook, but how many ways are there of describing what the teaching is like? It's the bit about making it reflect the school – 'Teachers should recognise their own school'. How do you accomplish that?"

"They don't want people just lifting bits from other reports and using the same words. They want …. What is the term Henry used last time? Telling examples."

"Exactly, 'telling examples', that's the bit I find difficult – 'the lesson was satisfactory – the teacher stood in front of the class and spouted on for about twenty minutes about Henry the Eighth's wives, while the children fell asleep.' Will that do for a telling example?"

I laughed and said that I would try and re-phrase that to make it into a telling example. "The teaching was satisfactory, but sometimes the teacher's explanations were too long, and pupils' interest was lost. For example, in a lesson on Henry the Eighth in Year 5, the teacher told the class about the king's wives instead of letting the children (I mean pupils, of course) research these for themselves."

"Well thanks Jane, I think that will just do nicely for my history para. The trouble is when I get home, I can't remember, half the time, what the lessons were about."

"I know. The other thing is that too many telling examples make the thing too long and then you're in trouble. What I find the most difficult is trying to write about what the children with special needs did."

"Oh don't," groaned Trevor. "You can't put, they did the same as everyone else, just less of it and not so well."

"Oh and you can't just say 'they make satisfactory progress', you have to put 'they make satisfactory progress in re-lation to their prior attainment'. We know what that means, vaguely, but I am sure parents don't and we are supposed to be writing in plain understandable English that parents can under-stand. There are all these contradictions – that's what makes the writing difficult. You've got to make it easy to read, but you must use this phrase and that term, you must put in this and include the other but it mustn't be too long."

"I know what will happen when I get my stuff out tomor-row and start to write," said Trevor standing up ready to make his way back to the car. "I will look at the blank paper and not know where to start."

No.34 Spinney Bank Walk: Six months after the inspection of Higham Infant and Junior School

"Steve, Megan. Your breakfast's on the table" Steven tumbled down the stairs and grinned at his Mam. She was back to making breakfast now that Jason had gone, and most mornings she cooked sausages which was Steven's all time favourite. Megan came downstairs and said she didn't want sausages – didn't Mam remember she was a vegetarian?

Mam said, "Oh Megan – where the bloody 'ell 'ave you got that from?"

"Mam, I don't know how you got the job of dinner lady speaking like that," Megan answered.

"And I don't know how you got to be such a stuck up little madam. You'd better watch it, it's your birthday next week."

Megan felt a flutter of excitement at the mention of her birthday, but wasn't going to let on. "What are you getting me?"

"New clothes, of course, but a surprise as well." New clothes was all Megan wanted. She wasn't much a one for dolls or the like. She could spend hours amusing herself with colouring or writing, she didn't need toys, but she loved new clothes.

"Come on Meg we'll be late," Steven said. He rummaged in the veg rack and came up with his reading book and handed Megan hers.

"I'll see you in school at eleven o'clock Steve," said his Mam, that's the time it says on your letter for your assessment with what's 'er name?"

"Mrs. Sharples," said Steven, "and she said it was important for you to come."

"Yes – well, I'll be there. You know Steven, I am proud you've stuck with this thing you do with the coloured bits of plastic."

"Its cellophane and they're called overlays," said Steven, "and they stop the words jiggling about when I look at them." His mother nodded and shoved them out the door.

Steven walked to school with Megan. It was the last but one week of the term. He'd had a whole term without Mrs. Mason. She'd left at Christmas. He could still remember the feeling he

161

had had when everyone clapped and gave her a present on the last assembly. He had felt as if he had been suddenly freed from a deep dark place. He had smiled and clapped after everyone else had stopped and Carl had given him a kick and whispered to stop clapping. None of the other kids were sorry she was going, not even her Miss Perfect favourite, Charlotte, and Danielle had even said she was glad she was going.

Miss Stansfield, who came to take their class after Christmas, was the best teacher ever. It was down to her that Mrs. Sharples had been asked to come in to test Steven and one or two other kids to see if their reading problem was caused by something called 'dsilexier' with another word, which Steven had trouble remembering. It was something to do with the way his eyes worked. Mrs.Sharples said that his was one of the most severe cases she had ever met. When Steven had told her that when he looked at a page in a book, the words seemed to fall off the page or to jiggle up and down, she had just nodded as if she understood.

Mystifyingly she had said: "Of course, Steven they would seem to be doing that with your condition."

How come no one had believed him before?

Chapter 17

The next morning, while I was trying to sort out the seemingly huge pile of papers that the Higham inspection had generated, the phone rang. It was Abby.

"Hi, did you get back OK?" she asked.

"Absolutely fine – Trevor and I stopped for a meal." I wanted to add 'and talked about you' to hurt her. I didn't like her anodyne greeting. What right had she to phone me up all bright and breezy, as if she had just got back from a school trip to the museum?

"Oh did you, we did too," she enthused, and then there was a short silence. She was probably wishing she hadn't said that as it brought Phil obliquely into the conversation, but it had been such a natural rejoinder. Now she was feeling awkward as she wasn't sure what to say about the meal she had had with Phil. She carried on with, "I was wondering if you would like to come round one evening – not this evening, of course, I know you'll want to be with Kate – but perhaps tomorrow? I could cook something and we could share a bottle of wine?"

"That's very nice of you." I made a non-committal comment not actually accepting the invitation.

"You will come, won't you? I was thinking I would make something from a recipe book Sam brought me last time he came down from Oxford. It's Thai recipes and I've not done one yet." There was another long pause.

I said "That sounds nice," again not actually accepting, and I knew that Abby was getting the message that I was annoyed.

"I feel I need to say sorry to you – It's an olive branch." There was a slight pleading in her voice.

"I gathered that, but what is it you're saying sorry about?"

"Letting you walk up the cliff path on your own, of

course."

"That's not what I'm annoyed about."

"Oh, then what is it?" Abby asked the question in a very quiet voice, probably worried that I was going to say something like 'you having an affair with someone else's husband.'

"I'm annoyed that you didn't tell me that you weren't driving back with me and Trevor – going back with Phil without saying." I stopped for a moment and there was silence at the other end. "It must have been miles out of his way."

"Oh Jane, I'm really sorry – I just didn't think. Really what can I say? I can see now why you were upset." The relief in her voice was obvious – my annoyance being over something trivial like travelling arrangements.

"Abby, I will come round," I started to be conciliatory. "But not tomorrow – I want to spend a few days with Kate. She's beginning to find it hard, my being away so much, and anyhow, there's masses of cleaning to catch up with. It's not so bad for you with Sam being away at Uni."

"The place still gets dirty – where does it all come from? And he brings piles of washing for me to do when he does come back. I think I've got about three loads of washing to do this morning." Abby was warming to her subject of motherly duties and I helped her out by concurring over the loads of washing. We were both happy to be on safe ground, talking about household chores – what a relief. "Well what about Monday or Tuesday evening?"

"Monday will be fine, and Abby," I pursued, determined to make sure she understood that my truce was only temporary. "I think we need to have a really honest talk about everything."

"Yes," she agreed, "we will."

When I put the phone down, I felt too unsettled to concentrate on paper work. I got out the vacuum cleaner and spent the next hour going over every bit of carpet in the house. One of the strange things about working on inspection is that housework becomes very therapeutic, almost a pleasure to be enjoyed guiltily. All the time I was cleaning, I was conscious of the fact that I had not started on my writing, which had to be in by Tuesday morning.

By Monday evening, Kate and I were back to talking in the short sentences that teenagers and parents generally use to communicate. Over the previous two days, we had indulged in long talks, Kate confiding in me her worries about girl friends, boy friends and the inevitable coursework. I told her about the inspection which, of course, she wasn't really interested in but made great efforts to appear so. But when I told her about the flasher on the cliff path, she got very angry, looking at me with righteous wrath. She made me promise that I wouldn't do anything stupid like that again – walk back on my own in a strange place at that time of the night. I couldn't help thinking that I was quite glad of the event. It went towards the list of things that might make her more cautious in similar circumstances. There had only recently been the case of a student going missing, a lovely, joyous girl being foolish enough to get into a passing taxi after a night out in Manchester city centre. Her mutilated body had been found a few days later on waste ground behind a factory building. Every mother felt for the parents of that girl, and then almost guiltily knew that they would use it as an example of what not to do, so their own daughter would stay safe.

On my way to Abby's that evening, I stopped at the off-licence and bought a bottle of red wine, paying slightly more than I usually did. All I wanted to do was sit down with Abby and while the evening away without having to tackle the immorality of her liaison with Phil.

Abby's flat was in Didsbury, about a mile from my house.

Historically, this fashionable South Manchester area has been the home of intellectuals and academics since early Victorian times. Abby had a second floor flat in a stylishly converted Victorian mansion. In the small hallway, family photographs were profuse and expertly framed – lots of Sam as a baby, toddler and young boy. There was one with a very beautiful woman in a fashion shot; it looked like something out of Vogue. Abby indicated, as I paused to look at it, that it was her mother.

"Your mother was a model?" I asked unable to keep the amazement out of my voice.

"Yes one of the beautiful people," was all she said, and I remembered how she had spoken of her mother that evening on our walk down the cliff.

I didn't ask any more, although intrigued. Instead I said, "there's a gorgeous smell. It's making my mouth water. I'm really hungry."

"I'm glad, because I've cooked loads. But first have a cocktail. I've made us New York Slingers, my husband used to make them – about the only thing of use that I learnt from him." Abby handed me a cocktail glass.

"Thanks, that looks gorgeous. Where was…is your husband from? He isn't English is he?"

"No he's American but he spent a lot of time in London as a child. His parents were divorced. We had that in common."

"That often makes couples try hard to stay together, so as not to repeat the mistakes of their parents."

"I tried – it was just that Marc didn't. He wasn't really the marrying type – not really his fault. It was in his genes. His dad was a womaniser, and Marc was too."

We sat and ate in a small dining area at the end of a long lounge. Abby's flat was not very large but it was well-designed and beautifully furnished. The Thai curry was delicious. Abby had taken a lot of trouble with the cooking. We talked about the inspection and about our writing – we had both finished it in time, ready to hand in to Nigel the following day. After we had finished the cocktails, Abby poured us glasses of a white wine that she had chilled. We laughed about Nigel, and about how he had reacted to my six for Mrs. Mason.

"Didn't I tell you, I wouldn't want him inspecting my school?" asked Abby.

"Yes, but I thought you meant he would be too harsh, not that he would bend over backwards to make everything look good."

"Ah that was just on this inspection, because that was the easy way. The data was saying that things were good, and he was leading. It suited him for judgements to be good. It would be quite a different story if someone else was leading and the data looked a little dodgy, then he would have no hesitation in giving harsh judgements. Nigel is one of those people who quickly assimilates systems – he knows how to play the Ofsted system already, while we're still struggling to 'do the right thing', as ever. But we mustn't be too harsh on him, you know. He did do a good job of building a relationship with the school, and the teachers really liked him. That's important."

"I bet they had a good giggle over his squeaky voice," I said, grinning.

"You know – I like that about him, makes him seem more human."

"Well, there are times when I illogically feel sorry for him – he's so earnest and his voice just makes him funny at times. I think Henry was happy with his leadership of the inspection, overall, even if Nigel isn't quite the blue-eyed boy Henry thought he would be."

"Oh I'm sure you're right, and don't forget he was the first to lead. We would have all found that a bit daunting." I nodded my agreement.

"By the way, Henry rang me today to tell me that I would be leading the next one. It's December sixth, just before Christmas, of all times."

"Abby. For goodness sake! Fancy telling me you're next to lead as if it was of no consequence!" I exclaimed. "How can you be so calm about it? Where is it?"

"Liverpool."

"Are we going back to the same hotel?"

"No. Well, I'm not sure, but you'll not be coming – remember what was said about the two teams mixing after half term? That's because Ofsted want Matthew and Henry to monitor each other's trainees, and also to bring in inspectors from outside, team inspectors who have already done a good number of inspections to work alongside us, basically so we can do more inspections."

"Oh, yes I remember that being spoken about. I am disappointed that I'm not coming with you though, really disappointed. Do you know who is on your team?"

"I know that Phil will be with me, Henry said I should get him to act as a sort of deputy. Apparently lots of people do that when they work for contractors, go around in twos so that one can lead and the other deputise and then they switch for the next inspection."

"How convenient," I said, a touch of sarcasm in my voice.

Abby ignored it, and told me that the other people on her team, as far as she knew, would be Nigel and a woman from Matthew Longton's group called Margaret. "She seems nice, a bit quiet," Abby said. "Do you know who I mean?"

"Margaret Williams isn't it? Yes, she does seem nice. But what about Trevor, Mary, and me? Do you know where we'll be going?"

"No. Henry didn't say, but I expect he'll tell you tomorrow when we meet to go over the Higham inspection."

"So you'll be with Phil." I said unnecessarily.

"Yes." We both went quiet. I felt a surge of annoyance at the situation. How could Henry have got things so wrong?

"You know," I said, "I'm supposed to be asking what the bloody hell you are doing?" The alcohol was taking hold of my words and releasing me from the restrictions of social niceties. Abby didn't say anything, but just lent across and poured the last of the wine into my glass. She stood up holding the empty bottle and went into the kitchen to get another one, or perhaps it was to escape from what I was saying.

"I mean it's not a good idea and it's not at all what should be happening, what was meant to happen," I continued, shouting out the ineffectual and not entirely logical words towards the kitchen door. When she returned with a full bottle in her hand, she stood by the table and just nodded.

"I don't know what I am doing," she said, sitting back down with a defiant plonk.

"But you're a grown woman – a responsible person, you should know what you're doing." I almost shouted.

"I'm having an affair with Phil." Abby's voice was loud too.

"But, what about his wife?"

"I'm not harming her – I'll never harm her. Is that what you are thinking that I might split them up – that I would get Phil to leave his wife?"

"It happens."

"Never, never. If Phil left his wife, I wouldn't be with him – never." She was slightly hysterical, out-of-control, a wild Bronte heroine of the moors. "Please believe me, I would never get Phil to leave his wife and children, please Jane believe me." She said it again and again that she would not ask Phil to leave his wife, that she would never speak to him again if he did.

"Calm down Abby, I don't want to upset you – I am not trying to be critical you know – it's just that I care about you and I don't know why that is even – I don't know why I should care what you do." All I wanted now was to get her to calm down. She was crying, almost uncontrollably dabbing at her eyes with a soggy tissue. After a few minutes she stopped with lots of sniffs and nose blowing. Then she got up and once more went towards the kitchen.

"I've got a pudding in the fridge," she said.

"How lovely. Is it a gooey chocolaty one?" I tried to say something normal, something to distance us from the emotion, but I realised my words just sounded patronising.

"No. Strawberry Pavlova, actually."

She came back into the room with two cut-glass dishes filled with meringue, strawberries and cream, which happened to be my favourite. She was much calmer so we ate the pudding and I asked Abby to tell me more about her marriage.

"I was so lonely when I was growing up, and when I met Marc he seemed to be wonderful. I was just dazzled by him. I didn't see the person he was inside. He had loads of friends and such a social life." Then she told me how her husband had gradually and insidiously drained her of her self-confidence, how he had always been a womaniser and how in his high-flying life style he thought that was normal.

"I never had any self-esteem, my mother made sure of that, but he took away any vestiges I had. But I want you to know Jane that I 'm not being with Phil to repair the damage Marc did to me. I put that right myself."

"I'm sure you did," I said. " Please Abby, don't think I'm against you. I am trying to understand. When I see you together, you look," I paused not wanting to use one of the hackneyed phrases that came to mind, "You look so close, as if a magic circle is encompassing you. I know I am only saying this because I'm drunk but I want you to know, I do understand, even if I don't really want to."

"I 'm so grateful for you saying that, because I know that is not what other people will say about us. I don't feel as if I chose to do this – or that Phil chose it – it's as if it was something outside of us that has propelled us together."

"Trevor would think you were mad, if you explained it like that."

"Everyone I know, except you, would think I am mad."

"There are lots of trite worn-out phrases that you could use like 'love is madness'."

"Yes and lots of trite worn out phrases that are not so nice as that, and I often think of them. Phrases like – she's having 'a sordid little affair with a married man she works with'. That's what most people would say." I acknowledged the truth of this.

"The thing is not to let other people know, Abby. It's other people who give things these labels and if they don't know about it then they can't do that. Be careful. You must be really, really careful. I know about you and Phil, and Trevor does but, at the moment, no one else. Keep it that way."

"You're right, I know you're right, but sometimes it's difficult."

"Well, Henry must not have noticed, otherwise he wouldn't have put you together on your lead."

"That's true."

I had a feeling that I had not said all the things I had meant to say. Part of me wanted to believe in a love that was a true passion; something that seemed to transcend the cosy comfort, the sensible go to work, watch telly of modern life – fill in your forms, shop at the supermarket, stop at the red light and do your gardening at the week-ends everyday boring life.

I left the rest of my drink in the glass and phoned for a taxi to take me home.

In the morning, I had a horribly bad head. All the fanciful things that I had said to Abby seemed ridiculous and the words that stuck in my mind were...'a sordid little affair'.

The next day, Wednesday, we all met at the offices in Trafford Park. Henry said we didn't need to get in until after lunch. I had a nice leisurely start to the day, having breakfast with Kate and feeling like a proper mum for a while. After she left for college, I switched the computer on and looked over the writing I had done for Higham and spotted one or two mistakes. I started re-writing and before I knew it I had nearly over shot the time for leaving. As usual I ended up driving to Trafford Park like a demented taxi driver with my eye on the clock the whole of the way. I was the last to arrive and Henry said with his customary sarcasm, "your consistency Jane is very commendable."

"It's reassuring," added Phil. "I always know I'm not going to be the last."

"Or be the only person to leave something behind." Trevor chipped in.

"I wasn't late." I said defensively,but not really minding the teasing.

"No," said Henry."You arrived with a good ten seconds to spare."

For this meeting, our group was joined by the five remaining members of Matthew Longton's group. We learnt that they were down to five because one of their number, a woman called Shirley had, as Matthew put it; "found things too difficult." Later when Abby and I were having a girls-in-the-toilet gossip, Margaret Williams, the woman who was going to be joining Abby on her lead, told us that Shirley had upset nearly every teacher in the last school their group had inspected. When she left, Abby and I agreed that Margaret seemed nice. Except for her, most of the Longton lot seemed a bit strange. They were definitely stand-offish. Margaret had been the only one that had spoken to us that day.

"They make Nigel and Mary seem normal," Abby said.

"Just about," I agreed. "Do you think inspection attracts strange bods?" I queried.

"Very probably – us included."

Henry and Matthew had important things to impart to us. Matthew took charge of explaining how things were to happen over the next few months. A small dapper man, he was a much busier sort of fellow than Henry, and unlike Henry clearly took his duties with Ofsted very seriously. We were given a smart folder on which the word 'MILESTONES' was embossed. Milestones were to dominate our existence for the next six months and to some extent the rest of our working time with Ofsted. They were dates that had to be given very careful attention so that they were never passed without whatever it was that was supposed to happen on that date happening.

Ofsted imposed strict timings for inspection events, and milestones were intended to keep those new to inspection, such as ourselves, on the straight and narrow pathway. Whereas Henry would have started us out on the pathway, and then left us to work out our own route, Matthew insisted on explaining every inch of the way with such painstaking care that those, such as myself, with a low boredom threshold had soon strayed. I spent most of my time wondering what the team members in Matthew's group were like.

Later on that day, I found out that the week when Abby was leading an inspection, the week beginning the sixth of December, I was to join an inspection led by Sarah Pennington who seemed to be a Matthew Longton favourite. I looked across at her when this information was given and she gave me a small but not very enthusiastic smile. Mary was coming on that inspection as well, while Trevor was off with someone else from Matthew's group. Sarah Pennington's inspection was in Coventry.

When Mary and I discussed how we were going to get there, I realised with a sense of dread that I would have to drive the ninety odd miles to Coventry down the M6 motorway on my own. Mary was going to spend the preceding week with her son in London.

PART 4

TWO INSPECTIONS,
COVENTRY AND WEST YORKSHIRE

Chapter 18

<u>18 Grange Road, Coventry</u>

Shelley Thomas woke up and scrunched her eyes up at the light. She sat up and felt sick. It was Monday. She got out of bed and said, 'I wish it wasn't Monday', over and over in her head as she went to the bathroom. She sat on the toilet and heard her mum calling from downstairs.

"Jason, Shelley, come on time to get up." Shelley got off the toilet and flushed. Bumping and banging noises came from Jason's room and then he pounded on the bathroom door. She let him in. He gave her a grin and flicked her hair as she went past.

"Hey Shell – Monday again." Jason said. He enjoyed weekends but he didn't mind school. Jason was always happy. At fourteen, he was set to do well in his GCSE's; he had a load of mates and to Shelley his life seemed wonderful. She struggled with her work, was in the bottom group for maths and she had no friends.

She flopped down the stairs holding her pyjamas in a screwed up bunch round her stomach and found her mum sitting at the table in the dining recess, a cup of coffee in front of her.

"I've got a pain, my tummy really hurts. I feel sick."

"Oh no Shell, not again," her mum said. "Not a Monday pain." While Linda Thomas had been sitting having her coffee she had been wondering if Shelley was going to be all right. Things had been back to normal for a week or two. She had seemed OK when she came home Friday and she had gone to school quite OK for a couple of weeks. Now here she was, not wanting to go to school again. It was as if, the day was suddenly spoilt before it had even started. Linda Thomas put down her coffee cup and went over to her daughter. She put her arms round her.

"You can't be ill every Monday, darling," she said, but what she was thinking was, 'I can't be off work every Monday, and Mum won't want to come round again, she grumbled last time.'

"I've got a tummy ache, honestly I have." Shelley turned away from her mother, the tears in her eyes smudging the world. She knew her mum knew; she knew she hated it as much as she did, only it wasn't her having to go to St James's. She was. She was the one that was going to have to go out to play and be alone on that playground, that cold, wet, horrid playground, where everyone had a friend but her.

Ever since she had started school, playing with other children had been a little difficult for Shelly but this year it had got worse, much, much worse. When she had been in, Mrs. Parker's class, things had been better. Mrs. Parker had been kind. She had listened to her and told the others to make friends. Besides there had been Samantha then. They had played together all the time, her and Sam. Sam had come round for tea and Shelley had gone for tea at Sam's house. It was the best thing in the world having a friend. But Samantha's dad had got a job in another town. They had moved house and Samantha had left at the end of Year 3, and now Shelley was in Year 4. Mr. Hughes wasn't like Mrs Parker. He didn't seem to notice anything, even when Bethany Stevens flapped her hand in front of her face as if there was a bad smell whenever Shelley walked past. Mrs. Parker had caught her out doing that and had been very cross, but Mr. Hughes didn't notice. Last Friday, he had acted as if she was clumsy idiot, as if it was her fault, when Donna had tripped her up walking into assembly. 'Do try to look where you're going Shelley,' he had hissed. He made her feel as if she was always barging around, too fat, too stupid to be careful. Donna and Bethany had been giggling but he didn't see that.

"I will ask to speak to Mrs. Butler, again BUT," her mother paused, "Shelley you must go in to school today." Her Mum was looking into her eyes – cupping her face in her hands, and Shelley just nodded. She knew it was no use. She knew her Mum couldn't help her. She had got to go in to school. It was her fault that no one liked her – she didn't deserve to be liked. She was the one who was useless and stupid.

"And I'm filling in that form, the one that you brought home on Friday with that letter about those people – what are they called, Ofsted? – people from the government coming to inspect the school. It's got a question on it about bullying, they're asking if your child is being bullied and if you're happy about how the school is dealing with bullying. Well I've ticked the box to say I am not happy. I mean what does Mrs. Butler do about it? She makes out she is very concerned and tells me that something will be done, but nothing is. She even gave me a copy of their bullying policy, what use is that? She said that Mr. Hughes was very good about dealing with upsets and that there was no bullying in his class. She never says a word to the children that are causing the problem, well not that I can see anyway."

"Mum, don't go and see Mrs. Butler. It doesn't help. I'll be OK, honestly." Shelley walked out of the room and went upstairs. The night before as always, her mum had put a pile of neatly ironed school clothes, shirt, green cardigan and grey skirt on the chair in her room. She began to put on each item, slowly, mechanically. She did not pause for a second. A hard feeling in the pit of her stomach solidified. And as she stared at her reflection in the mirror it was as if she was not there at all.

I was uncomfortable for much of the time that I spent on the inspection led by Sarah Pennington. The school was St. James's Church of England Primary School in Coventry. It didn't help that I seemed to have caught a 24-hour virus, which started to make itself felt on my drive to Coventry on the Sunday evening. Sarah Pennington had booked accommodation for the whole team in a very reasonably priced Bed & Breakfast, the Rosedale which was situated almost in the city centre, in a small side road just off the strange antiquated ring road that circles Coventry. This ring road has such a small circumference that traffic banks round the corners like cars on a racing circuit. Circumnavigating it, you almost feel as if you are getting dizzy. That evening, it made me think of the Parisian Periphique (not yet in 1996, enshrined in the minds of the British public as the scene of Princess Diana's death, but still the scariest road most Vauxhall Astra drivers ever experienced). I went round the Coventry ring road twice before finding the correct exit – my ability to spot the required exit number impaired by the increasing pain behind my eyes and an unpleasant nauseous feeling. By the time I had lugged my baggage up to the second floor of the Rosedale, I had only seconds to spare before being sick in the shared bathroom, two doors down the corridor from my room.

I spent the first day of the inspection in a blur of misery, my eyes sore, a dull pain in the part of me that was supposed to be my head and a throat bristling with sharp edges. Illness of inspectors is not factored in by Ofsted, or anyone else to do with inspection. The best you can hope for is a brief moment of sympathy from a colleague who may suggest that you sit down, have a drink and take an asprin or such like. School staff behave very much as children do when they learn of an adult's affliction; they murmur something in acknowledgement and then no less that five seconds later go on treating you in exactly the same way as they would an inspector enjoying robust health – i.e. you are some kind of a God and therefore do not suffer the ills which afflict common mortals. No one wants to think about the possibility of a sick inspector. If the correct number of inspectors do not present themselves in school at the appointed time, the whole inspection is null and void and arrangements have to be made to do the inspection again. It is unthinkable.

It was not only, however, my state of health that was making me feel bad on this inspection, it was Sarah's style of leadership. I did not dislike her, and I was far too inexperienced to consider that she was wrong in her approach, I just found her methods depressing. She was a petite, tidy person. Her heart-shaped face, still attractive had, without a doubt, been very pretty when she was younger, and her smile was delightful. But, unlike Mary's, it rarely appeared. Mostly, she looked very serious and detached as if she had just heard news of the demise of a distant relative, unsure whether to be uninterested or upset. When we arrived in the inspection room for the first time on Monday morning, we discovered that she had been there some while before us, preparing everything to her liking. Laid out in very specific places were the inspection forms, school documents and stationery equipment such as, rulers, rubbers, stapler and hole-punch. She made it clear that she expected everything to be kept in its allotted place. There could be no excuse for untidiness in this inspection room.

"I don't want to waste time looking for things, when it only takes a few seconds to put things back where they belong," she told us as we looked round at her handiwork.

The team was smaller now because we no longer had any extra people as dispensation for being trainees – we were working up to speed. It meant a lot more pressure, and consequently the need to work more efficiently, so it should have made sense to me that Sarah had organised the room well. But it didn't: it just made me feel grouchy, and sure that I would never be able to achieve such administrative brilliance.

Matthew Longton was to be with us for the first day as part of his monitoring, and I got the distinct impression that he thought a great deal of Sarah's organisational skills. A believer in duplication as a means of checking that everything was as it should be, Sarah had provided a quantity of files. Each one of these had a neatly printed front sheet on to which we were to transfer various pieces of data from our completed observation forms. Although Matthew joked with us about the perils of putting an item in the wrong place, or not recording correctly, it was obvious that he fully endorsed Sarah's methods. At the first team meeting on the Monday morning, I sat in the circle of inspectors on uncomfortable, child-sized chairs, with a handkerchief clutched to my now dripping nose. Sarah's flat, unenthusiastic voice described in careful detail exactly what she wanted from us, and the sheer efficiency of it all was overwhelming me. I could see Matthew Longton looking at her with satisfaction, like a teacher watching a talented pupil leading an assembly.

At one point, I realised that she was speaking about the importance of keeping a check on the time that we were in each lesson and of recording this time accurately. "Too many people simply put down a guess, say half an hour when in actual fact the observation lasted 35 minutes. This happens because they have not made careful note of the time when entering the room, and then they wonder why their calculations go awry." I was stupefied. Did it really matter if five minutes was not accounted for? She went on with more, "I personally think it is very important for us to be spot on with our timing. This gives us the right to check the school's time keeping procedures. If they say that children are to have fifteen minutes play – do they actually keep to this? I will be responsible for checking the times that children go out and come in from play and I would like you to check whether teachers start lessons promptly, or whether there is any time-wasting." As she spoke, I thought of all the times that I had sent children out to play late because we had been engrossed in a lesson, and equally the numerous times I had let them have a few minutes extra on the playground when the sun was shining and the world was laughing. I knew that, in some deep basic way, I was very different to Sarah Pennington, but that under no account should I make this fact known. I must watch my time-keeping.

She had not organised the 'getting to know you meeting' with the teachers as Nigel had done, and when she spoke about the staff she seemed quite disparaging. Remembering Nigel's friendly, joking attitude with the staff at Scarborough, I whispered to Mary, "come back Nigel all is forgiven." She gave me a half smile and carried on jotting down notes as Sarah spoke. I realised that she was worried about forgetting some of Sarah's very precise and exacting stipulations, and I started note-taking as well. However much I disagreed with what she was saying in principle, in practice I needed to be able to toe the line, or Matthew Longton might give me a bad report.

Although we had been introduced to the headteacher, a Mrs Butler, on our arrival at the school, neither Sarah nor the head had seemed to think it important for her to spend any time with us lesser mortals, mere team members. We had not, for instance, been given a tour of the school and Mrs. Butler had left it to Sarah to show us the whereabouts of the inspection base. I realised that this lack of social courtesy had made me feel under-valued, and I wondered whether the teachers in the school felt the same.

After spending over half an hour outlining her expectations regarding our work, Sarah finally got on to highlighting the main points about the school. She spoke quite approvingly of the head. "She has tried to implement a lot of good changes in the two years since her appointment here and her policies are of a very high standard, but some of the staff are difficult, unwilling to change." We were to hear a great deal more about the good quality of this headteacher's policies over the next few days and I began to see that in Sarah's estimation, a well-kept file and a properly documented policy would rate more highly as a qualification for leadership than inspiring the staff, engaging children's interest or making school life enjoyable.

One thing Sarah did that I thought was good was her organisation of the daily timetable. On a wall in the inspection room, she had pinned up a large timetable indicating our visits to different classes which she had worked out prior to the inspection so that there would be no clashes and no teacher seen too little or too much. Remembering how long Henry had spent on sorting out the timetable, I couldn't help giving Sarah credit for this.

As well as Mary, Sarah and a quiet inoffensive man called

Peter Morrison from Matthew Longton's group, a team inspector from the outside contracting world called Michael Slater was to join us for Wednesday and Thursday. The lay inspector, a woman called Sharon Clarke had been allocated three days. A team member like Michael Slater got paid by the day, and in 1996 that would have been around £400.00 per day. His responsibilities were IT and design and technology together with the aspect of Staffing, Accommodation and Resources. To those of us on school salaries with expenses, Malcolm appeared to be making a fortune, which when I talked to him later in the week, I discovered was not far from the truth.

Although we thought we had worked hard on our previous two inspections, on this one we were to find out just what a slog inspection could be. I was doing English again, but with it I had history, geography and physical education. I was also responsible for the aspect that encompassed Behaviour, Attitudes and Personal Development, which, of course, I had done before at Higham. On that Monday, there was no respite, one lesson followed another in agonising rapidity, followed by meetings in the evening with co-ordinators. I kept going by taking as many painkillers as possible, cutting the recommended four hourly interval as much as I dared. Somehow, I got through the day. By six o'clock, I had one last torture ahead, the end of day team meeting led, of course, by Sarah. I thought she might cut short my agony – tell me to go home. But when I tentatively broached the subject of not being well, she simply said that the meeting would not take long. It took an hour, at the end of which I was seriously wondering if I would live for another day.

I felt so poorly I didn't want to drive back to the Rosedale so I asked if anyone would let me go back with them, expecting Mary or Sarah to offer. But it was Peter Morrison who picked up my brief case and said; "come with me, Jane." Peter was a pleasant man, but totally in awe of Sarah. He kept saying how good she was, and how much he was learning from her. All of which irritated me enough to increase the pain in my head by several notches, making me less grateful for his lift than I should have been.

As soon as we got back, everyone got ready to go out for a much needed evening meal. All I wanted to do was lie down and never move again, so I said I wouldn't be joining them. Sarah's lack of sympathy was beginning to upset me. She made no comment at all when others exclaimed about me not going for something to eat. "You would be much better with some food inside you," said Mary in her motherly way. I just shook my head and turned away. Ridiculously, I felt like crying at what seemed like callousness on the part of these healthy monsters who could wander off out at eight o'clock at night and eat in a restaurant.

We had been told that the landlady would allow us to use the tables in the breakfast room to work at, as there were no facilities in our rooms. I sat at one of the many tables in this empty room, trying my best to organise my work. Then, just after everyone had left, I realised that I had got through all of my paracetamol tablets. The thought added to my irrational feelings of dislike towards my colleagues – they couldn't even supply me with another painkiller. I decided to seek succour elsewhere. Perhaps the landlady would be kind? I was not wrong. When I knocked tentatively on the 'private' door a friendly, smiling woman opened it.

"I say you don't look so good," she said. She gave me some painkillers with a cup of tea, fussed and tut-tuted over me carrying on working and said that I should have spent the day in bed instead of going into the school which was music to my ears and instantly made me feel better.

I told her that I had to do another half hour of work, but

that then I would be going to bed. About ten minutes later, I looked up to see her place a bowl of hot tomato soup on my table with two slices of buttered toast. Heinz Tomato soup from a tin, the most perfect comfort food ever devised by man. I spooned down every last mouthful with gratitude. Over the next few days, we became friends. She was called Mandy, and at around thirty years old, was very young to be a landlady. But it turned out that she had been brought up in the Rosedale as a child and was following in her mother's footsteps as a landlady, her mother having taken herself off with her new husband to a life on one of the Spanish costas. In subsequent evenings after I had finally finished work, we chatted about everything and nothing over a bedtime cup of cocoa. She was my touchstone of ordinariness in this new inspection world, which I was finding increasingly mystifying and unsettling.

Chapter 19

Towards the end of the inspection, almost everything at St James's C of E was looking as if it was average and that equates with the word 'satisfactory' in Ofsted terms. At the evening meeting on Wednesday, Sarah asked us all to indicate what we thought would be our final judgements on our different subjects. In my subjects, I had satisfactory teaching, satisfactory progress for children, satisfactory standards and co-ordinators who did a satisfactory job of leading their subject. Some years later Chief HMI Andrew Bell was to hit the headlines by saying that satisfactory was not good enough, which sounds a contradiction in terms, but I understood what he meant; St. James's was a perfect example of it. Although in 1996, we were placating teachers who were disappointed by only being given a 'satisfactory' with words such as: 'satisfactory is fine – it's what you are paid to do, anything else is the icing on the cake', there was already a nagging feeling that it wasn't what children should be getting. There was something lacklustre about it, especially when almost everything in a school was satisfactory. It was workaday, as if life promised no sparkle, excitement or opportunity to achieve the unexpected.

There were also occasions when evidence was very borderline, and so a judgement of satisfactory had to be given in the absence of more concrete evidence to the contrary. At St. James's I was finding physical education fell into this category. The two lessons I had seen had been satisfactory, both of them following a rather worn-out but acceptable formula. I knew, from seeing those lessons, that children in this school were not being challenged enough to run fast, jump high, kick balls accurately and hard, or vault over apparatus so that one day they might compete in a national arena. No ex-pupils of St. James's would be winning

Olympic medals. Many may not even learn to love sport or physical exercise enough to keep it up after school and so stay healthy for the rest of their lives. But lessons were organised properly and there was an appropriate programme of work, following national guidance. There were a couple of clubs, football for boys and a swimming club run by parents, involving no more than 30 or 40 pupils of this 260 admissions school. The co-ordinator, Mr. Hughes, a Year 4 teacher, said that teachers were no longer willing to lead clubs after school because of the enormous increase in planning and paper work they were expected to do. He had looked at me angrily when he said this, as if I was to blame for this state of affairs. He was a thin rather unprepossessing individual who looked as if he had always done just enough, but never any more in his life, and wondered why he was getting nowhere fast.

I knew that what the school was providing was just enough, but I wanted to shake him and shout – 'this is not good enough! Where are the opportunities for excellence?' I wanted to stay behind for a week and take lessons in PE, dance and games and say – 'see that's how it's done'. Yes, you are right in thinking that I am very crusading about the benefits of sport, gymnastics and dance, and slightly big-headed about my own ability to teach them. However, what was noticeably lacking in the approach of the co-ordinator was any enthusiasm or passion for his subject. He seemed to be saying 'I'm doing enough and that is all I am going to do'. On Sarah's inspection, I meekly followed suit and, instead of saying what I really thought, I matched my findings against the criteria, doing enough but no more. When Sarah asked me at the evening meeting about the overall grade, I said PE was satisfactory. I felt as if I was letting the children down and it was not a nice feeling.

Michael Slater, who had only been in the school for a day,

amazed us all by declaring IT to be unsatisfactory. When Sarah suggested he might change his mind after spending Thursday in school, as after all he had only been at the school the one day, he shook his head and said no, he was quite experienced enough to know that what he had seen that day was unsatisfactory. He made the point about being experienced very deliberately and I saw Sarah flush a little at this allusion to her trainee status. He was a stocky man of about fifty, quite good-looking, with a tan that spoke of frequent holidays in warm places, and until this rather cheap gibe at Sarah's newness in the world of inspection, I had rather liked him. He intrigued me – the first outside inspector, other than the lay inspectors, John Ainsworth and Sharon Clarke, with whom I had worked.

Sarah then asked me if I could make my final judgements about my aspect, 'Pupils' Behaviour, Attitudes and Personal Development.' I reported that behaviour in class seemed balanced between satisfactory and good while around school it seemed to be good with no running on corridors and respectful listening in assemblies. My judgement was, therefore good overall for behaviour. Sarah gave a slight incline of her head to indicate agreement.

"But, I am a bit worried about how well the children get on with each other." I stopped for a moment to look down at the list I had prepared. "At play, there is little mixing between the sexes and between age groups. There is quite a bit of rough play, especially among the boys. There are no strategies for older children to help younger ones, such as the 'buddies' scheme, or anything like it that lots of schools are using now." I stopped. Sarah looked at me blankly as if I was talking another language.

"One boy in Year 2 had told me that he was bullied by older boys," I continued, beginning to feel more as if I was having to justify myself, rather than report findings. "I have seen several children seemingly on their own at playtimes, especially a rather plump girl in the juniors. I was about to speak to her when the whistle went and the children lined up. I just get the feeling that there is cattiness amongst the girls." I finished lamely.

"If you are saying that relationships are unsatisfactory, I think you need more evidence than this Jane. You have already said that behaviour at lunchtimes is good, and those two things don't stand besides one another at all, do they – good behaviour at lunchtime and unsatisfactory relationships at play? Have you talked to the lunch-time staff?"

"Well no, but I'm not talking about behaviour, I'm talking about relationships, the way children are with each other." I looked round at the other members of the team, hoping that one of them might support what I was saying.

"I'm sure there are some children who are bullied," Sharon Clarke, the lay inspector spoke up, "that happens in every school, and of course, there are always those who fall out with friends." She sounded very reasonable, as if I was a slightly over-excitable person who needed calming down. "The headteacher has a very good policy on bullying. She has told me that she deals with all incidents immediately they arise… I have some examples here." She pointed at her open file. "I spent quite a while today going over this with her."

I felt a spurt of annoyance at this glib, adult way of looking at the issue, good policy in place, authoritative headteacher telling you everything is dealt with: things must be fine and dandy – no need to bother with what children say.

"I' m sure that is what she has told you," I said. "But we are here to take into account what the children tell us."

"Yes, Jane, is absolutely right." Michael Slater, much to my amazement, joined the discussion. "Schools, that is headteachers and staff can tell you all sorts. It is, after all, in their interest to do so. But it's our job to verify what they say. I seem to remember that there was some mention of bullying at the parents' meeting and wasn't the percentage of concerns from the parents' question-naire above average?"

Sharon looked at him sharply, annoyed that he was en-croaching on her ground. "The percentage was, as you say above average, but only very marginally. And, yes there were one or two parents at the meeting who voiced concerns about bullying, but there were also many who said that it was dealt with very well and that they were very pleased with the discipline in the school."

I looked at Sarah. She showed no sign of taking part, or favouring one argument over the other. She had distanced herself from the discussion, as if the outcome was of no consequence to her, knowing full well that she held the upper hand. She played it.

"Jane," she said, "perhaps you would come back to this to-morrow, I don't want to keep the team here all night. If you could get more evidence to substantiate your hypothesis, we will be in a much better position to consider the grade." Without even rais-ing her voice, Sarah had managed to manoeuvre me into two un-favourable positions, firstly one of delaying the meeting and, secondly one of causing a postponement on a grade decision be-cause I had not gathered enough evidence. She neatly fielded the problem – it was my problem and not one that that needed the full weight of the team to get it sorted. There was nothing I could do but agree to defer until the next day. As compensation, I asked if I could have some help in getting evidence.

"Of course, Jane, Sharon and I will help you out. We can both talk to some children tomorrow. Can you find time for that Sharon?"

"Oh yes, I can fit it in, I'm sure I can." With their fitting in and helping out, both ladies sounded eminently well-organised and professional, unlike the person who needed their help.

"Thank you Sarah, I would appreciate that." I felt as if I said the words through gritted teeth, but in fact they came out as if I really was grateful. I had given up the fight.

At the end of the meeting, Michael Slater asked if anyone could help him with directions to the Rosedale.

"I could come with you in your car if you like," I offered. I had scrounged a lift with Peter Morrison that day so my car was not at the school. I was glad of an opportunity to thank Michael Slater for speaking up on my behalf at the meeting, besides which he was a welcome breath of fresh air from the Sarah Pennington gang. Mary was now a fully paid-up member, she had even told me that she thought Sarah's lead was very good. When we had got in the car and I had made sure that Michael was heading in the right direction, I turned to him and thanked him for his support.

"Well, I'm quite sure you are probably right in your assumptions. It's never easy to get to grips with whether there is any bullying going on, but there is no way that lady is going to tackle such a thorny issue."

"I'm sure if Sarah had directed the whole team to spend a little time on it, we might get somewhere near the truth."

"No doubt, but then she would have to confront the head with it and heads fight tooth and nail over that one. Even when it's staring them in the face, they stick with their 'we have a policy' stuff as if bits of paper are going to make the slightest difference."

"Well, anyway thanks again for your support."

"I do feel very strongly about the issues around bullying, and about the way so many inspectors and leads brush the whole thing under the carpet, but I must confess that on this occasion, I probably spoke up to get up that supercilious, irritating woman's nose."

"Goodness Michael, Sarah's not quite that bad is she?"

"Let's put it this way, she is definitely going down in my little black book."

"Your black book?"

"Yes, many of us full time team chaps have one. It's a list of leads we don't want to work with. All her bloody files and record sheets are a bit much, I can tell you. She might think they are efficient, but in reality, they are counter-productive. On inspection, you need to be well-organised, I'm not disputing that, and I am sure you have to check up on some people, there's some really weak inspectors out there, but the main thing is to have a system that takes up as little of people's time as possible. What inspectors need to do is think about what they have seen and not spend time feeding in data into a bewildering array of systems. I know tomorrow's meeting is going to go on forever."

"Yes probably until about eight o'clock."

"Oh Gawd. I should be home and getting on with my paragraph by eight o'clock."

"What starting writing the night you get back?"

"How else would I be ready to go to another inspection on Monday morning?"

"Is that what you do?" I looked at him in amazement.

"Yup, an inspection every week, for eleven weeks of most terms. Gets me up to about fifty thousand a year, pounds that is. I only took this two day one on because I had a family wedding to go to last weekend."

"Well, you do amaze me," was all I could say as we pulled up outside the Rosedale. At this time headteachers of a medium sized school were only on around thirty thousand pounds.

That evening, I went out with everyone for a meal in the place they had been frequenting all week. It was a nice reasonably priced wine bar just a few streets away from the Cathedral, which we walked past – the sight of its gaunt, shattered walls still able to evoke thoughts of bombs screaming down from a night sky. I would have liked to have sat next to Michael Slater, he had been so interesting to talk to, but instead I was sandwiched between Sharon and Peter. Peter was a kind man who spent most of his time on inspection missing his wife and family. I heard a full account of his daughter's latest frightening bout of asthma, her brilliant grades at the end of the summer term and his wife's success in landing the job of deputy at the school where she had worked for fifteen years.

Thursday was a nightmare day. Having spent most of the previous days working a little under par, I had innumerable jobs to catch up on. I missed the mid-morning break. At lunch-time, however, I managed to talk to a group of girls on the corridor just on their way out to play. They looked at me blankly when I asked them about bullying and they only gave me one word answers to all my questions. After I left them, they ran off to the toilets so I followed them. There was much giggling going on. I stopped just outside the door, listening.

"She asked if anyone ever called us names!" A shriek of laughter. "As if anyone would dare!"

When I put my head round the door, they looked sheepish.

"Oh it's you lot again," I said, "I was looking for people I haven't talked to yet, so I'll leave you in peace." I walked away. I had a nasty suspicion I had just been talking to the bullies.

When I got outside, the playground struck me as particularly bleak. I could imagine how daunting it must be for any child that lacked confidence or had no friend to play with. First, I spoke to some Year 6 girls sitting on one of the thin benches dotted along the playground periphery. One of them said she had been bullied in Year 5, but it was over now. Then, I spotted the plump girl who I had seen wondering about on her own on the Monday. She was on her own again, just standing near the fence and looking down at her feet. I went over to her and asked her if she wouldn't mind talking to me. I chatted to her for a bit about being an inspector at the school and showed her my name badge. Her response was very minimal, but she did tell me her name was Shelley.

"I was wondering," I said cautiously, "why you are on your own. Don't you have anyone to play with?"

"Not today."

"Oh. Do you have someone to play with on other days?"

"Yes, my best friend Samantha, but she is away today."

"Oh, I see. You must miss her."

"I do a lot." Then Shelley started to tell me everything about her friend, the colour of her hair, her birthday, her favourite games, what she did when she came to her house for tea. I couldn't stop her talking. She had turned into a different girl. I was just beginning to feel I could ask her about bullying when the whistled signalled the end of play. Shelley stopped talking, and the blank look that I had seen on her face at the start came down like a shutter. She turned away from me and walked to her class line. As I watched her go, I knew there was reluctance in every step.

Sarah and Sharon both gave me neatly written observation forms on which they had recorded discussions with children, all of whom said they had friends and were not bullied. Sharon had underlined these words. In the end at the final team meeting, I grudgingly had to agree that relationships were satisfactory.

I had a nagging feeling that I was not right, and the nagging stayed with me all the time that I drove home. I kept thinking about how I could have found out more, what I should have said to Sarah and how I should have been more assertive, until I reached the welcome sight of my own front door when thoughts of St. James's vanished in the pleasure of my homecoming.

18, Grange Road, Coventry: Three weeks after the inspection of St. James's Church of England Primary School

Shelley Thomas sat on the side of her bed and pressed the pin from her lucky-dip badge into her left arm until blood came out in a little droplet. She looked down at it and pressed the pin in again and made another droplet appear just to the right of it. She stared at both of them, watching the blood ooze, until she heard her brother Jason call to her to come down for tea. She patted the blood off with a tissue, but some more came so she stuck the tissue on to stop it staining the sleeve of her blouse. She went downstairs for tea.

Later that evening, she sat next to her mum on the settee watching Emmerdale.

"Everything OK at school Shell?" her Mum asked. She was very casual, as if she was asking about the weather.

"Yes, everything's fine Mum."

"Must have been those inspector people who came to the school the other week – made Mrs. Butler sort things out." Shelley didn't say anything. She stared at the screen. She stayed beside her Mum, as close as she could, until it was time to go to bed. She didn't want to go upstairs to her room on her own.

"Mum will you come upstairs with me?"

"Big girl like you, needing her Mum to come to put her to bed." Her Mum laughed and gave her a little shove. "Don't be daft. Your dad's in soon, needing his tea." Shelley's dad worked unsociable hours at a nearby factor, one while nine and most weekends. It paid better than the proper daytime shift, but it meant Shelley hardly ever saw him. "You know Dad will be upset if you're not in bed – he'll come up to kiss you goodnight."

"Promise – don't let him forget."

"I promise."

18, Grange Road, Coventry: Six weeks after the inspection

"What are you telling me? Graham Thomas was looking at his wife as if she had gone mad. "I don't understand what's happening?" He was almost shouting which was unusual for him because he was a mild-natured man.

"I took Shelley to the doctors today and he said that she needs to see a child psychiatrist."

"What? You took her to the doctors today?" he repeated – " a child bloody psychiatrist for goodness sake! What's the matter with her?"

"I found a lot of blood on the sleeve of Shelley's school blouse."

"So she had fallen over? Had an accident? Had a fight?"

"No, she had been pricking her arm with a pin, for some time it seems, and then she used a pair of scissors." As she said the word scissors, Linda Thomas began crying, loud sobs that shook her shoulders, and Graham sat down and put his arm round her which made Linda cry even more. When she stopped, they sat in bemused silence for some while.

"Look love, we'll sort it out – whatever it is, we'll sort it out. We're a family we'll stick together. We'll get Sharon right."

"I've let her down. I kept telling her to go to school. I didn't really want to hear about it. I thought that the school had dealt with it, but I should've noticed. I should've seen she was just getting more and more strange. She was clingy all the time, even in the evenings. But she went into school each morning and didn't say anything to me."

"You reckon it's that bullying you were telling me about?"

"Of course, it is. The doctor was really good. It was a new young chap I've never seen before. He said straight off – what she's been doing, self-harming," she choked a little as she said the words. "It's a classic symptom of a child being bullied, only it's usually older children that do it."

"I'm going into that school myself to see that Mrs. Butler, and Shelley's not going back, not for one day. Do you hear me? I don't care if you have to give up your job. She's not going into that school. We'll get her into another school somehow or other." Graham Thomas was deeply, horribly angry.

4, Kingston Drive, Coventry: Twelve weeks after the inspection

It was Monday morning and Mrs. Stevens was looking into the lovely, wide, new mirror above the dressing table of her very recently installed bedroom suite. She was putting on her make-up. When she had finished she gave a satisfied smile at her reflection. She liked the way the over-lapping top she had chosen neatly defined her figure, still good after three children. Then she caught sight of Bethany's face in the mirror as she stood behind her.

"What's up love, whatever is the matter?"

"Mum, I don't feel well – I really don't feel well." Mrs. Stevens swivelled round in her chair to face her daughter.

"Bethany this is the third Monday you've told me you don't feel well – what is up with you? You never ailed from one year to the next and now you seem to have something wrong with you every week. What is going on at school? Is it the work?"

After every question that she asked, Mrs. Stevens paused, waiting for an answer, but Bethany just stood looking at her, not speaking. Then suddenly, her lower lip started trembling and tears were flooding down her cheeks.

"It's Donna, Mum, she's turned 'em all against me. They keep picking on me, saying I'm daft. It all started because I went down in the spelling group – I do different spellings to them now – easy ones."

"Well that's no reason for them to pick on you."

"They say I'm daft and, and Donna says…." she paused, "she says nasty things about you."

"What things?"

"That you're a tart, and I'm a slag." Bethany choked on the last word and the crying became hysterical. Her mother moved towards her and put her arms round her daughter.

"Hush darling, hush," and then puzzled: " but Bethany, love, Donna? She's your friend!"

Chapter 20

Phone calls figure prominently in the lives of inspectors because team members, contractors and schools are nearly always some distance from each other. On the Monday after I got back from Coventry, I spent much of the day on the telephone.

Henry was the first person to call me in the morning. I thought he had rung to ask how things had gone in Coventry and to tell me that the next inspection I would go on would be led by Trevor. This was the case, but then there was more.

"Have you got a pen and paper handy there Jane?" he asked.

"Yes, yes I have."

"Well I would like you to take down these details now – it's the name and address of the school for your lead."

"My lead?" I repeated, as if such a thing had never entered my head, which of course it had, but somehow it had always been in the distant future.

"It's in February, two weeks after you get back from Trevor's. Ofsted is really packing them in now – they want to get as many done as possible before April for some reason."

Then he was telling me a name; the headteacher was a Mr. Westcote, which I wrote down, and then the name and address of the school – Home Farm Primary, Brewer Street, Spittalshaw, Birmingham, but by the time I started to write the 'S' of the oddly named Spittalshaw my hand had began to shake, as if I was in the arctic without an overcoat, making it almost impossible to write

"How is Spittalshaw spelt?" I asked, playing for time.

Henry spelt it out. Then he added: "It's a pretty impoverished area on the west side of the city. Lots of drug-related crime."

Oh, great, I thought, just what I wanted for my first school as a lead inspector.

"Here's the phone number," Henry continued unconcerned.

"Just a moment," I said, relieved that the shaking hadn't transmitted itself to my vocal chords. "I haven't quite got the address of the school down yet."

When he reeled off the telephone number, I had to ask him to repeat that several times as well. Panic was scattering my brain cells. I heard him ask me if I was sure of my ground with regard to the initial meeting with the school and the organisation of the parents' meeting. I had managed to say a weak yes, though not feeling sure of any ground, let alone that pertaining to leading an inspection. Then he went on to give numerous instructions, most of which I barely registered. Fortunately, towards the end, I heard him telling me to remind the headteacher of all the documents the school should have ready for me on my arrival.

"They so often leave things out," he said, "even though the handbook clearly lists what's needed. I sometimes ask myself if they bother to read it. You've got to spoon-feed them most of the time, you know. I think it's because most of the time, they put it out of their minds and when the brown envelope arrives they just go into a panic. Anyway you've got all that, Jane, haven't you?"

"Yes, I'm fine with all that, I was just writing it all down so as not to forget anything." I lied. The words brown envelope went round in my mind – what did he mean? But I thought it would sound too stupid to ask.

"Good, good." There was an encouraging tone to his voice and then: "You've no need to worry, you know. You'll be fine. You've made a great deal of progress over this term."

"Thank you." His calm voice was beginning to have an effect. "I'm sure I will be all right, once I get into it."

"Absolutely, first time is always a bit strange. As I said Jane, you'll be fine." I thought he was going to say goodbye then but he carried on: "Oh by the way, you know Phil has organised a Christmas do for us don't you?"

"No, I hadn't heard."

"Well he will no doubt get round to ringing you soon, but apparently, his wife Stephanie offered to do an evening buffet for us, partners invited, of course. I asked Phil if he was sure about it and he said that Stephanie loves entertaining. Madeleine is not at all into that kind of thing." Madeleine, Henry's wife, was very academic and worked on obscure research at the British Museum.

"It's very kind of Phil and Stephanie,"

"Yes, it certainly is. Of course, we'll all take a bottle, or something. Oh my goodness, Jane I nearly forgot to tell you to ring Trevor. I've told him that you should accompany him on his initial visit to his school. It's Barleydale Primary near Halifax; Matthew Longton is going to be monitoring the visit." I smiled then at Henry forgetting these rather pressing and important pieces of information.

"Right I'll phone Trevor right away," I said, a little surprised that Trevor hadn't phoned me already.

When I put the phone down, I sat for a while staring at it, as if it could explain to me why such terror had engulfed me so completely. When I was a child I had learned to play the piano to an average level of competency. Thus when I started teaching I was often asked to play for assemblies and concerts. The accompaniments for songs such as "I love the sun it shines on me" and "Morning has broken" are not masterpieces, they do not even remotely reach the standard of the easier works of Schubert or Chopin which I had mastered as a teenager. But when I was sitting at the piano stool with the school silently waiting for the first notes to tinkle forth, panic would grip me. There was no explaining it, it just descended, taking me over like some alien force; it manifested itself by my hands shaking, sometimes uncontrollably, a distinct disadvantage when you are about to play the piano. I used to sit at the piano, ostensibly in control, a smile on my face and not the smallest of tremble in any part of my body, and then the moment that I raised my hands to the keyboard, the shaking would start. Duff notes in my piano accompaniments during assemblies cheered up many a bored colleague.

When I dialled Trevor's number, there was no answer. It left me with no option but to ring Mr.Westcote, the headteacher of Home Farm Primary. Again, I sat looking at the phone for some time and then decided to write down everything I should say, starting with the first 'hello' to the school secretary. Half an hour later, I had my script ready so I picked up the phone and dialled. My hands were only shaking slightly and my head felt reasonably clear. The number rang about four times and then someone picked up:

"Home Farm Primary School, can I help you?" said a voice with a strong Birmingham accent in flat disinterested tones that belied the offer of help.

"Hello. My name is Jane Schaffer, may I speak to Mr. Westcote." There was only the smallest tremor in my voice.

"He's not in the office at the moment." The short response somehow managed to convey that the speaker was not about to divulge more about his whereabouts or to suggest anything so helpful as to find him.

"Perhaps you would like to call back later."

"Is he out of school today?"

"Who's calling?"

To answer, I looked down at my script and read: "I am phoning to introduce myself to Mr. Westcote as the lead inspector of his forthcoming Ofsted inspection in February." There was silence at the other end of the phone, a lengthy silence.

"Hello, are you still there?" I asked. It was at this moment that I realised the power of the 'O' word in schools. There wasn't just a sea change, the whole tidal flow of the school altered. Suddenly it seemed that Mr. Westcote had just been spotted coming down the corridor, and the next minute I was told that I was being put through to his extension in his office. As the school changed so did I – I was no longer a casual caller, I was an Ofsted inspector who had just discovered that most school staff were in awe of such a person. I didn't need my crib sheet any more. When I spoke to Mr. Westcote, I introduced myself with confidence, smiling all the time to make myself sound friendly; and now, I got the distinct impression that it might be the other person on the end of the phone who had the shakes.

I took charge, sounding authoritative, calming some of Mr. Westcote's most pressing fears....no it didn't matter that there was a supply teacher in Year 4 and of course we would understand that the new deputy they were appointing at Christmas would have little experience of the school by the time we came in February, and yes we would do our best to be understanding about why the school development plan wasn't finished yet. (Well that might be a problem but I wasn't going to say so just then). I efficiently trotted out the list of documents the school needed to prepare for us.

Right at the end of the call Mr.Westcote said, "Well I am glad to have got that over, I have been dreading this phone call ever since I got the brown envelope and now I see you are quite an understanding person." (There it was again, I thought, the brown envelope.) I said my goodbyes, reassuring Mr. Westcote that I was understanding and that I was greatly looking forward to my visit to his school. The phone call had taken nearly thirty minutes, but when I hung up, I was feeling pleased. It had gone well, and Mr.Westcote sounded nice. What did it matter if the school was in a poor area? Dedicated teachers worked in such places – I of all people should know that.

After a stop for coffee, I managed to get through to Trevor. I was still puzzled as to why he hadn't contacted me about the visit to his school. I soon realised that he hadn't thought he needed to. He had just assumed that I would accompany him whatever date he arranged. When I chided him for leaving it to me to phone him, he seemed genuinely puzzled as to why I needed to know the dates so soon. Trevor, despite his generosity and kindness on occasions, had some blind spots. He also had some irritating ways. One of which was to explain things more than once, as if you could not possibly be following his drift. Consequently, my phone call to him went on for a long time and I had to keep shifting the receiver from ear to ear, as he gave me a detailed description of the school in triplicate.

Finally through fear of paralysed ear, I said: "Thanks Trevor, that's really helpful. I'm really looking forward to coming with you on the initial visit, even if Matthew Longton is monitoring us – by the way, did you know about the Christmas do at Phil's house?"

"Oh yes, Phil phoned me yesterday. He said that Stephanie had suggested it and he had to go along with it, but I don't think he was too happy about it – his two women in the same room together – his wife and his mistress!"

"Trevor that's a terrible way to describe it," I said.

"Well you can say that, but it's true."

"Do you think you'll be going?"

"Oh yes, I wouldn't miss it for anything." My sympathy for Trevor as a man, lonely through the recent loss of his wife, diminished. Was he jealous of Phil? Despite his obvious once very happy monogamous situation, did Trevor wish he was a man with a mistress, especially one so lovely as Abby? In the event though, Trevor did miss the evening at Phil's; he went down with the 'flu.

After my talk with Trevor, I got on with tidying up the last of my papers from Coventry. I had spent Saturday and Sunday writing my paragraphs to send to Sarah Pennington. They were saved on my Compaq and now I opened up my document file and checked over the text. There were lots of small errors – commas left out, sentences too long and the inevitable missed apostrophe. I put them right. The drill, in this pre e-mail attachment era, was to print up a final draft as a hard copy and also to save it on to a floppy disc. Then the hard copy and the disc had to be sent to the lead inspector, to arrive not later than the Wednesday following the inspection. The lead inspector would then use the disc to copy, cut and paste the team inspector's writing into the full report. In 1996, this simple procedure did not always go smoothly. People saved things in the wrong format, or the disc itself might be corrupted, and then leads would get discs they could not open. After many attempts to read gobbledegook, the lead would get very annoyed, phone the offending team member, who if sensible was out, and then have no recourse but to use the hard copy to type out the paragraphs themselves. Naturally, Penny's wrath would be great if this fate should befall her, so I copied my stuff twice on two separate discs to be on the safe side, listening to the reassuring whirr as the Compaq recorded my work.

As the day wore on, I found myself expecting a phone call from Abby. Surely she would want to tell me how her lead had gone? I had been too busy on Saturday and Sunday to think about phoning her. I had presumed that that was how it was for her, but by now, she must be able to spare a few moments for a chat. I started to feel faintly aggrieved. Then a little worried, perhaps things had gone terribly wrong? Supposing Henry had failed her? I picked up the phone and dialled Abby's number.

After a few rings, she answered sounding incredibly jolly. "Jane, how lovely to hear from you – how was your inspection with Sarah Pennington?"

"It was OK," I said, suddenly not feeling like talking about Coventry. "I take it everything went well with you?"

"Oh the school was wonderful, just wonderful. Sister Mary is the most fantastic headteacher – the children are so happy there. They come from poor homes you know. It wasn't that far from Beswick Street – a slightly better part of Liverpool but not much. The results they get are incredible."

"Lucky to get a school like that for your first lead," I said.

"I know, I was really lucky, and I had a good team, well except for one person."

"Who was that?"

"It was the lay inspector. He was awful. He had no idea, and I dread to think what his writing is going to be like. He kept calling me the boss, which made me want to hit him over the head, and he got it all wrong on health and safety. Then he only just made it for his meeting with the governor who had come in especially to see him. I had to go and find him."

"Oh dear, that was bad. How was it with Phil?"

"It was great." Abby was quiet for a moment. "We work really well together. We're thinking of working together as a partnership. Phil has a friend who has a contracting business in Leicester. He thinks it might be a good thing to sign up with him." The more cheerful and enthusiastic Abby was getting, the more deflated I began feeling.

"You are looking ahead. I've not even got round to thinking about the end of this term."

"Oh it's not me, it's Phil. He plans all the time."

"I thought he was going to go back to his school after this year."

"Well, he had thought that to start with, but now he has worked out that he could make so much more money in inspection he is not so sure and well…"

"He wants to be with you."

"Yes, of course that comes into it. But come on Jane, you've not told me anything about Sarah Pennington. What was she like as a lead? I bet she was a bit of a fussy type."

After all that happiness and good fortune, I didn't feel like moaning about Sarah so I just told her about being ill and she was full of sympathy. Then I quickly went on to the subject of the Christmas do and for the first time Abby stopped being so overflowingly happy.

"I don't know what I am going to do. I really don't think I can face going."

"Perhaps you could get the sickness I've just got rid of," I suggested. She laughed and said she might do just that and then we said our good-byes and how we had to get back to work. Before I managed to get on with anything though, I had to reason with myself about the feeling that had come over me during that conversation. I knew it was jealousy, just jealousy. And I had had the nerve to criticise Trevor for the same thing! Half an hour later the phone rang and it was Abby again.

"I've just had a great idea. We could go together. One of us could drive and the other get sloshed." I was glad Abby had phoned again. I could cope with her happiness now, and in any case, it was not as if it was perfect for her.

"Or we could get a train to Bolton and a taxi from the station so we could both get sloshed," I said.

"A brilliant idea that Jane. We could start having a party before we went, so we were in the mood – spend the day treating ourselves at the shops – do some Christmas shopping have lunch out, all that stuff." Abby was getting enthusiastically into a mood of defiance, a devil-may-care disrespect for the situation confronting her. "What do you say Jane?"

"OK you're on. We'll sort out the details nearer the time – now don't you go changing your mind and backing out,"

"I wouldn't dream of it."

"Oh by the way Abby, can you tell me, what is the brown envelope?"

"Haven't you heard of it? Goodness. Oh I forgot you had that strange head. Well it's become a sort of shorthand for saying Ofsted have informed you of the date for your inspection. Heads ring each other up and say: 'The brown envelope arrived today'. And then they scream, very loudly down the phone to their friend. It's one of Ofsted's little foibles to use re-cycled brown envelopes for this communication; mustn't waste money on white ones you see."

When the day came for the do at Phil's house, Abby and I went Christmas shopping in the city centre, muffled up with gloves and scarves against the cold bright air. Festive cheer was in full swing. The tinsel brightness of the shops beckoned to us enticingly. It did not take much to get us in the mood. We gathered up armfuls of clothes to try on, tight pants, spangly tops, soft cashmere jumpers that we couldn't afford. A late lunch with several drinks kept us giggling through the afternoon. Then we headed back to my house to get changed.

Kate fell under Abby's spell. "I never had any teachers that looked like Abby," she whispered at me while Abby was in the bathroom applying make-up to her already perfect face. Luckily Kate had an invite for the evening as well, so we were all getting ready at the same time.

"You are so lucky to have had girls," Abby said showing Kate how to put her eye make-up on, a skill I had never mastered. "I never had a chance, of course, to do any of this sort of thing with Sam." We both admired Kate's outfit. I was proud of how lovely she looked, fortunately taking after her father with much of her looks.

"She's so lovely," Abby said when we left the house, and I felt warm with pride. On the train to Bolton, where Phil lived, we sobered up. I could see Abby was getting nervous.

"Stop worrying, there's nothing to worry about." I reassured. And there wasn't. The evening was one of those pleasant, restrained, adult affairs when everyone nibbles, sips and talks on general topics. It was, though, the kind of occasion when only couples feel really comfortable. Most people had come as a couple. Except for Abby and me, only the nice Margaret Williams from Matthew Longton's group was on her own. Trevor had gone down with a virus, similar to the one that I had had, so could not come. Inexplicably, I missed him, not because there was ever any notion of me being a couple with him, but just because Trevor was now so much part of our group. Nigel, of course had brought his trophy glamour girl. He stood beside her for most of the evening as if someone might pinch her. Mary's husband was very pleasant and jovial. I spent some time talking to him and discovered for the first time that Mary was an accomplished musician, playing both the violin and the piano to a high standard. I teased her for being so reticent and she in turn told her husband off for his husbandly pride. I thought they made a nice couple. Sarah Pennington's husband matched her perfectly, slim and suavely good-looking. They were both smartly dressed and smartly uninterested in talking to anyone other than Matthew Longton and Henry and their respective wives, certainly not a singleton like me.

Stephanie and Madeleine, Henry's wife, seemed quite taken up with each other. They talked together a lot. When I joined them at one point, they were discussing some proposed changes to hospital administration. They both seemed to know a great deal about the government white paper on the subject, although neither worked in that field. I knew nothing and could only contribute smiles and nods to the conversation. Feeling stupid, I edged away as soon as I could. Why could they not talk about something normal people talked about – like the price of fish or what their children were up to?

Stephanie Docherty was not at all how I had imagined her. I had imagined a home-loving, comfortably pretty Irish woman, maybe plump. She was very English, tall and confident. Everything about her, the way she dressed, her voice and manner spoke of a privileged upbringing. Her features were individually quite good but her face was pleasant rather than attractive. When thanked for putting the evening on, she smiled as if it had given her very little trouble, and probably it hadn't. I tried not to watch her too much, but as the evening went on, I began to understand why Phil had strayed. Even as she gently laid a hand on his arm to ask him to bring something in from the kitchen, her manner implied 'this is mine and I am in charge.' The 'in charge' and the implied ownership would irk a man like Phil, although he would never admit it. Yes, I thought looking at them together, Phil would stray but no, he would never leave. Stephanie had his measure.

Abby and Phil were careful not to avoid each other completely and, conversely, not to spend too much time in each other's company. I saw Abby move over to take my place with Stephanie and Madeleine when I moved away. She was fortunate that now the conversation had moved on to the latest show at the Whitworth Art Gallery. Abby talked animatedly; she would have no shortage of things to say about an art exhibition.

Peter Morrison and his friendly wife Jill were ensconced on a sofa in one corner of the room. When I went over to say 'hello', I naturally congratulated Jill on her recent promotion, so I only had myself to blame at having to hear Peter's blow by blow account of her stiff interview and his happy pride at describing the other applicants she had trounced. I talked to Matthew Longton and his wife about the 'flu from which Matthew was recovering. (No doubt, I thought caught from me in Coventry). It had been instrumental in his cancelling his monitoring visit to Barleydale, which had given Trevor so much joy at the time. Now Matthew asked me about the school and said he was sorry to hear that Trevor was down with the dreaded bug from which he himself had just recovered.

When I later described the evening to Kate, I said that there had been riotous dancing on the tables. Her mouth had fallen open, and then we started laughing as I told her the truth that I had enjoyed a riveting evening in which a discussion on the number of meals Matthew Longton had not eaten during his recent bout of 'flu, as recounted to me by his wife, had been a highlight.

Chapter 22

<u>23 Broomfield Crescent, Barleydale</u>

"Come on, Daniel, sweetheart, put your trainers on. We've got to get off to school now."

Daniel made no move to get off the settee where he was happily watching that morning's episode of ' Bob the Builder'. His mother disappeared. She cleared the cereal dishes off the table and rinsed them under the tap. She was just about to start taking some of the clothes out of the tumble dryer when she glanced up at the clock. It was twenty-five to nine. It took them no more than ten minutes to walk to school, but today there was dinner money and the book bag to take in, and she would need to find a scarf for Danny. It had felt really cold when she had nipped out with the rubbish. If they didn't make a start soon they would be late. She moved purposefully into the lounge again. Switching off the TV she stood in front of Daniel.

"I told you to put your trainers on, Danny."

Daniel got off the settee. He pulled a sulky face, but stuffed his feet into his trainers. When he had done up the Velcro straps she ruffled his hair and gave him a kiss.

"Good boy, you don't want to be late do you?" Daniel shook his head and ran to the front door. His mother hurried back into the kitchen and found the change she had put ready to slip into one of the special dinner money envelopes. Then she retrieved his book bag from the unit in the lounge.

Daniel reached up and opened the front door an inch. He peeped out. He wasn't supposed to open the door and he pushed it to again before his Mum came to put his coat on. He liked school. His friend, Jack would be there and Benji. They played together all the time. They thought up really good games and, even when they fell out over something, they soon forgot about it. Suddenly, he remembered that Mrs. Whitehead had said they needed more empty boxes for the making table.

"Mummy, I've got to take dum boxes to dool, Mrs. Whitehead ded."

"Daniel it's too late now, I'll sort you some out for tomorrow."

His mother put his coat on, struggling for several minutes to pull up the zipper. She started putting his scarf on, but he didn't want it. He shouted "No" when she tried to tie it up. He tugged at it and threw it on the floor, so she gave up.

His mother held his hand as they walked to school. There was a cold wind. It swirled up the last of the brown leaves still scattered on the pavement. Daniel remembered last Friday at story time, Mrs. Whitehead had got really cross with the class because they hadn't been quiet. She had complained that they were not listening properly.

"Why is a witch coming to tool today Mummy?" He asked.

"Witch? What do you mean, witch?

"Mrs. Whitehead ded that on Friday – she ded that we had to be very good on Monday, or we would be turned into frogs by the lady who was coming to vidit – It must be a witch mustn't it?"

"Oh I don't know, Daniel. But it sounds as if Mrs. Whitehead was joking or maybe you've got it muddled up somehow."

"Witches turn people into frogs." Daniel persisted. His mother frowned a little. What a peculiar thing? Surely Mrs. Whitehead didn't need to threaten the children with some silly imaginary visitor to make them behave? Jill, who had helped out in the class, had said that the children were often very noisy, that they got a little out-of-hand sometimes. Still, she liked Mrs. Whitehead and Daniel loved school. His reading had come on, even though he never seemed to do any writing, not like Lucy, Jill's little girl, who was always using pencils and crayons. Daniel's mother sighed, but that was boys for you.

"Are witches bad?"

"Witches are only in stories Daniel. Perhaps some actors are coming to the school today to do a play about witches." Daniel's mother wondered if she had missed a letter about some school event. It was always happening. She would have to ask Jill when she saw her. Jill was much better at keeping up with things than she was. They turned in at the school gate and when they got to the path leading to Daniel's classroom she let him run ahead. He was soon at the classroom door. Into his second term in Reception, Daniel was perfectly happy to leave her now, without a backward glance – so different from the first few weeks when he hadn't wanted to let go of her hand and she had spent sleepless nights worrying that he would never get used to school. She went in and unzipped his coat. She hung it up on his peg. Mrs. Whitehead looked really busy and flustered so she didn't bother to ask her what Daniel might have meant about the witch.

Our inspection room at Barleydale Primary School was unusually comfortable and bright. That was because it was Mrs Evans' office which she had given up for our use. When we had visited in December (unaccompanied by Matthew Longton), Trevor and I had done our best to dissuade the headteacher from this course of action, but she had been adamant.

"You will work better if you are comfortable and there's plenty of room for me in Joyce's office," she had said with her hearty good humour. Her generosity seemed genuine, not extended to us in deference to our position, but because that was how she treated everyone connected with the school.

Sheila Evans was a tall, very attractive woman with a warm smile; her larger than usual figure suited to her personality. She had answered all our questions, on that first visit, with an openness that had startled us because we were not expecting it. Trevor and I had looked at each other on several occasions with eyebrows slightly raised because of her straightforward answers and manner. It seemed that, at this school, we would achieve the hitherto unattainable, but always expected, Ofsted concept of 'working alongside school staff to bring about improvement.' We had only been in the school a short while before we all agreed to using first names and dispensing with unnecessary formalities. This friendly headteacher seemed to be embracing inspection with enthusiasm.

She had been headteacher for two years and was fiercely proud of how much progress her staff, parents and children had made since her appointment. Prior to her arrival, things had been allowed to run down by a head who had often been absent through illness, and had become increasingly out-of-touch with the changes in education going on around him. In the time since she took up the headship, there had been a considerable amount of change, but she had done things at a sensible pace and thereby kept the support and now obvious affection of the staff.

"Not like that chap at Beswick Street who just got everyone's back up by bringing in too many changes, resulting in his own downfall," Trevor had remarked.

To start with, Sheila's main aim had been to improve the behaviour of the children and the relationships in the school, which we were told had become very poor. To do this, she had instigated a programme of behaviour management that incorporated raising pupils' self-esteem. Next she had sorted out the dismally bleak accommodation so that corridors were now freshly painted and carpeted and classrooms bright and cheerful. Finally a programme of monitoring and evaluating the quality of teaching in English and mathematics was beginning to show results in improvements in the school's National Curriculum test results.

Parents gave a resounding endorsement to Sheila's leadership at the parents' meeting and the post-bag had been full of letters praising the changes that she had brought in. It all meant that Trevor was in the comfortable position of leading an inspection where a strong headteacher was happy for inspectors to add weight to her own judgements and so help to bring about further improvements. This was one of the easiest inspection scenarios, and also one of the most satisfying. Trevor had been lucky. I was relieved and glad for him, but also slightly peeved. Despite being happy to support and help Trevor with leading, it seemed unfair that he should get such an easy ride. I found myself getting annoyed with him because he seemed so obtuse at times about simple things, like making sure that he would not have trouble with coverage or with team members being able to get the evidence they needed.

On our first morning, we appeared to be a cosy team, everyone happy to be in such a well-managed school. Besides Trevor and myself, we had been joined by non-other than Sarah Pennington who now seemed to smile much more than she did as a lead inspector. The fourth team member was a man called Tom Bikerstaff whom none of us had met before. The lay inspector was to join us on Wednesday.

Sarah and I greeted each other like old buddies and we each settled our bags down besides one of the comfortable armchairs. Tom Bikerstaff commandeered the head's desk, declaring that he couldn't work unless he had ample room. He was an elderly man, very tall, with a pronounced stoop. He peered at you over his glasses in absent-minded, dotty professor mode. Typically, Trevor let him get away with his selfishness manoeuvre. It meant that Trevor's own things, including the inspection documentation, were consigned to a side shelf already half-full of items belonging to the school. I smiled to myself thinking of how Sarah had set up the inspection room exactly to her liking. She would have brooked no such take-over by a mere team member, and here was Trevor cramped up in a corner of the room, laying out piles of documents in what could only be described as an untidy heap. I had to busy myself so as not laugh out loud at Sarah's deadpan expression that, despite her attempts at disinterest, grew more and more incredulous as Trevor tried to squash everything on to a small shelf.

Following Nigel's example, Trevor had arranged a meeting

with the staff, which was definitely a point in his favour. He spoilt the effect a little by forgetting that he had done so. He suddenly jumped up and told us about the meeting, but we were already a few minutes late, so we had to scurry off down the corridors, past the lovely displays that adorned every wall, arriving at the staff-room door out of breath. 'Ooops', I thought, there's good time-keeping by inspectors, as per Sarah's model, already compromised.

The staffroom was quite cramped and we four had to squeeze round the door to fit in, standing too close to each other for comfort. The staff appeared relaxed, and laughed in a jolly way at our squash, telling us there was never any room for meetings. One after the other, we introduced ourselves and told them what our responsibilities were to be. I was doing English again, the elderly chap Tom Bikerstaff was responsible for maths and Trevor was doing science, his preferred subject. Sarah was going to be looking at the provision for the under fives. I scanned the faces to see which lucky teacher was to be the recipient of Sarah's observations. A kindly faced middle-aged lady called Mrs White-head seemed to be the one. I felt like going over and telling her to be sure to watch her time-keeping. I could imagine Sarah standing with a stopwatch at the door timing how long it took her small charges to divest themselves of their winter coats after play. Woe betide Mrs. Whitehead if any tardy infant lingered about on the toilet. Trevor finished off the short meeting by giving the staff good wishes for a successful inspection. It all seemed very friendly.

As we made our way back to the inspection base to finish off our meeting, Sarah and I walked along the corridor together. She was gracious enough to say that she thought Trevor had done well with the introductory meeting, and even said that she might include something of the sort on her next lead. I was just begin-ning to think kindly thoughts towards her when she added:

"But I don't know what Matthew will think of his inspection room. It really is dreadful, and I am afraid, I shall have to say so. The only saving grace is that he has done a nice clear timetable, although, I am not sure if he has crossed checked it for coverage. There seem to be very few lessons of RE for me to see."

"That's because RE is mostly taught on Fridays," I said. "And yes, he has checked it for coverage." I knew this to be the case, because I had done it for him the night before, but I didn't say that to Sarah. Trevor had only produced the timetable because I had insisted that he did, and when I had scanned it on Sunday evening at our arrival at the bed and breakfast where we were staying, I had spotted a couple of coverage errors. Trevor had corrected them, I was sure of that. Despite my growing irritation with him, I thought I had better warn him about Sarah's criticism of the room so that she would not be able to grumble to Matthew on Thursday.

Matthew Longton was coming to monitor on the last day of the inspection. Unfortunately for Trevor, this was just about the worst time possible for a monitoring visit. The reason being, that Matthew would be able to look through all of the evidence forms and check that Trevor had been through them properly himself. Checking the observation forms written by your team, in the evening after the inspection, was a formidable task for the lead inspector. Many skimped it. No chance of that, however, on the inspection of Barleydale. Trevor spent long hours into the night reading every word people had written for fear of what Matthew might come up with if he hadn't noticed an error or weakness. The thing was to put your signature on the form if you were happy with an observation, or to write a comment, preferably in red ink, if you thought it was not good enough, or if one of the fiddly boxes had not been filled in. The other unpleasant thing about Matthew coming on the last day was that he would sit through the final team meeting and be able to see whether all the appropriate judgements had been arrived at properly. The only person who was looking forward to Matthew's arrival was Sarah.

Trevor had taken little notice of my grumbles about Sarah Pennington when I had hoped for sympathy after being with her on the Coventry inspection. Now, I felt guiltily pleased that, as the days went by, he got more and more irritated and uptight about her. He would find me on the corridor to whisper in agitation: 'Do you know what she has just said now?' Or, 'that woman has been complaining about....' And I would murmur some soothing response, but occasionally I couldn't help thinking Sarah was right. More and more, I was noticing how ineffectual Trevor could be. He was often indecisive, and worse than that, he sometimes missed obvious signs that something needed following up.

Sarah never made a fuss or caused an argument; she merely let you know, in a small but damning phrase, that something was not to her liking. Somehow or other, she would then extricate herself from whatever issue she had raised and leave you with no comeback, feeling frustrated or annoyed. At team meetings, when all were in agreement that an aspect of school life should be judged good, and at Barleydale, most things were good, Sarah would sometimes say, without any explanation: "I think it is no more than satisfactory." Trevor should have been more forceful in asking her to explain her reasons, but he wasn't. Although her views went against those of the majority, she managed to create an unsettled feeling, so that even if you had been sure in the first instance about your own judgements, doubt would set in.

Fortunately, Tom Bikerstaff, hit it off with Trevor. His dotty absent-minded professor appearance belied a very quick mind, and there was not much that he missed. When Sarah came up with one of her roadblocks, Tom would save the day for Trevor. He knew the handbook back to front and he could accurately quote a sentence or two from it that would, amazingly, silence Sarah. When, for instance, she had said that the school did not have something termed a curriculum 'map' and that this, of course, was not a satisfactory situation, Tom quoted: "…judgements should be based on how well the organisation of the curriculum and assessment contribute to pupils' attainment, progress and response rather than on predetermined notions of what is desirable in curriculum organisation." Obviously consigning Sarah's curriculum map to a 'predetermined notion' not to be argued over, he added with a flourish, "Ofsted Handbook for Inspection, Page 76," mightily pleased with himself.

After that all Trevor had to do was say: "Well, we are all in agreement then, such and such is good," and mark down the grade in the appropriate box acting as a secretary, rather than the lead. On Tuesday evening I made a mental note that I would need to suggest to Trevor that I would record the grades at future meetings. At least, this would give the semblance of him being in charge.

Chapter 23

On Wednesday lunchtime, Sarah and I found common ground. It was on the issue of writing. We were both working in the inspector base as was the lay inspector who had arrived that morning. He was a tall, very attractive man called Hamza Choudray. I had just finished looking through the children's writing books. Although writing in the junior classes was good, writing in the younger classes was bothering me.

"Oh dear," I moaned, "there's just too much copying going on in the infants and there is no real link between them learning the letter sounds and using them."

"Exactly," Sarah said, managing to irritate even when she agreed with you; her one word somehow conveying that she had been the first to identify this matter.

"Is that what you've found in the Reception?" I asked, ignoring my irritation.

"Oh, it is not a literate environment at all. There are far too few opportunities for children to use pencils. Some of them don't write very much at all. Some of the boys just about write their names and that's it."

"Does the Reception class teacher have a programme to teach letter sounds?"

"Yes, but it's a very slow process and not done well at all. She told me that they have a 'letter of the week' but it's done rather like a fun time. She uses the big book and they spot words beginning with the letter, which is all very well and good, but there are lots of children that don't really connect and so do not commit the letter to memory. None of them realize that the letter sound they are learning for their reading is what they need to write. She needs to have a short, sharp focused session every day on letter sounds. It's fine to have a focus letter for the week, but you need to recap on letters previously learnt. Some will learn far more than one a week, and those that find it difficult need to have plenty of re-enforcement."

I looked at Sarah with a new respect – she had just put into words, what I had been thinking for some time about the 'letter of the week' sessions that were very popular in infant classes at the time. I said as much and for once Sarah flashed her very nice smile.

Just then, the newly arrived lay inspector, who was going through the files to get up to speed on the inspection, paused in his perusal of them and looked up. "It sounds as if this teacher should be at least sent to the penitentiary for her misdemeanours, if not actually hung from the gallows." He spoke with an Asian accent which, with his slightly old-world English, was very appealing. His expression was so serious, that for a second you were not sure how to take what he said.

"I know you are joking, Mr. Choudray," said Sarah, "but it is what we are here for, you know, to help schools to see where they are going wrong."

Hamza Choudray, gave a small bow in Sarah's direction, and a beaming smile. "Oh yes, Mrs. Pennington, I absolutely agree. I am sure that you are very good at helping schools to see where they are going wrong. You must not take the slightest notice of what someone like me, an ignorant lay inspector is saying." Although these condescending comments might have caused offence, if made by someone else, his teasing was done in such a charming manner I could see that Sarah was disarmed, almost unsure of what to say next.

"I don't just find fault, you know," she said, "I have praised many things about this Reception class."

This was news to me as I could not remember her saying one good thing about the Reception, so I chipped in with. "There

221

does seem to be a lot going on. Are the children stimulated by the activities offered?" I asked innocently. I had noticed in passing that the room overflowed with interesting displays. There were paintings hung from every conceivable surface, almost a forest of plants at different stages of growth and a large tank of African snails that chomped their way through the leaves of some of said plants. That week the Reception had been baking bread. This activity had filled the infant department with a mouth-watering smell. Towards the end of the afternoon, Reception children had wavered their way round the school corridors proudly carrying in their small hands what looked like huge plates piled with chunks of buttered hot bread to offer to everyone.

"She gives the children a secure environment and they respond to her activities very well. Yes, as you say, some of her activities are very interesting," was Sarah's faint praise.

"Ah, I can see that you are indeed a lady who is even…what is the expression, I am looking for, even… ?"

"Handed, even handed." I supplied.

"Ah, yes an even-handed lady, and I am sure I will learn a great deal from you – I am still learning you see. Schools are such fascinating places and you ladies have so much knowledge. You have been in teaching all your lives and know so much." Sarah looked slightly pained, not to be taken in by this effusive praise of our talents.

"What was your profession, Mr. Choudray before being a lay inspector?"

"Oh do call me Hamza. I was an accountant, that is why a lot of lead inspectors like me to check on the efficiency aspect."

"Oh that would be very helpful," I said. "I'm sure I would be asking you to do that aspect if you came on an inspection with me. I'm not very good with the intricacies of financial management, let alone aware of what makes it efficient." Sarah gave me a pitying look.

"It is one of my strengths," she said.

"Well, I knew we had much in common, Mrs Pennington!" Hamza Choudray smiled broadly. For once, Sarah looked wrong-footed, but unsure as to why. Then Hamza walked to the door and said he was off to eat lunch with the children.

"A very attractive man," Sarah remarked when he had closed the door. "We're fortunate to get ethnic minorities coming into inspection – it's so important don't you think?" I agreed with her on both points.

Later that day, I discovered that Hamza Choudray was not only skilled in financial matters; he was also very good at getting on with people. By mid-afternoon, he was on first name terms with everyone from the caretaker to the chair of governors. He and Sheila Evans reached the swapping of notes about the problems of teenagers, elderly parents, and getting a good plumber in just about as long as it takes most people to say, 'How are you?' I passed them on the corridor as I was on my way to an afternoon lesson, discussing the ingredients for a good lamb curry. Joyce the secretary became his unofficial assistant for the day, her kindly middle-aged face flushed with excitement at her sudden importance. She hurried to get Hamza such things as registers, fire drill records, lists of absentees and budget details, delving into dark recesses of the office and cupboards on corridors to do so.

Hamza would say, "do not bother yourself, Joyce, just when you have a moment free will do," in reference to needing a certain document, and then two minutes later Joyce would be putting it in his hand.

At the evening meeting, he declared that his areas (care, guidance and pupils' welfare and the school's relationship with its parents) were all very good and no one, including Sarah, disagreed with him.

At the hotel on that last evening, I sat in Trevor's room, calming him down about the imminent visit of Matthew Longton, and going over all the judgements we had reached so far. He had spread papers out all over the room and was busy picking them up and putting them down again – I was not sure to what purpose. On the last evening, the lead inspector has to draw all the team's judgements together, come up with headings for the main findings and list the key issues if any of the findings are unsatisfactory. At Barleydale, all was very straightforward because most things were good or very good. Trevor really had very little to do and nothing to agonise over. Sarah and I had made our concerns known about the teaching of writing to the English co-ordinator and she had relayed them to Sheila Evans. She had understood what we were saying and agreed that it would be helpful to the school to have writing in the early years identified as an area for development. I had explained this to Trevor, at least three times, but he had got into such a state of anxiety that he was no longer taking things in properly.

The only other area that was not strong enough in the school was Information and Communication Technology. It was no surprise or worry, as Sheila had highlighted it at our first meeting. Trevor, however, was not content with having just two key issues. He kept going through the record of corporate judgement and reading corresponding bits of the handbook. I knew it was because he was thinking about Matthew's visit rather than the needs of the school. I wanted to shake him – hadn't he been handed the easiest school in the world to inspect and here he was making such a meal of it? Finally, he explained that he was concerned because the data showed teaching in the whole school as good, but only satisfactory in the Reception class.

"Surely," I said, "you don't think that the Reception class is an issue do you?"

"Well the teaching is not as good as in the rest of the school."

"Trevor. It's skewed because of the writing." I was suddenly really worried that he was going to suggest something draconian for the poor teacher in Reception.

"Let's just look at how the other areas in the Reception class come out." I suggested. When we looked through all the observation forms, the other areas came out as good. "I think this has happened because Sarah has weighted her decision towards the unsatisfactory she gave for writing, and that obscures the good for mathematics, and all the other areas. These little ones are mostly doing well. You can't make an issue of the under fives just because of one area of weakness." I argued the case strenuously.

"I can see what you are saying, Jane" said Trevor, slowly and without too much conviction. "Now that I've actually looked through the Reception observations all together, I can see that teaching is mainly good."

"The teacher in Reception, Mrs. Whitehead is a lovely person – she really cares about the children and they love school." I said. Trevor nodded. "It would destroy her if she was picked out as the one failing the school. I am sure that is not what Sarah intended anyway. Don't you think she might have said so by now?"

"Well, I thought she might be just standing back and letting me fall into a trap, waiting to speak up tomorrow at the meeting and show me up in front of Matthew."

"Oh Trevor, you have let her get to you! She is pretty irritating I know, but she wouldn't do a thing like that."

"I think I've just been panicking."

"Yes, that's the first sensible thing you have said. Come on, everything's fine, let's go down to the bar and have a drink. It will

225

calm you down. You'll be fine tomorrow. Matthew Longton's not an ogre. This is one inspection when we should enjoy the last day."

Trevor looked at me as if I were mad, but, much to my relief, started packing up his papers. He found his room key and patted his pocket to check his wallet was there, obviously deciding to follow my advice to go down to the bar. When we got there, we found Tom Bikerstaff sitting on his own in the small lounge area, which was fortunate. He and Trevor spent a happy half hour chatting about fishing, the shared hobby that had sparked off their friendship in the first place.

I sat staring at pictures of deer in ancient forests and frigates on the high seas that someone had incomprehensibly chosen as embellishments for the walls. I started fretting about Home Farm Primary, thinking about my telephone call before Christmas and reassured myself that, although the secretary had not been very friendly, Mr. Westcote, the headteacher, had sounded nice. His voice had been deep and quite sonorous. It made me imagine him a thickset man, perhaps a little rotund. He had sounded a capable man, one who would be friendly with the children and staff. The school was probably fine. Surely Ofsted wouldn't give you a problem school on your first lead? The date for my initial visit to Home Farm was the coming Wednesday, hardly anytime after returning from Barleydale. Margaret Williams, who was going to be on the team, was to accompany me. Phil had been supposed to come, but the date had clashed with the feedback date of his own inspection.

"I say, Trevor," I leaned across and broke into his conversation with Tom, "I wonder how Phil has gone on with his lead?"

"Oh I am sure it will have been fine. His school had really good grades."

"Where was it?"

"Some posh part of Harrogate."

Hmm, I thought, Phil gets sent to Harrogate and I get inner city Birmingham. It added to my sense of foreboding. Perhaps all the good schools had been used up by the time they got to me? Then I remembered that Mary was leading on the same week as me and I thought that, when I got home, I might ring her to swap notes before my visit.

On the last morning, because the situation in the school was so good, there were only a few lesson observations to cover, and general tidy up jobs to do. At lunchtime, Sarah and I both made our way down to the infant department. We were on a mission to hand back the huge piles of records and children's work that had amassed in the team room. All the classes in the infants, including the Reception class, were situated round a central cloakroom area. When we arrived, staggering under our burdens, there were a few children getting their coats on after having eaten their lunch. Mrs. Whitehead bustled out of her room chatting with one of the classroom assistants. On seeing Sarah, she stopped immediately, and her good-natured smile did not falter. Sarah managed one of her lovely smiles in return, being gracious now it was time to say 'goodbye'. Just as Sarah was about to speak to Mrs. Whitehead, a small boy pushed his way in front of her. He obviously had something to say. Sarah bent down and smiled at him, perhaps expecting a nice compliment.

"Are you really a witch? he asked in a loud cheery voice. "You haven't done any dells yet. Witches should do magic dells. Are you going to do one?"

"A witch?" Sarah's smile vanished as if switched off by a tap.

I noticed a red flush spreading over the faces of the two members of staff.

"Oh Daniel, what are you saying?" said Mrs. Whitehead very loudly, too loudly. "Of course Mrs. Pennington is not a witch."

Daniel was not to be dismissed so lightly. He looked up at the now stony face of the inspector.

"I would have really liked it if you had managed a dell. My mummy doesn't believe you're a witch." He started walking away towards the outside door, but turned before reaching it and looked solemnly at Sarah, "but I know, you are." With this last enigmatic statement, Daniel, who was probably one of the boys who could 'only write his name', ran out to play.

In the end, everything went well for the school, and Matthew Longton's monitoring of Trevor's work also went reasonably well, although there were numerous items for improvement. Matthew gave Trevor a list of neatly written commandments, saying that they all needed to be sorted out before his next lead. And who could doubt him? Trevor had said with a sigh. As for the school, we gave Sheila Evans a glowing endorsement as a 'very good headteacher' and, at our last meeting with her, the two areas for improvement, the teaching of ICT and writing in the Reception and infant classes were accepted without complaint.

As I drove away with Trevor in the evening I said, "lovely school, but I will always remember it for the witch."

"What on earth? What witch?" asked Trevor and I told him the story of the small boy from the Reception class who, (for some unknown reason, though possibly implicating certain adults) was sure Sarah was a witch. It cheered him up for the whole drive home.

The Reception Class: Six months after the inspection of Barleydale Primary School

Good headteachers act upon Ofsted findings quickly and very good ones act upon them very quickly. When Daniel's mother came to see her child's books at the end of the summer term, she was very pleasantly surprised.

"Goodness Mrs. Whitehead," she said, I didn't know Daniel could write all these words."

Mrs. Whitehead said "Oh after Ofsted left, I was sent on a brilliant course on early writing, and I have to say, I learnt so much."

Daniel's mum smiled warmly at her. It was so typical of the nice Mrs. Whitehead to own up to needing to go on a course. Daniel had drawn a picture of a car. Underneath in large shaky letters he had written: 'My daddy car goes fst'. There was a blue line under the word 'goes'. Daniel's Mum noticed that there were blue lines under other words in Daniel's book.

"What are the blue lines for?" she asked.

"Oh that's where Daniel has been given that word. It's so that we know which words he can write himself and which ones he needed help with. Then Mrs. Whitehead turned back to the beginning of the book to a picture of a person – large head with a few smudges of hair, two points for eyes, a straight line for a mouth, a round egg body and two stick legs and two stick arms, Daniel's standard drawing of a person.

"Daniel drew the lady who came to inspect us," she said.

"She looks a bit of a witch," said Daniel's Mum laughing.

"She was," said Mrs. Whitehead going faintly red, but smiling as well. "She knew her stuff, but do you know? She stood with a stop-watch to check how long it took us to bring the children in after play!" Mrs. Whitehead enjoyed sharing this little moan with Daniel's Mum, but she knew she had blushed at the mention of the word 'witch'. She had always blushed easily.

PART FIVE

MY FIRST LEAD, HOME FARM PRIMARY SCHOOL, BIRMINGHAM

Chapter 24

Before I went on my visit to Home Farm, I had rung Mary to find out what kind of school she had for her first lead. I did not get through then, but on my return, I rang her again. I was hoping that someone else out of my group might be facing problems like those I now knew I would be facing at Home Farm, but no such luck. Mary burbled on, full of enthusiasm for her school. It was a small country school in Cumbria where the children seemed to belong to 'one big happy family'. I put down the phone and felt hard done to. What had I done to deserve Home Farm, and Mr.Westcote? Was it a sign that I shouldn't be doing inspections? Had I offended the gods of pedagogues living and dead?

After I spoke to Mary, I rang Phil. He was full of his experiences at Harrogate. When I told him how lucky he had been with a school in such a nice area. He said: "No, don't be fooled. It was in a nice area but we had a tough time, they were not pushing those bright kids anywhere near enough."

"Oh so it wasn't an easy ride, like Trevor's place?"

"Oh for sure no – easy if you were prepared to turn a blind eye, take things at face value and just see the things the school wanted you to see, but I'm not Nigel you know."

"I know, Phil, I know. Actually, I've rung to tell you about Home Farm."

"Oh what's it like then? Is it going to be a tough one?"

"Well, I think I might just have met that English co-ordinator you pointed out to me on our first week of training."

"Who? " Phil asked, puzzled and then the memory came. "Oh you mean the one I said might be over the hill, thinking her job was ordering new books and arranging them nicely on the shelves?"

"Yes that's the one."
"Oh b' Jeesuz."

On the evening before the visit, Margaret Williams and I had spent some time talking to each other on the phone. Home Farm Primary School, buried in the inner city sprawl north of the centre, was not going to be easy to find. In these days before satellite navigation systems, we were reliant on maps and the frequently incomprehensible directions given to us by school secretaries. Fortunately Margaret had an A to Z of Birmingham and this saved us a great deal of trouble.

We arranged to meet outside the school ten minutes before we were due to meet the headteacher. Although I got slightly lost at one point, I still managed to arrive only a few minutes after Margaret and parked up behind her. The aspect was bleak. Spittalshaw was a scrufffy run-down area that had not yet been identified by the City Council for development. There were boarded up shops, small, ill-kept terraced houses and huge bleak walls behind which lurked the occasional factory but, more often than not, derelict buildings and waste ground. Both of us had set off at a very early hour. Margaret had waited until I arrived and then we got out of our cars, stiffly stretching after nearly a three and a half hour drive from our respective homes, glad to see each other.

The school, visible through heavy Victorian iron railings, stood in the obligatory expanse of tarmac, a gaunt, two-storey building. Its gloomy aspect heightened by the weariness of its surroundings. At the front, a cluster of trees poked their gnarled winter branches towards the sky. Staff cars were parked under them, haphazardly, with no proper markings for a car park.

"At least there's a notice board with the entrance clearly marked," remarked Margaret.

"Yes, perhaps the inside will be a pleasant surprise. After

all it's not the school's fault that they have such a dreary old building." I said.

"Oh no not at all." We were both trying to put as positive a slant on the start of our visit as possible.

I could not have been more wrong in my imaginings, based on our phone conversation, regarding the appearance of Mr. Westcote. He was not at all robust or rotund. He was beanpole thin, with slightly hunched shoulders and a sharp, pinched face, bringing to mind a Dickensian character. He looked a sufferer from ill-health, an impression that was enhanced by a frequent nervous cough. Despite his unprepossessing looks, I found myself warming to him. His shy, diffident smile made me think of a small boy peering out from a grown-up's face.

His office was pristine, almost as if no one worked there. There were two notice boards, both impeccably neat. On one board all the staff's timetables were displayed. The space between the sheets of A4 was exact. On the other, there was a large map of the world. Coloured wools attached to drawing pins ran from a point on the map to a post card pinned up in the area of the board around the map.

"I am very glad to meet you at last Mrs. Schaffer, and you Mrs. Williams. I have got everything you asked for ready in those two boxes." Mr. Westcote led the way into his office and indicated two large plastic boxes neatly filled with a quantity of flap files and the larger box files.

"Thank you Mr.Westcote, that looks exactly what is required."

He motioned us towards two chairs and we sat down. He looked at me expectantly, as if I was about to open a magic Ofsted box and present him with the key to everlasting educational success. I started on my talk, encompassing the main purpose of inspection and a detailed explanation of procedures. I had rehearsed this so often, I could have been reading from a script, but I had thought that the headteacher might ask questions or contribute opinions. Mr. Westcote did neither. In just over an hour I went through everything and the headteacher of Home Farm Primary wrote everything down in an exercise book. I felt as if I was giving dictation. I peppered my presentation with phrases such as; 'Do you want a more detailed explanation about that?' and 'Is that acceptable?' And the only response I got was a nod, slight smile or 'as you wish Mrs. Schaffer'.

We had not been offered a cup of tea or coffee, but when the bell went, a shrill, loud buzzing, at 12 o'clock, Mr. Westcote got up and said; "I hope you don't mind but I took the liberty of ordering you lunch. The cook will bring it in on a tray. It is what she does for me every lunch-time."

"That's very kind of you." We both hurried to say.

"Of course, we will pay for our lunches before we leave." I added.

"I have asked my secretary to organise that for you. She will be in, in a minute." Once again our thanks were effusive. When the secretary arrived, she noticed that we had not yet been offered a drink. She chided Mr. Westcote on this omission, promising to bring us a drink straight away. Poor Mr. Westcote looked startled and abashed.

"I don't know what I was thinking of!" he exclaimed. "You must think me dreadfully thoughtless."

"Oh not at all, Mr. Westcote. We never gave it a thought," Margaret hastily lied. "There's just so much to think about at these meetings, something is bound to get forgotten." We were, of course, extremely glad to see the secretary back with cups of coffee and when our dinner trays came, salad with tuna and baked potato, standard school dinner food, we tucked in with almost unbecoming haste as we were so hungry.

"I always insist that my staff take time off to eat a proper lunch," said Mr. Westcote. "I ban talking about work during lunch."

We commended him on this thoughtfulness for his staff and I said, hastily swallowing a mouthful of tuna and mayonnaise, "perhaps we should follow that rule. I was wondering about your interesting display with the world map. Is it the countries of origin of your children, or places where people have visited on holiday?"

"Oh no, not at all. I'm glad you have noticed it. The postcards were all sent to me by my sister. She had a very important and interesting job that took her to many different parts of the world. She always sent postcards and sometimes very interesting artefacts from her journeys – you may see some of them during your time here in our school. She takes a very real interest in the school and the children. When a postcard arrives, I share it with the children at assembly time. It is one way of helping them understand the countries of the world." (Their very own adult Barnaby Bear, Margaret later joked.) "I always choose a child who has worked very hard to come to my office to fix the postcard with the coloured wool. They take it as a great honour."

Then he reached into his drawer and took out a framed photograph. He passed it to us. We looked at the photo of a tall, grey-haired woman standing under a palm tree in bright sunshine. You could see the family resemblance. "My sister is quite a bit older than me. She is my only living relative. In fact she is retired now. She lives in New South Wales, so we mainly get postcards from Australia now."

"So you don't have any children of your own then, Mr. Westcote?" asked Margaret.

"No, no, I was never married. I'm afraid I never found the right lady." We smiled and murmured the kind of things that turn such information into a fortunate occurrence, rather than a misfortune.

On the tour round the school, which we made not long after lunch, the most noticeable thing was tidiness. Displays were double or triple mounted and looked as if staff had spent hours getting every picture square in its frame. Bookcases were neat and children's coats were all hung up on pegs. Every now and again, a flowerless plant or cactus was strategically placed on a window ledge with a small mat underneath, needless to say too high to be seen properly by most children.

"I think it is so important for children to learn to be tidy, to take care of things and to be punctual, which is why I ask staff to always keep good time and to arrive on time to such things as assembly. At Home Farm, children learn to be tidy and to respect each other's property and we have a good record for punctuality."

I wanted to say, but they don't learn very much else, but of course I didn't. I did, however, take the opportunity of pointing out that the data in the PICSI showed very high rates of absence. When I mentioned this, Mr.Westcote twitched slightly. He displayed this mannerism, we noticed, every time something unpleasant was broached.

"We can do nothing about the lackadaisical ways of our parents, Mrs. Schaffer."

Classroom doors were very tidy, each one with the teacher's name displayed in exactly the same manner. We didn't get to see inside the classrooms as Mr. Westcote said he was not keen to interrupt his staff, and I thought it better not to press for this. Of course, if I had been more experienced, I would have over-ruled his decision and asked to meet not only the teachers but the children as well. As we made our way along the featureless corridors, I felt the building's emptiness, as if its purpose was to quell activity, rather than encourage productivity. The place seemed damp and arid at the same time and I couldn't help letting out a small sigh.

When we got back to the office and got round to discussing the school's results in national tests, a great deal of Mr.Westcote's twitching occurred.

"Mr. Westcote, we have looked at your results for 1996 and I am afraid that they are even lower than those of 1995," said Margaret who had taken over the discussion to give me a few minutes break. Mr. Westcote nodded and twitched.

"Our year sixes were a very poor year group all the way up school." He said this as if, at their birth, these particular children had been visited by the wicked fairy who had wished poor cognitive ability on them for life; their poor academic achievements throughout their schooling having nothing whatsoever to do with his staff.

"We were wondering, what action you took to improve results last year?" Margaret persisted. Mr. Westcote looked startled, twitched and then came up with a bright idea.

"Ah well many of them, yes very many of them were on our special needs register."

We did not say and what difference did that make, which was the question that begged to be asked, because it was becoming very obvious that this would be much too confrontational at this juncture. We were both beginning to realise that Mr. Westcoe had little understanding of the current expectations that headteachers should monitor their school's test results.

"One of our team members, a lady called Mrs. Pendlebury, who is very experienced and qualified in the area of special needs will discuss matters with your SENCO," I said, "and I am sure that will clarify things," not, of course, being very sure at all.

"I'm sure it will. My SENCO is a very hard working member of staff."

"Can we just go back to the analysis of your results," continued Margaret. "We have, of course, noticed that for the last two years science has been much better than maths or English. In fact your science results are only just below the national average."

"I am so glad you have spotted that. We have a wonderful science co-ordinator, Mr. Green. He is responsible for this improvement. He takes all the science lessons in Years 4, 5 and 6 and he is very good."

I had wanted to point out that if the school could raise the standards in science, there was no reason why they should not do it at least in mathematics, if not in English. With so many children having English as a second language, there was good reason for the very low standards in English, but the same did not apply to mathematics. Margaret made an attempt to talk about this, but Mr.Westcote could not, would not, see the correlation. He made his explanations either by giving a eulogy to his staff or an apology for his pupils' lack of achievement caused either by their many needs or, on one or two occasions, the shortcomings of their parents.

At four fifteen it was time for our meeting with the staff. We left the headteacher's office promptly. On my way to the staffroom, nervousness began, and I started to worry that my shaking would beset me. I was about to talk to a room full of some twenty or so teachers on the organisation of their inspection, surely a reason for panic? But when I got in there, I was so taken aback by the state of the room, that I forgot any apprehension. There were clutter and bits and pieces everywhere, just like any other staffroom. It amused me so much – the staffroom was the only place in the school that was untidy, a small but significant rebellion against the tyranny of triple mounting.

I sat down on a lumpy staff room chair and smiled at the assembled faces. Quite a few smiled back. I introduced Margaret

and myself, and set off on my much-rehearsed piece. The staff behaved exactly as Mr.Westcote had done, they listened and wrote
notes. To start with no one asked questions, which was unnerv-
ing, but I carried on without mishap. Towards the end thankfully,
the new deputy, a lively, friendly thirty-year-old, put some sensible questions to me and I smiled broadly at her to show how
grateful I was for her interruptions.

At the end of my talk, I asked the staff to introduce themselves and to name their subject responsibility. As they did, I explained which inspector they would meet with for their subject
interview. This helped me to start to commit their names and
roles to memory. I first noticed the chirpy chap who was the miracle worker with science. I told him he would meet with Margaret. He was so animated he got up and shook her hand, saying
what a pleasure it was to meet her. Easy to see why he was a good
teacher. Then there was a young attractive Asian girl who was the
PE co-ordinator. She gave me a warm smile when I said that she
would be meeting me, and that PE was one of my favourite subjects. A middle-aged lady, whose plump arms had been folded
tightly in front of her all through the meeting in an expression of
'I'm always right and I have been for thirty years', turned out to
be the co-ordinator for English. She had not smiled once. I wondered how she would get on with Phil, who was leading on English.

The meeting over, Mr.Westcote took us down to his office
again. He left us to go and arrange with the caretaker for the
chairs to be set out for the parents' meeting at six thirty. There
was nearly an hour for me to catch my breath. The nice deputy
appeared at the door and offered to go out and buy me a sandwich, which I gratefully accepted. Margaret was going home because the lay inspector, Hamza Choudray was coming to take the
minutes of the parents' meeting. It was the preferred Ofsted

arrangement for the lay inspector to do this. Before she left, she chatted with me about the day, trying to give me encouragement and support.

"You don't know, Jane, things might turn out much better than they look. There's the science after all."

"Yes, and you're the lucky person doing science!"

After she left, the deputy, who was called Mrs. Young returned with the sandwiches, and I sorted out what I owed her. I realised how hungry I was and glad to have a snack to give me energy before the start of another meeting.

"You must be getting exhausted," she said, which was kind.

"It is a long day, but it's so interesting meeting new people. I don't think I've thought about being tired."

After she said goodnight, I waited for Hamza Choudray to arrive. I had been very pleased to see his name on the team allocation form, indicating that he was the lay inspector for this inspection, and glad that I had met him already at Barleydale. To pass the time, I looked through some of the files in the plastic boxes that were ready for me to take away. I came to the minutes of the finance committee, with the reconciliation for the budget of the previous year – even I could see that there was something amiss. This school had a huge budget surplus of over seventy thousand pounds! That was enough to fund two extra teachers for a year and still leave a surplus.

When Hamza Choudray arrived, and after we had exchanged greetings and the usual pleasantries, I told him about the surplus, and he shook his head. "They have no idea about budget management, or accountability for public funds." He frowned, "that money is intended for the use of the children currently at the school – it is not meant to be hoarded up."

"Well, perhaps you will be able to help them understand

this. I took you up on your suggestion at Barleydale; you're down to do efficiency."

"Fine, Jane, I'm fine with that. I enjoy it."

Then we talked about the parents' meeting and Hamza asked if I wanted him to translate. He was happy to speak to the parents in Urdu, Punjabi or Hindi, if needs be. I said I would be grateful if he did, and if he would butt in if he saw me making any obvious mistakes, or leaving anything out. He laughingly agreed but reassured me that I would no doubt remember everything. By this time, there was less than ten minutes before the start of the meeting. We had been expecting Mr. Westcote to come and find us to take us to the hall, but obviously, he meant us to find our own way.

When we got there, Mr. Westcote was chatting to the caretaker. Just two women, dressed in the traditional Asian shalwar camise were seated amongst row upon row of empty chairs. These were placed at perfectly even intervals upon a hall floor that was as shiny and polished as any hall floor could be. Obviously the caretaker and Mr. Westcote were twin souls. We went over to them and I introduced Hamza Choudray.

"I am so pleased to meet you Mr.Westcote, and I must congratulate you on the appearance of your school. It is a pleasure to see," Hamza paused. "Such a clean and tidy place – am I right in thinking it's largely down to this gentleman's excellent efforts?" Hamza nodded towards the caretaker, a grey-haired man as big and burly as Mr. Westcote was insubstantially thin, and Mr Westcote beamed, already falling under Hamza Choudray's charm offensive.

"Yes John does a splendid job." Then Hamza asked if Mr. Westcote was going home. It was not permitted for any member of staff, including the headteacher to stay to the parents' meeting.

"Oh no, I've told John, he can go home. I'll wait in my office to lock up after you have finished." That's how he copes, I thought, doing everyone else's job in lieu of his own. I asked if him if he thought there would be more parents coming.

"Our parents are always late," he said. "They have no idea of punctuality. That is why the fact that our children come to school on time is such an achievement. Those two, are two of our dinner ladies but, yes, I think more will come."

I wondered what strategy the school used to encourage punctuality, but didn't want to ask about it just then. Perhaps absences were so high because a fuss was made if you arrived late, and so it was better not to go to school at all than arrive late. As I watched the thin figure of the headmaster leave on the dot of seven o'clock with John the caretaker in tow, I felt a moment of pity for this strange man, so obviously out of his depth as a head-teacher in a large, inner city, multi-ethnic school.

A small table was set out in the front facing the sea of empty chairs. It was bare with none of the cheering touches, such as a vase of flowers or even a carafe of water, that schools like Higham and Barleydale had provided. I sat down and placed the handbook for inspection and my agenda side by side on the table to make it look as if something was going to happen. Hamza had gone over to talk to the two Asian women. I could hear that they were speaking in Punjabi and occasional bursts of laughter skittered across the shiny floor.

Then some more people arrived. Two tall, very striking African women dressed in bright African cottons covered by dull English winter coats entered the hall and stood just inside the door. One of them held the hand of a small boy. He looked so fearful, clutching her hand like a lifeline. They had come with an English woman, a plump, smiling middle-aged person who came towards me. She introduced herself as a social worker assigned to the refugees in the area.

"Is it all right if I stay? I know the meeting is only for parents but I've come with Mrs. Akanu and Mrs. Matabelee because they speak very little English, not that I can speak their language, but they know me."

"Of course, of course, please stay." I said.

"I did try to explain that they didn't need to attend," the social worker continued, "but they were so keen to do the right thing, and the little boy, Mrs. Matabelee couldn't leave him behind – they are on their own here, so sad." I reassured her again that it was quite all right. I went over to them and motioned towards the seats at the front. Then I crouched down to say 'hello' to the small boy. He stared back at me with his wide-open, frightened eyes. I felt a rush of annoyance with the school for not having made any arrangements for children such as this. Many schools put on a crèche for parents' meetings. There was not even a box of children's books to offer him.

While this was going on, quite a number of people entered the hall and filled up the rows at the back. Most of them appeared to be of Asian, Pakistani origin. There were just four parents of seemingly white UK heritage and a man and a wife who were possibly from Africa or maybe the West Indies. We now had an audience of three people and one small boy sitting in the front row, the two dinner ladies in the middle and about twenty people at the back, separated by rows of empty chairs.

"Jane, I will move people forward for you if you want." Hamza came over to say to me. "It's not a good idea to have all those people at the back." I nodded in agreement, acknowledging his greater experience in the matter. We both stood at the front making move forward gestures, laughing and asking for brave souls to change their seats. One very large, obviously English chap whose bulky frame almost filled two seats came to our rescue. He got up and said in a good brummie accent:

"Curm on you lot, nur good being where we can't 'ear the lady speak, shift yer bums." Those that understood laughed, while those who didn't looked mystified but got up just the same and followed him down to the front. After about five minutes of disturbance with coats and bags causing problems, people were settled in their new seat. I started the meeting feeling quite pleased. My opening words, thanking them for giving up their time to come, and all the other introductory pleasantries were translated into Punjabi by Hamza. All seemed to be going the way it should.

When I moved on to the agenda questions, though, it was a different matter. I started off by asking whether they were happy with how their child was doing in reading and writing. Hamza translated. No one answered. I waited. Now there was a small awkward silence. I repeated the question. Nobody volunteered so much as a nod or shake of the head. I went on to the next question about progress in mathematics. Nothing. And then, the next about science. Nothing. It was like talking to a wall. Getting desperate, I asked about whether they were happy about their child's use of IT. At this, to my intense relief, a man spoke up. He was an Asian man of around fifty, perhaps owning a small business, hard-working and a little tired. He identified himself as a governor and said that he did not think his son was doing as well as he should. He was particularly worried about IT.

"If my son does not learn how to use computers he will be left behind when he wants to find a job. IT is the new world." He spoke good English, if rather quickly, and his accent was pronounced, so I found it difficult to follow everything he was saying. Others seemed to be looking at him with respect. I wondered if he was a community leader. Some appeared to be nodding their agreement. He went on for a while, describing how he, as a governor, had tried to get more computers from nearby businesses

244

for the school but teachers did not make enough use of them.

When he had finished speaking, it was as if he had opened the floodgates. People started speaking all at once, but not necessarily to me. Some spoke to their neighbours, some leant across to the person in front of them or turned round to the person behind, others addressed their comments to Hamza in Punjabi. Several people tried to attract my attention at the same time, and none of them waited for anyone else to stop speaking before speaking themselves. It was chaotic. Not the way an Ofsted parents' meeting was meant to be conducted. I looked across at Hamza and he shrugged his shoulder as if to say, don't worry about it. I decided to go with the flow, judging that it was better to get chaotic response than no response at all. After all it was no good following the agenda if no one spoke up. I learnt from a quietly spoken woman, who said she was from Iran, that her daughter was doing very well and she was happy. The large English chap was worried about his son because he couldn't read. The nature of his son's problems seemed quite serious but the man didn't know if he had been identified as having special educational needs or even what benefit that might be, an indictment of the school's methods of communication, if not their provision.

The two African women with the social worker said nothing but then I saw that the woman who had come in with her husband, who I had thought to be possibly African had gone over to speak to them. They obviously understood her. Then she came to me to say that the two were happy with their children's education (they had been in school all of six weeks); she had acted as a voluntary translator and I thanked her for her efforts. She added that she was not so happy herself. Her son was clever but got away with doing just the bare minimum. She seemed a very educated and intelligent woman, and I had the instinctive feeling that what she was saying was right.

After that I requested quiet. Gradually, the noise subsided and some semblance of a meeting was established. I ventured to ask some more general questions and asked people to speak in turn. This time I got some response but after about ten minutes, people were getting up and sidling out of the door. I decided to quit while in front and thanked them all for coming, closing the meeting with quite a number of questions not having been deal with properly.

After saying our 'goodbyes' to Mr. Westcote, Hamza and I left the school. We walked into the dark night to find our cars, thankfully still parked on the side road where we had left them earlier that day. We laughed together about the unconventional nature of our meeting. I was obviously more worried than Hamza, that had I been observed by Ofsted, it would have been pronounced a failure.

"But you had to carry on," Hamza said. "What good would it have done to have insisted on conducting the meeting in the manner Ofsted expects? No one would have said anything. At least we heard their views."

We shook hands and wished each other a safe journey. As I made the long, weary drive back to Manchester, I felt the responsibility for this school weigh heavily on me. One small face from the parents' meeting kept intruding on my mind, as it would do over and over again for the next few weeks. It was the sad little face of the African boy who had sat as still as Lot's wife turned to a pillar of salt on the chair beside his mother – a stillness so unnatural for a boy of his age.

Chapter 25

A decision that a school requires special measures will depend on the combined weight of features. It is unlikely that one feature alone will result in such a decision, but where there is widespread and significantly poor attainment and progress, risk to pupils or the likelihood of a breakdown of discipline, the school will normally be judged to require special measures. In all such cases the headteacher and the governing body should be informed of the registered inspector's concern.

Handbook for Inspection Crown Copyright 1995

The Randolph Hotel is in central Birmingham. It has a strange history. Owned by the City Council, it was once a doss house; its many floors and interminably long corridors once gave shelter to the city's poor. Nowadays, the large, verging on luxurious, lounge and dinning areas give no hint of this, but from the outside its huge bulk and hundreds of slit windows placed very close together give away its origins. Booking accommodation in Birmingham is always tricky because of the many fairs and business conferences held in the city, so I thought myself fortunate to be able to book rooms for all the team at the popular Randolph. Although not as close as I would have liked to the school, which was situated north-west of the centre, it was reasonably priced, a very important consideration. Booking accommodation for the team is one of those quirky little jobs that falls to the lead inspector. It requires nothing more than diligence, but some leads pride themselves on their ability to suss out the best bargains going in the hotel sector. While I was far from joining this illustrious group of bargain getters, I was satisfied that the team would be reasonably happy with my efforts.

In the week running-up to the inspection, my feelings of being hard-done to at having been allocated Home Farm had modified. I had been made quite a fuss of. When Henry got my pre-inspection commentary, which clearly identified the many problems at the school, he had rung me straight away. He told me that he would be in constant touch throughout the inspection, I was to ring him every evening, and that he had arranged for Phil to act as my deputy. This would mean that Phil would help me read through and check the team's observation forms, something I was beginning to dread because of the size of the team. Henry himself would visit for the whole of Thursday and be there for the final team meeting. Phil had rung and said that he would take charge of the journey. He would come on Sunday to pick me up, with all the inspection paraphernalia and drive us down to Birmingham. Then Abby had come round on Friday afternoon. She arrived unexpectedly with a huge bunch of flowers and a welcome hug.

"You poor thing, the school sounds a mess. Phil showed me your pre-inspection work. It's really good." She poured sympathy and praise on me in equal measure, and insisted to Kate that they took me out for lunch the next day, Saturday: "to make sure she doesn't spend the whole day working." They both looked at me as if I was a lost cause because I worked such long hours. I did work long hours, but that was because I was a slow worker and had to check and re-check everything I did meticulously.

We went to a local wine bar. It was a lovely lunch and I enjoyed being with the two of them. Kate seemed to be so grown-up in Abby's company. My other two daughters, who were in their twenties, lived in London. Alerted by Kate, they had sent me good luck cards and found time from their own exciting and busy lives to phone me.

Sunday dawned bright and fresh. Despite waves of panic and trepidation about my own ability to do this unbelievable thing – lead six much more qualified and experienced people in making life-altering decisions about all the professional staff at a school, I woke up feeling as if I was at the start of a new dawn. Simple things, such as packing enough tights, knickers and shoes, choosing which top to go with which suit and popping a few bits of make-up into a sponge bag, happily diverted my attention. Although I had tried my best to be ready on time, when Phil arrived, panic bubbled to the surface and I started double checking the files that I was taking, and finding things that I had not put in which I might need. Phil stood about in the hall, chatting with Kate, waiting for me to finish. As I dashed passed them to get something from upstairs, I was amused to see both of them wearing the same colluding expressions that I had seen on Kate's and Abby's faces on Friday – 'it's not her fault she's too dizzy to take care of her life properly' looks. Phil enjoyed himself enumerating to Kate how many times I had been late for meetings, and Kate whose own time-keeping was just as bad as mine, elaborated on how many times she used to wait for me when I was supposed to be picking her up from school events.

On the drive down, Phil and I gossiped about the others, not Abby of course, although I did tell Phil about our lunch together on Saturday. He had smiled a happy smile at the mention of her name. Phil had had Mary on his team in Harrogate and he couldn't wait to tell me how irritating and exasperating she had been. "She just does her own thing and doesn't pull together with the team."

"I am surprised," I said. "Although perhaps there were signs of it. I remember her being so selfish about wanting people to help her with English at Beswick Street, so I suppose I'm not that surprised." I was eager to have my own moan about Trevor at Barleydale, and how often his prevaricating had irritated me, and then for good measure I added the bit about Sarah and the child who had called her a witch. Phil laughed almost as much as

Trevor had done.

"Well, it doesn't look as if our group is such good mates after all," Phil said a little sadly.

"It's only to be expected. When people first get together, its easy to be friends, but then when work starts getting serious, you can't afford to be with people who are not up to scratch, just because you feel some kind of loyalty to them, or sorry for them."

"Yes, you're right. As things get tougher you have to look after your own interests and make sure you are working with people you can trust. But then there's the problem of the people you know nothing about. You've got three people who are unknown quantities on this inspection. I must say I hadn't bargained for this aspect of inspection – having to rely on people who you may or may not get on with, or who may or may not be any good. It's a gamble."

"Oh but I have met one of the three; I worked with Michael Slater in Coventry. He came for two days on Sarah's inspection." I spoke casually, not wanting Phil to pick up on the fact that I had been pleased to see his name on the team plan.

"What's he like?" asked Phil.

"I thought he was really nice - he certainly knows his job."

"Well that's a relief. But that still leaves two we know nothing about."

As it turned out, these two unknown team members were ones I would have willingly swapped for Trevor or Mary. A lead inspector receives all the CVs for their team before the inspection in order to allocate responsibilities appropriately. Unfortunately, the CVs often bear no correlation to the efficiency, insight and overall capability of an inspector, and certainly give you no clue as to whether or not you might like the person to which they relate.

Steven Linklater had an impressive CV. He had high-powered letters after his name, such as a master's degree in education, and besides working for a local authority as an adviser for ICT, he was a lead inspector in his own right. After a while though, it became all too apparent that he had only come on the Home Farm inspection because of the other team member I could have done without. This was a woman called Jackie Pendlebury who worked for the same local authority as Steven Linklater. Jackie wore the highest heels I have ever seen teeter down a school corridor. It did not take long to work out that the two of them were much more interested in each other than they were in the inspection. Margaret took an instant dislike to Jackie. They were both specialists in early years and whenever anything came up about provision for the under fives the two of them would take opposing stands. The main reason for her dislike though, was because of the barely disguised intimate nature of Jackie's relationship with Steven Linklater. Steven and Jackie always sat together, came down to the bar together and shared lots of whispered jokes, confidences or whatever.

"I cannot stand people who bring their personal lives into inspection. They should be here for the children, not for the chance to share a glass of wine with each other and whatever else it is they share behind closed doors." She had said to Phil and me one morning on the inspection, just after Steven Linklater had left the inspection base. I couldn't help giving Phil a bit of a hard stare as she said those words, and he did look slightly uncomfortable.

The team had all agreed to my holding the pre-inspection meeting on Sunday evening in the hotel lounge. Everyone would be present, except for Hamza Choudray who, as lay inspector was only in school for three days, not four like everyone else. The meeting was arranged for seven thirty. Phil and I had arrived at the hotel with plenty of time to unpack the car and settle into our rooms before this meeting. I also needed to introduce myself to the two team members, who I had not met before, as soon as possible. From an enquiry at reception, I discovered the number for their rooms. I noted with surprise that they were 314 and 316, on the same corridor next to each other. Had they rang up and requested this after I had made the booking, or was it just a co-incidence? I knocked on Steven Linklater's door first and a tall man in his early fifties, in casual but expensive looking clothes, opened the door and shook my hand vigorously. I thanked him for agreeing to come on the inspection and said that I hoped he would give me the benefit of his experience. He had laughed jovially and said he was sure I would not need it. Jackie was also full of smiles and good humour. It was impossible not to notice that she was a very attractive woman – the sort of person who looked as if she had been born wearing make-up and nail varnish and who, when she passed you, left a waft of perfume that, on anyone else would seem too much but which with Jackie, seemed a natural accompaniment to her being.

After meeting these two, I scurried back to my room conscious that the team meeting was not long off. I rehearsed what I was going to say at the start, and scanned down the agenda that I had prepared, even though I had done this several times at home. I realised with pleasure that I was not suffering with nerves, I felt more excited than nervous. Anxious not to be late, I set off in good time for the meeting carrying a large plastic box of papers, but half way down the long corridor from my room on the way to the lift, a thought nagged at me, had I forgotten one of the information sheets for the team? This resulted in me stopping, putting down the things I was carrying and checking through the paper work which I had packed in neatly segmented sections in the plastic box. When I couldn't find what I was looking for, I returned to my room for a frantic hunt; taking the whole pile of papers out of the box, I found that the missing ones had slipped down under the other papers and were lying snugly at the bottom. In consequence of this quite unnecessary search, I managed to arrive several minutes late.

Phil couldn't resist the opportunity to make a comment about my unsuccessful time-keeping, "You're so lucky Jane, you'll have a few extra minutes of life, beings as you'll be late for your own funeral."

"Which will no doubt make us early for ours," said Steven Linklater, a witty comment that drew a guffaw of laughter from everyone, Jackie laughing the most.

"At least she won't have the stop-watch out timing our entrances and exits as per some lead inspectors I could name," said Michael Slater. I smiled at him, grateful for his good-natured support.

We sat in the hotel lounge having drawn up enough armchairs for us all and talked in low voices, conscious that we must not be overheard by any passing guest. Despite my disparaging views of some of Sarah's methods, I had copied one of her ideas in that I provided each team member with a timetable of the week's events, listing everything that was to happen on each day of the inspection. I had also assembled the agendas for all team meetings, night and morning and a timetable for the meetings with co-ordinators. Producing these items had taken me several days of work and I was very pleased when Phil had said: "Oh well, that's all very clear – everything we need to get us going, thanks Jane." And everyone else murmured approval.

This good start on my part was not maintained, as what followed was much less successful. I got out the large timetable of lesson observations that I had made ready to stick on the wall in the inspection base and put it down on the low table in front of us, suggesting that people could copy down the parts relating to their observations, if they wished.

"Well you might have let us know you were going to do that," said Steven Linklater. "I spent a couple of hours yesterday, drawing up my own timetable and now it's no use."

"I'm, sorry about that Steven, I didn't think about it, but you can cross-reference yours with mine and that will be useful, don't you think?"

"Waste of bloody time."

I had to admit that I had made a mistake in not letting people know that I was drawing up a timetable. Everyone had done their own like Steven, and I could tell that they were miffed, although no one complained as vociferously as he had done. Also, it was not an entirely successful exercise for them to transfer the information from my timetable to theirs. There was a scrum as everyone tried to check their observations. There were people crossing out what they had previously written, not being able to see properly and pulling the sheet round while someone else on the other side of the table was trying to copy something down.

There were several complaints of: 'Oh but I really wanted to see that lesson' and 'I don't want to be in for just half an hour, I hate short times like that.'

Phil came to my rescue.

"I say, hang on a minute everyone. I think it would be better if Jane just calls out people's observations, (the way we did it with Henry, Jane). Use your big timetable here and then if anyone wants any changes, they can discuss it with you."

"Thanks Phil, that's a good idea. I'm sorry this has been such a muddle." I was abashed by this setback, but not too abject, after all I was bound to make mistakes. After a tiresome half-hour, it was sorted out to most people's satisfaction.

Before we adjourned, we managed a short discussion about the main areas of concern in the school. An in-depth consideration of the main issues should have taken up the major part of the meeting, but in 1996, nearly all pre-inspection team meetings were spent fussing over aspects of inspection administration rather than focusing on the school's needs. By this time, I was more worried about how I was going to manage Steven Linklater than how I was going to manage the next few days in school. When we turned to my pre-inspection commentary, he spoke up straightaway.

"Well it's a pretty cut and dried case. The data says it all, but your pre-inspec, (not a bad job that Jane) just finishes it off. This school is headed for special measures – it will be my third in twelve months, not as team member of course, the other two were my leads. The last one was the one I did three weeks ago and the school didn't half kick up a fuss." Despite his slight compliment, his words shocked me.

"I think Steve, we shouldn't be jumping to conclusion just yet," Phil said quickly. "I know Jane's pre-inspection makes a case for special measures, or serious weaknesses, as a possibility, but she does make it quite clear that the children come from very poor backgrounds and that there is a huge proportion of second language kids and don't forget there are refugee children as well. We mustn't forget that what we find at the school, especially with the teaching, is the deciding factor."

"Yes, but Phil, there is little to support the view that the leadership is doing much to raise standards," said Margaret, surprisingly backing up Steven.

"I know, but we are here to carry out a fair and unbiased inspection, not damn them before we start," said Phil.

"Phil is absolutely right" I joined in. "I have identified some strong *possible* weaknesses." (I emphasised the word possible) "But surely inspection is about testing the hypotheses in the pre-inspection? They are, at this stage, only hypotheses. There are clear indications of strengths as well." Suddenly I was feeling that I wanted to protect the school. I didn't want to just summarily damn them, and with this feeling came a wave of tiredness. We would get nowhere at this point. "Perhaps we should pack up now? Try to relax for the rest of the evening."

"Best thing I've heard you say all night," said Steven. Even this hearty agreement grated on me. Into my mind flashed Abby's comment about how she had felt like slapping an irritating team member. He added insult to injury by coming over and clapping me on the shoulder.

"Don't take it to heart, my love. It's great to see such lack of cynicism, but I know, exactly what I'm going to find tomorrow – boring, dull teaching with kids that don't want to learn." I squirmed under his patronising manner but spotted the expression on Phil's face which was 'don't get annoyed.' I laughed and said, contrary to the way I was feeling:

"Oh I shan't take it to heart. It's amazing what a good stiff drink will do for one."

"We'll all take you up on that one," he said and headed off quickly, with Jackie in tow, no doubt to find a drinking place in the city centre.

Margaret declared that she was turning in for an early night, saying how tired she was. "Goodnight, see you in the morning," she said. "Don't lie awake worrying, Jane, it will be all right, you'll see."

Michael came over and asked if he could get Phil and me a drink. Phil got up and the two of them went through to the bar. I sat in the armchair staring into space. Irrationally, I felt an overwhelming desire for the Home Farm staff to come up trumps; to prove my hypotheses wrong. It was partly because I was so against Steven Linklater's attitude – how could he talk so uncaringly about putting schools into special measures? I wanted the staff to do well and for us to leave saying that the teaching was good and that, although there were some weaknesses that needed sorting out, there was much to praise about the school. The faces of some of the staff came to mind – the new young deputy, so enthusiastic and kind, the chirpy science man so eager to meet Margaret and the lovely Asian girl in charge of PE Why was I going to their school to disrupt their lives? Could I be the sort of person who could destroy people, tell them that what they have been doing for the last twenty years was not good enough?

Michael doubled back and said, "I forgot completely to ask you what you would like to drink."

"Oh a half of lager will be nice, thank you, but shouldn't it be me buying the drinks?"

"Don't worry about it, I've an idea I'm earning more than you two anyway." He gave a cheery smile. They came back a few minutes later with the drinks and settled themselves down in the armchairs.

"Who do you work for?" asked Phil.

"Well, I'm with several contractors at the moment but mostly I work with Northern Inspections. They are the ones who've been asked by Ofsted to fill the gaps on these inspections led by you trainees."

Phil asked him about the rates Northern Inspections were offering and told him about the smaller contractor he and Abby were planning to work for.

"A friend of mine runs it; they're called Forward Education. Have you heard of them?"

"Yes, I have. They've quite a good reputation, I think. But I haven't worked for them. The trouble sometimes with smaller companies is that they take a long time to pay, and a few have gone out of business when they've not had the contracts from Ofsted."

"I've talked to my friend about that a lot. He has to put in

257

a tremendous amount of time and effort with his bids to Ofsted. It's getting very involved with quality control measures now, which wasn't a factor a few years ago. Even so, I'm thinking of going into business with him."

"Are you Phil? I hadn't realised that," I said.

"Yes, I think I would enjoy the challenge."

"Well good luck to you," said Michael. "And what about you Jane, which contractor do you think you might go with?"

"I've hardly given it a thought," I said. "I've got to get through this inspection first, you know. We get marked on all the inspections we do. If I don't meet requirements when our HMI monitors the inspection on Thursday, and if I don't pass our final assessment, I shall be back at school."

"Don't be silly Jane, you'll pass for sure," said Phil.

"I'm sure you will," said Michael, "and when you get round to thinking about what you want to do, give me a ring, I'd be glad to give you advice. If you want to go with Northern Inspections, I know the chap who runs it pretty well and I could introduce you. They're a solid, well-organised lot there and the admin back-up is very good, that's what counts with me."

"Thank you very much. That's if you've not put me in your little 'black book' by the end of this inspection." I joked.

"Black book? queried Phil. "Oh yes, I've heard that some team inspectiors keep a list of leads they don't want to work with, is that what the black book is?"

"Yup, it is, and very useful it is too."

"I bet Geoffrey Owen is in yours." Phil said.

"Well actually no he isn't,"

"Who's Geoffrey Owen?" I asked.

"Haven't you heard of him? He's hit the national press a few times because he has a bit of a bad habit of putting schools into special measures," said Michael.

"Oh, I see an axe-man like Steven."

"Well, I don't know about Steven Linklater, but Geoffrey is not at all like him. He is in fact, a very clever man. (I'm not saying Steven isn't clever, mind you, but he has certainly got some very irritating ways.) Geoffrey is a quiet man, but lethal when needs be. He can sum a situation up in a flash. When other people are still thinking about something, he's moved on to the next thing. But he doesn't suffer fools gladly and that makes him disliked by some team members, especially those that are a bit weak – not to mention weak headteachers."

"Sounds like you quite approve of him," said Phil.

"Yes, and no. The thing is Ofsted are a tricky lot you know – they want someone to do their dirty work for them – Geoffrey gets more than his fair share of the problem inspections, but then they don't back you up when the shit hits the fan. I quite accept that his inter-personal skills are wanting."

"Well I wish Home Farm's problems had been handed to him rather than me," I said dismally.

"You'll be fine," said Michael. "Just remember Jane that you can't be nice to everyone in this line of work. If you brush stuff under the carpet, it's the children that suffer – a bad school just goes on being bad."

"I know," I said. "But if you cause disruption, that can't be good either."

"No, but at least the problems can be faced, and hopefully fixed," said Phil.

I stood up to go, "Thanks for that you two, and for the drink, I'm going up now. I need an early night."

"Oh, I think we might just have another pint," said Phil with Michael nodding agreement. "We can talk about really important things like football."

Chapter 26

The teaching was a roller coaster ride. Every night Phil and I got together to read through the lesson observations of the day and to collate the findings from the data. We worked together to do the job of monitoring the quality of each inspector's work from the observation forms that they handed in, both teaching ones and those referring to other events. In this way we gained on overview of two things; the quality of the school's work and the quality of the work of our own team.

Monday Night

On this our first night at the job, we were unexpectedly and happily surprised at what we found. Looking at each other with an almost covert delight that things seemed to be turning out much better than we could have hoped for, we noted that there had not been a single unsatisfactory lesson. In total, twenty six lesson observations had been completed by the team. Of that number, twelve had been good, thirteen had been satisfactory and there were two very goods, one for a science lesson taken by the co-ordinator in one of the Year 4 classes and one for a lesson given by the deputy headteacher in Year 2.

Although we were both pleased, we played down our mounting optimism. "If this keeps up for the rest of the week, it's going to make a big difference," said Phil. "It is looking much more hopeful than I thought possible."

I agreed. We were going to be able to tell Mr. Westcote, at our meeting with him at eight o'clock the following morning, that for the time being, he had nothing to worry about as far as the teaching was concerned. These were the percentages for teaching that we would report at that meeting:

- ✓ 4% very good
- ✓ 46% good
- ✓ 50% satisfactory.

"The behaviour is looking all right as well," said Phil. "Margaret saw the assembly and she's put that behaviour was good – the children attentive. It was a good effort by Mr. Westcote apparently. He had five or six children acting out the story of the Good Samaritan."

"The children seem to like him."

"Mmm, I'm not sure I would go as far as to say that. I asked several of the older ones who their headteacher was and what did he do – they seemed a little vague. They knew his name, of course, but I couldn't say there was a great deal of enthusiasm. I had to give them quite a few prompts, and then one of them said that he lets them play football but they have to take turns with the kids in Years 3 and 4 and they don't think that's fair."

"Well it is fair, isn't it?"

"Of course it is, but the fact that they don't think it is might mean that Westtie hasn't really got them on his side."

"Yes, I see what you mean." I looked back at the observation forms. " Do you realize, that for mathematics, Steven has given a good, a very good (in the deputy's class) and one satisfactory this morning," I exclaimed.

"Yes but look, his observations were all done in the younger classes, and one of them, as we might expect in the deputy's class." I looked at the observation forms again.

"They are well written," I remarked.

"Very well written," Phil agreed. "And look what he puts for the children's attainment. He's put a four for the deputy's class and very good progress that means he is saying that they are on their way to reaching the expected standard by the end of the year."

I felt a sense of foreboding. There was something in that statistic that was ringing alarm bells, but for the time being, I was ready to pack up and try and get a good night's sleep. It was getting on for ten o'clock. Phil and I had met for this reckoning after our evening meal and doing all the other inspection jobs that needed doing. Just as I was about to say goodnight to Phil, there was a knock on the door. When I opened it, there was Jackie, expensive high heels still on her feet and lipstick still perfectly applied. Had she just touched it up? I mused to myself, fascinated by this vision of glamour before me.

"Jane, I'm awfully sorry," she said. "But I've got one more observation form here that I forgot to give you earlier on."

"Oh thank you Jackie, we have just finished tallying them all up." I said hoping by my tone that she would understand the inconvenience of her late visit.

"I am really, really sorry." She looked at me pleading mock forgiveness.

"I'll forgive you," I said, "as long as it's not a five."

"Oh no, its just a jolly bog standard four." She handed it to me, blithely unconcerned that she had just thrown out all our carefully calculated data.

Tuesday Night

The thunder clouds began to gather, and rain poured down all over my parade, which of course, was really Mr.Westcote's parade. The unsatisfactory lessons had started to appear. Steven had given two fives, one in Year 3 and one in Year 4; Margaret saw a session taken by a teaching assistant in Year 5 that was unsatisfactory; Michael gave an unsatisfactory for an IT lesson in Year 6, and Phil gave an unsatisfactory for English in Year 4. The data for Tuesday was very different to that of Monday night and our bubble of optimism burst.

Phil and I counted and recounted the pile of forms, checking over numbers in each grade to make certain our final count was correct. If people used an extra sheet to write more about a lesson, this could inadvertently be counted in twice or, as Jackie had done the previous night, someone might have forgotten to give you one of their forms and either of these errors could alter the now sensitive data. Once unsatisfactory lessons begin to accumulate, the lead inspector has to keep a very close eye on the percentages. Ofsted had ruled that anything over twenty per cent unsatisfactory teaching should automatically trigger special measures. There were now 57 lessons in total: 3 very good; 17 good; 32 satisfactory; 5 unsatisfactory. This meant our report on the percentages to Mr. Westcotte the next day would be:

- ✓ 91% satisfactory or better
- ✓ 5% very good
- ✓ 30% good
- ✓ 56% satisfactory
- ✓ 9% unsatisfactory.

We were not near to the dangerous 20 per cent, still quite a way off but, during the team meeting, problems had begun to stack up. Also, Phil had had a disastrous meeting with the English co-ordinator, who, as I had predicted, had little understanding of how to develop the subject and so raise standards through the school.

Once issues have been identified and confirmed as possible weaknesses at the evening team meeting, the lead inspector needed to tell the headteacher as soon as possible, so that there are no great shocks when the final report is given. The school can, at this early stage, bring evidence to show that inspectors are wrong in their judgements; they need an early warning in order to do this, so it was vital to get the feedback right at the morning meeting. There are, of course, problems in being too open and frank as the school could turn hostile. I would need to use as much tact as I could to broach the areas of concern with Mr. Westcote.

"Do you want me to go through what you need to say to Mr. Westcote tomorrow, Jane? It's all looking quite serious."

"Thanks Phil that would be a big help, although I think I've got a good idea about most of it. It was a good team meeting wasn't it? You know, ridiculously, I've almost got to like Jackie, although it's such a pain when she and Margaret argue, but she's doing a good job in the under fives. The teachers down there love her, bedazzled I think by the glamour, but she has taken time to look past the dreadfully shabby nursery and Reception class building – it is a disgrace, that outside mobile for those little children. But she has given them credit for what they do to encourage mums, lots of them come in to help."

"It's not too bad a team at all, and I think Hamza Choudray is magic. He's got this under-spending of theirs sorted out, despite all their nonsense about saving for re-building – they don't need to – they've bags of spare room, just a bit of re-modelling would do wonders. That eejit, Steven's not too bad really, although I will be really glad to see the back of him, the over-bearing sod. But he has pin-pointed what's wrong with their planning in mathematics really efficiently." Phil paused for a moment and then added, "and by the way, he's not married – he divorced his wife a couple of years ago – she went off with his best friend, which was nice."

"Well, his best friend was probably not as bombastic as Steven."

"Now whose, being an eejit? What would I be telling you about the private life of that man, for Jane? No, I'm talking about

Michael."

"Oh," I said.

"Well, don't you be giving me that 'Oh' and pretending you're not interested."

"Phil!"

"Well you are interested aren't you? And he likes you, you know. And just so that you know, I was only getting into conversation with him about marital problems because I happen to know Margaret Williams is going through a divorce at the moment. So I remarked to him that perhaps that was why she always looks so serious."

"Phil – you are impossible. How you get to know all these things about people, I don't know."

"It's what makes me a good inspector, me and chaps like Hamza, we're naturals."

Wednesday Night

On this penultimate evening, the teaching data continued to slide. I had decided not to go to the hotel restaurant to eat a meal with the team, even though Henry had joined us, but had asked the hotel for one of their bar sandwiches to be sent up to my room. Consequently, I had saved an hour or so and by the time Phil put his head round my door, I had already worked out the data for teaching.

"Hey sneaky, missing dinner – how do you think the team managed without their leader?" joked Phil.

"Absolutely fine, I should think. Did you look after Henry?" Henry had arrived at school in time for the evening meeting and was staying at the hotel. I had had to push any worries about how he had judged my performance as team leader to the back of my mind, as I had so much to think about with regard to the school and the inspection. Keeping my worries in check had been one of the factors in my deciding not to have dinner with the team. Just sitting next to Henry would have made it difficult not to start surmising about what he had thought. He was not going to give me an assessment until the inspection was over.

"Oh – I looked after him fine. He was very professional, didn't say anything about the school or the meeting over dinner. He is busy re-doing his garden, landscaping it with his wife, so we talked about gardens."

"Thanks Phil – I knew you would stand in for me. I was just worried that I would not manage to get through all the work this evening. I have to be on top of things for tomorrow."

"For sure, Jane, I understand, I'd be the same."

"I've done the data for tomorrow. " I showed Phil the results of my efforts. On Thursday morning's feedback we would be reporting the following percentages:

- ✓ 84% satisfactory or better
- ✓ 6% very good
- ✓ 32% good
- ✓ 46% satisfactory
- ✓ 16% unsatisfactory.

While the figures for the whole school looked as if teaching overall was satisfactory, one of the points of discussion at the team meeting had been the disparity between the infants and junior school. The infant department was much stronger than the juniors.

"The problem is," said Phil, "the true picture of what is happening with the teaching is being obscured by the good grades that the teachers in the infants are getting."

"I think we had better work out separate figures for the infants and juniors." I said.

"Agreed." We set to, dividing the forms up according to

the two stages. I worked out the infant scores while Phil did the juniors. Unsatisfactory in the infants was down to five per cent, and sixty per cent was good or better. In the juniors, the percentage of unsatisfactory lessons was up to the unacceptable level of 20 per cent.

"We can't ignore this twenty per cent in the juniors, it explains the lack of progress in this stage and it's mostly in Years 3 and 4, with some in one of the Year 5 classes." I said. "Is this enough to justify failing the school?"

"I think it is, Jane, I think it is. What's happening in the juniors is cancelling out all that good work in the infants. That is what is happening, and you can't ignore it."

I shook my head. "You know, I just can't believe that I am going to be failing a school. It just seems unfair to those who are working so hard and doing so well. They are going to suffer with the others." I could not believe how bad I was feeling.

I had spent most of my time in the Infant department. Most of the teachers in the Infants were well motivated, hard working and enthusiastic. Granted, there was one, a stodgy lady in her middle forties who looked as if her enthusiasm for teaching had long since slipped away, whose classroom was as dull and uninspired as herself. But all of the other classrooms were bright and cheerful, with children who spoke little English learning the language from each other, and skilled staff, as they played in a make-believe shop or went out on visits to real shops. Classrooms in the juniors, in contrast were dull and uninspiring; the one display board with the latest artwork, triple-mounted of course, being the only thing to catch the eye. Just three teachers out of the eight in the juniors were any good. One was the science co-ordinator. In contrast to the others, his classroom was packed with things to interest, from a row of healthy plants, to colourful charts and pictures done by the children of planets in the solar system. He shone like a beacon in the mist of mediocrity on the junior corridor. The other two good teachers in the juniors were the Year 6 teachers. One of these was the young PE co-ordinator (I had not seen her teach yet).

"What I cannot understand," I said, "is why the good practice in some parts of the school is not used as an example to those whose teaching is weak?"

"That's because the headteacher hasn't got enough guts to take on the bad eggs and, I'm not sure he really knows who is rubbish, and that goes for some of his senior staff. Not, of course, that nice new deputy. But how is she going to tackle some of the huge management problems? Such as an English co-ordinator who doesn't understand that you can't teach children about complex sentences or adjectival clauses when they don't know the basics – like a sentence needs to have a verb in it, or even that it should start with a capital letter and end with a full-stop?" Phil's anger at the ineptitude of the English co-ordinator was making his voice harsh, and he synchronised a thump with his fist on the worktop when he got to the word 'stop'.

"The English co-ordinator has got to you, hasn't she?" I said with some amusement, remembering my thoughts at the initial staff meeting.

"I could fail the school just for employing that woman."

"Yes but Phil, the whole point is we haven't come to a decision to fail the school as yet."

"No we haven't and there are reasons, of course, but I think we have been prevaricating – putting off what we know needs to be done."

"And that's my fault?"

"No, you are just trying to be as fair as you can be."

"But you gave reasons at the meeting why you are not sure about unsatisfactory progress in the juniors."

"I know, I did, I'm just the same as you Jane, I keep seeing another side to the matter. With progress it's what I said at the meeting, the work the children are doing in Year 6 is definitely of a higher standard. The Mr. Green science chappy in Year 5 and those two teachers in Year 6, the Asian girl, Miss Ali and Mrs. Miller, the older lady are not at all bad and they have started to make a difference."

"That is what I mean – it's not clear cut, but I have got to make sense of it somehow. I know I am just finding it difficult with the concept of failing a school – telling them that they are a load of rubbish and making it public."

"You didn't have any trouble telling that woman at Higham that her lesson was unsatisfactory did you?"

"No, I know but that was different."

"Wait there," Phil jumped up and went out of the room. He came back a few minutes later with a small pile of exercise books. "These are books from Year 3 – the six children in the bottom group – have a look."

I sat down on the edge of the bed in the only small space that was free of papers, and took the books from him. I opened them up and leafed through the work the children had done this term. It did not take very long. These six children were busy each day copying out sentences that killed the English language stone dead. Written in careful print in each book, I could read:

'The knife on the table is sharp.'

'The flowers in the vase are pretty.'

'The hat on the peg is woolly.'

The reasons for the writing of the sentences could only be guessed at, but one could conjecture that a missing word had to be filled in as sometimes a happy transposing occurred: 'the flowers in the vase are woolly'; 'the knife on the table is pretty'; 'the hat on the peg is sharp', which made one think that now at least the reader's interest might be aroused. The work in each book mirrored that in all the others, the only difference being the size and aspect of the letters that formed the words.

"None of them could read the sentences to me. They didn't have the slightest understanding of what they were writing. In the lesson I saw, they were all busy writing the one about something being a colour 'The boy kicked a blue ball'. They were supposed to underline the sentence with the right colour, and they did, because the picture of the item was that colour – you couldn't miss."

"Were they working from an exercise book?"

"No, the teacher had a huge box of cards, all in sets with elastic bands round them – I think she must have made them all twenty years ago when she started teaching. But the thing was, Jane, they worked in silence. None of them said the words they were supposed to be learning and, as I said, none of them could read them, not even the sentences they were doing that day."

"Perhaps that was just as well." I said this with heavy sarcasm. I was beginning to feel a hot sense of anger at this teacher's incompetence. On some pages, the children had done pictures. Mostly these were stilted and ill-formed – they were the pictures of children who had not had pencils are crayons to play with when they were little – stick people, small box cars, lots of white paper and little exuberance. One child had covered over all his drawings with heavy black scribble, obliterating whatever he had first put on the paper. I looked at the name on the front: 'Joffrey Matabele'. I stared at the name for a while, and then I knew it was the little boy from the parents' meeting.

"You know Phil, you had better go and get on with your own work, you've still got loads to do to finish up your data on English. I can manage this myself now." He protested, but I said, "really its fine now Phil – I think I've got everything straight in my head." He was, I knew, anxious to get on with his own work, but didn't want to leave me in the lurch. I insisted and pushed him out of the room.

I meant what I had said to Phil, my thoughts were now much clearer. Seeing those books had graphically illustrated what I had been trying to ignore all along: the school was letting the children down, some of them badly. I knew that I could now compile a list of weaknesses that would be quite enough to put this school into special measures, the main one being that, in the juniors, those children with special needs and those who spoke English as an additional language were making unsatisfactory progress. After this would come the lack of leadership in helping to raise standards, no identification of weaknesses in teaching and insufficient curriculum planning to ensure progress, especially in mathematics. Steven was quite adamant that the maths curriculum was badly planned and children were repeating work. There were, of course, numerous other minor things that the team had identified.

I took out two sheets of A4 paper and wrote the heading 'Home Farm Primary School Main Findings and Key Issues.' I listed the school's main strengths and its weaknesses and then compiled the key issues which were the things it needed to do to put things right. At the bottom of the second page, I copied from the framework the wording which applied to a school that the lead inspector considered to be failing to provide a satisfactory education. In the morning I would photocopy the two sheets for each team member and, of course, Henry.

I finished in just over half an hour. I felt satisfied, not elated, not pleased at what I was going to have to do, but sure that it was the right thing. It was twenty two minutes past ten and the thought crept into my head that I could go down to the bar and just have a quiet drink before going to bed. I had been working since seven thirty in the morning.

As I made my way along the corridor to the lift, I suddenly felt as if I was rejoining the real world. At the bar, I smiled at the friendly bar tender and thought about ordering a short, perhaps a gin and tonic but then decided to go for a glass of red wine. The barman was just putting the glass down in front of me, when a voice behind me made turn round.

"Have you come up for air?" It was Michael Slater. He had walked over from one of the armchairs, a pint of beer, half finished in his hand.

"That's just what it feels like," I replied. "But I'm feeling pleased with myself. I've drawn up draft main findings and key issues for tomorrow."

"Goodness, you have been working hard."

"It was just a matter of putting together what everyone has been saying – everyone has been fairly solid about the lack of progress in the juniors, and that is the main issue. Of course, it means Mr. clever clogs was right at the pre-inspection meeting – it is a failing school."

"Yes, he was right in what he said, but not in the way he said it or in his attitude to the school. Unless you give the school every opportunity for a fair inspection, you're not going to be able to pinpoint why things are going wrong and that is the most important thing for them, so they can get it right in the future."

"Exactly – if we just went on what the data was saying, there wouldn't be much point in doing an inspection."

"And are you going to come and sit down for a while? I was sitting in one of those nice comfy armchairs when I saw you come in."

"That sounds like a good idea." We picked up our drinks and walked across the room to the armchairs. I was suddenly unsure of what to say next, aware that I wanted to say something personal but not sure of how to start.

"Phil told me that your group have become pretty good friends."

"Yes, I suppose we have, but I think inspection tends to split up working relationships, doesn't it? I mean teams get mixed up all the time by the contractors?"

"Yes, that's true. Sometimes you work with the same people a few times, but often you don't. It can get quite lonely, even though you're with people all the time." He paused and I was just about to make another middle of the road remark that no one could misinterpret as too personal when Michael spoke again. "I hope I'm not being a nuisance, or an embarrassment or anything, but I was wandering if you would like to meet up after this inspection's over – I mean socially – perhaps go for a meal or something?"

"Good heavens."

"I've never asked anyone that before on inspection and as a matter of fact I can't remember how long ago it was I asked someone when I wasn't on inspection. I'm really sorry if I've startled you – shocked you."

"No, honestly don't apologise. It's a really nice idea. I mean I'd like that."

"Oh good, I thought for a minute I'd made an awful gaffe."

"I was just surprised."

"Well, I was as well really. I don't know what got into me."

"I live on my own, except for my youngest daughter who's in her first year at college now," I said.

"Yes, Phil told me. I asked him if he knew about your background."

"What about you?"

"I'm on my own, but unlike you I don't have any children to fill my time, although I do spend a lot of time at my sister's place. She's got three under ten, and an uncle is always useful as a household extra."

I smiled at this, thinking what a lucky woman she was. We chatted on for a while about the places where we lived. Michael was in a small village just outside of Warrington. Then I got up, concerned that I needed to get to sleep so we said our good nights, Michael promising to phone me after the inspection. It was only after I got to my room that I realised that I hadn't asked him anything about how he thought the team meeting had gone and whether he thought Henry would have passed it. Then I realized that I hadn't asked Phil either.

Chapter 27

The next morning, the last morning of the inspection Phil and I arrived at Mr. Westcote's door five minutes before the appointed time of eight o'clock. We had been very careful to be punctual each morning. We sat on two small infant-sized chairs that were placed outside the door to the headteacher's office. Phil's knees stuck out in front of him and seemed much too close to his face, which made me want to laugh. We knew that Mr. Westcote was talking to Henry. Part of Henry's role in monitoring the inspection was to gain an understanding of how well the lead inspector had built a relationship with the headteacher. The difficulty with this, of course, was that no matter how nice you might try to be at the start of the inspection or how helpful, this will be forgotten or discounted once the head has heard some unwelcome news, and Mr. Westcote had had two days of unwelcome news, so I could imagine him detailing every small slip I might have made to Henry. The door to the office opened exactly at eight o'clock, and Henry came out, gave a brief nod to us and disappeared off up the corridor. Mr.Westcote did not get up from his desk to ask us to come in, so we just went in and shut the door behind us.

As I sat down in the sparse office, my file open on my lap, I tried hard not to be engulfed by a wave of sadness. Mr. Westcote had chosen not to have anyone with him at these meetings. He said that his deputy had too much to do and that she was not yet experienced enough. He looked more frail than ever, as if the shocks of the past three days had caused him to shrink, not in height, but in width, his spindly frame more angular than ever. His eyes strayed to the only colourful thing in the room, the world map with its surrounding postcards.

"I have just told Mr. Calderbank that I know you are going

275

to come in and tell me that the teaching statistics have worsened, that you and your team have made up your mind that this school should be put into special measures. I want you to know that I knew from the start that you would come to do this to my school." He finished speaking on a peevish note, accompanied by several quite sizeable twitches.

"Mr. Westcote, the teaching statistics have worsened, but that is not the main issue. The overall percentage of unsatisfactory lessons is 13 percent, and that does not necessarily trigger special measures. The problem is that much of the unsatisfactory teaching is in Key Stage 2. In the younger classes, teaching is much better and so the children make much better progress. This can be seen in last year's test results, but it is more pronounced this year because it looks as if, by the end of Year 2, most children will have reached the national average." I paused and waited for him to speak but he did not say anything.

I went on, "the real problem in the school is the lack of progress children make in the older classes." Again no response. "We outlined the main issues yesterday and they have not changed, I'll just list them again for you if you like."

"There is no need, Mrs. Schaffer, I have them all in front of me here." Mr. Westcote picked up a pen. "I would like to tell you my opinion of them now, if you do not mind."

"Of course," that is what this meeting is for.

Mr. Westcote ticked off items as he spoke. "I do not agree that our budget management has been in error. I do not agree that our special needs records are not kept up-to-date or that parents are not involved." (When he said this, I had a job to stop myself from interjecting but managed to distract myself by writing down what he was saying.) "I have had to agree with Mr. Choudray that there has been a lapse in our care by not providing evidence of accidents that occur at playtime, and I have to agree with Mr,

Choudray that I have been remiss in the manner in which records of unauthorised absences are kept, and this will be put right. I do not agree that the accommodation for the under fives, or their resources, are inadequate." Mr.Westcote stopped and we waited in silence. A few minutes seemed to go by, but it could only have been seconds. There were at least four other major issues that we reported as concerns the previous day.

Phil said very quietly, "but you do agree don't you, because you told Mrs. Schaffer about this on her first phone call to you, that the school development plan does not provide the staff with a clear mandate for development? And that the process of monitoring teaching is not in place?" Again there was a silence and then the killer admission came:

"I should have been checking up on everyone, but you just think they are doing the job they are paid to do, don't you?"

"Our greatest concern, Mr. Westcote is that the children in the juniors do not make enough progress – that they slip back after the good start they have made in the infants." I kept my eyes down, looking at my file, not daring to see any of Mr. Westcote's twitches that were adding a surreal element of bathos. "You know, there will be lots of good things for us to say about your school. The children's behaviour is a strength and, although there is not enough done to celebrate the different religions in your school, the children's relationships with each other and with the staff are a credit to you." As I said these calming words, I could feel the tension lift. I was tempted to add that the final decision regarding special measures had not yet been taken by the team, but all things considered, I didn't think it wise to give him false hopes. Instead, I said that I thought Mr. Choudray would like to have another quick word with him.

"Oh yes, I can see Mr, Choudray, anytime this morning," he said. "He is such a helpful man."

277

"I will also ask Mrs. Pendlebury to come and see you so that she can explain to you what she is saying regarding the special educational needs records and about the involvement of parents."

"Very well, if you must," he said, a very pained expression on his face. Clearly Jackie's charm had no effect on him; it did not compensate for the fact that she appeared to be making a bizarre suggestion – that the school should work with parents to help the children with special needs achieve.

I shut the door quietly behind us as we left, and Phil and I walked as quickly as we could to the inspection room to tell the team about the headteacher's reactions to the very heavy issues that the school was facing.

After the team meeting which went well, I thought, with everyone clear on their jobs for the final day and in agreement with the key issues that I had given out, Henry had called me over. He wanted to have a few words. As I waited for him to speak, while we settled back down into two chairs, and the last of the team left the room, I felt a lurch of anxiety. Was he going to start the process of letting me know that things were not good enough?

"I know we are going to have a full feedback, but I thought I would set you mind at rest before then. I am going to defer feedback from this evening, you'll be tired then – shattered I would think, after a week like this."

I nodded. "Yes, it's been hard, but Phil has helped me a lot."

"Yes, yes, of course. It was very fortunate that you had a strong team on this inspection, and Steven Linklater, he is a very experienced man. But, I want to let you know, Jane, you've done a good job. You've been fair, been thorough, no doubt about that;

the evidence base is very secure, but you've seen the bigger picture, and you have kept the respect of the headteacher. Of course, there are lots of things you need to improve and develop, and we'll go into those at another time. We'll have a proper meeting at the office on Monday."

I was stunned. I sat back and felt as if tears were very near the surface. All I could say was.

"Mr. Westcote didn't moan, say I was dreadful?"

"No. He likes you. He had a list of things to complain about, he wouldn't be human if he hadn't – apparently the parents' meeting was a bit of a shambles – you know heads always have their spies at those meetings but no, despite it all, he likes you."

"Have I passed?"

"You have definitely passed, and all I want to say now is conclude to-night's meeting as you did this morning's (much better than last night's when people rambled too much and you lost the drift on occasions) and I will see you in the office on Monday for a full feedback."

I walked out of the door feeling elated. When I had calmed down a bit in the ladies loo, I looked at my timetable to remind myself of what jobs I still had to get done that last day. It all seemed a little like an anti-climax, the last day's jobs had seemed so important when I had planned the timetable. They still had to be finished, all ends neatly tidied up, but what difference would they make, now that the decision had been made as to the school's future? First, I was going to spend some time checking out a nursery music session for Jackie in the hall; there was an English lesson in a Year 3 class, with a teacher who was already identified as weak; at lunchtime I had arranged to go out with Hamza to check on play; and then in the afternoon, I was finally going to get to see a lesson by the PE Co-ordinator, the young Asian girl that everyone said showed so much promise. She was taking a dance lesson at two o'clock.

The nursery music lesson was charming with small children marching round the hall following their teacher in a snaking circle. Some were chosen as musicians to 'play' the drums, tambourines and other percussion instruments in time to the beat. The enthusiasm was enormous, but the teaching of skills a little haphazard. I gave the lesson a good, mainly because there was so much enjoyment. The English lesson was as dreary as I had feared and the lack of progress in writing that was clearly apparent in the children's books confirmed for me that we had in fact made the right decision. At lunchtime, just as I was about to go and find Hamza for our walk round the playground, Mr. Westcote came and asked me if I would talk to one of the governors. Apparently he had come in especially to see me, unaware that he should have made an appointment. Mr. Westcote seemed very anxious that I should talk to him. It turned out to be the gentleman who had been so vocal in his condemnation of the school's provision for information technology. I listened and nodded as once again he condemned the school, and I was struck by the irony that Mr. Westcote had obviously thought he had come to sing the school's praises.

After my talk with the governor, I realised that I had better grab some lunch and forego my visit to the playground. I went into the dinning hall and got a plate of dubious school dinner, a large blob of pasta and red sauce that went by the name of lasagne, accompanied by a few anaemic pieces of lettuce and a wafer of tomato. I made my way to the team room to eat.

"Anyone seen Hamza?" I asked. "I was going to go out on the yard with him this lunchtime but I got delayed."

"Mmm, he waited for you," replied Margaret, "but I think he's gone out without you."

Hamza Choudray stood at the side of the school wall and watched the junior children surge out of the door to freedom. Some dashed headlong, heedless of where they were running, just running, arms open into the widest space they could find. Others gave a skip, a jump, a turn, talking to friends while still propelling themselves in the right direction. They came out in big noisy chattering groups, in threes, in twos, best friends, arms around each other. Then there were those that came out on their own. Hamza picked them out with an expert eye. Here at Home Farm, there were more loners than at most schools. After a few minutes the tall figures of the lunchtime staff could be seen, making their way out to separate sections of the playground, carrying wire baskets containing skipping ropes and balls of various sizes. When they put the baskets down, children swarmed round, selecting their chosen piece of equipment.

Home Farm playground was a huge L-shaped piece of tarmac, with little to break the monotony. One end, that went round the corner of the building, was graced by four picnic tables and benches and a few small trees, now bare of leaves and cheerless. A section was coned off to allow football to be played. Football playing was organised by the headteacher. There were two separate groups, the older juniors and the younger ones and they were allowed to play on alternate days. The older juniors, because of their seniority, had three days to the two days enjoyed by the younger group. Mr. Westcote had explained to Hamza how the right to have football had been linked to the behaviour policy. Serious infringement of school rules by a member of one of these groups would mean the loss of football rights. "Works like magic," the usually doleful chap had said with a wink. A third small football contingent was allowed on the edge of the specified area. The footballers in this group were from the recently arrived community of refugees from Uganda. Their football time was a concession to their settling in period.

Experience had taught Hamza to make sense of the willy-nilly scene in front of him. There was nothing untoward, particularly. The lunchtime staff were doing their job patrolling for potential difficulties, the football was enjoyed, and some girls lingering about the benches in the quiet area were chatting. Then again, there was nothing particularly good about it, nothing to counteract the bleak environment and it was clear that several individuals obviously just got through playtime, rather than enjoying it. Sometimes they tagged on to others, sometimes they stood about on their own, accepting their loneliness.

The little refugee boy was easy to see. He stood on the same spot of the playground as he had done the day before and as he did when his mum left him in the mornings. If he hadn't looked so sad, Hamza would have made a joke to himself and the other inspectors about how he must have squatters rights by now for that bit of playground. Hamza approached him. He stopped a few yards in front, not too close, and then he bent down so that the boy knew he must be talking to him and said:

"Hello, I am Mr. Choudray." He pointed to himself and said 'Mr. Choudray' several times. Then he pointed to the boy. The boy looked at him and said nothing. Hamza stood up straight and motioned to him to follow him, smiling. Much to his relief, the boy followed. Hamza led the way towards the group of refugee footballers. When he and the boy got close he held up his hand to one of them.

"May I borrow your ball?" he said loudly. Without waiting for an answer, he swiftly intercepted it on its way past his foot and bent down and picked the ball up. The four older boys looked at him with consternation.

"What have we done?" one asked slowly, his English

shaky.

"Nothing. I just wanted to borrow your ball." Hamza smiled at them, pointing at the ball and then pointing at the small boy who was standing on one side watching. "You are good boys, I know. You won't mind me borrowing your ball for just a minute will you?" He had no idea if they understood him. He put the ball down at his feet and tapped it carefully towards the younger boy. The small boy stopped it, and looked up at Hamza. He looked puzzled. Hamza motioned to him to kick it back to him. Slowly he brought his foot back and kicked the ball. It was not a very good kick, it went to one side, and Hamza had to run quite hard to retrieve it.

"Good, good what a good kick," Hamza clapped and turned to the older boys encouraging them to clap too. One got the idea and gave a few claps. Hamza kicked it back to the small boy. This time the boy kicked it hard, straight and true back to Hamza. The older boys clapped, loudly this time. Hamza and the boy kicked it back and forth to each other, again and again. Then Hamza picked up the ball, walked over to the boy, pointed to himself and said: "my name is Mr. Choudray." And then he pointed at the boy. The boy said, "Joffrey." Hamza motioned to the older boys.

"What are your names?" he said to them. The five boys all gave their names. "Look," he said, "this is Joffrey. He speaks your language doesn't he?"

"Yes, he does," said one of them. "My mum knows his mum."

"Then why don't you talk to him, why do you let him play on his own?"

They looked a little abashed. "He is too young for us."

"Would you like to be on your own?" Hamza asked. Then he bounced the ball a few times and kicked it to one of the older boys. After a moment's indecision, the older boy kicked it to Joffrey. A kick about started with Joffrey included. It lasted till the whistle went. Hamza began to walk away, calling over his shoulder, "I'm coming back tomorrow to see if any of you are good enough to play for Manchester United."

"Yeah, Manchester United," cheered one of the boys.

Of course, Mr. Choudray would not be back the next day, the inspection was ending, but he knew now that the school was failing, not just the slow learners, that had been proved by the subject inspectors, but also children like Joffrey, children who had come from goodness knows where and from goodness knows what horrors to stand on a windy patch of tarmac in Birmingham.

"Remember, Joffrey's playing tomorrow." Hamza's words blew back on the wind.

When I entered the hall, the dance lesson had been in progress for a while. The ten-year-old children were scattering, running about the hall criss-crossing each others' paths, whirling, twirling and just missing collision by a fraction. Their bodies reached up then swooped low, at one with the surging music, their movement expressing the rise and fall of waves. Involvement was complete, not a single child was adrift. When the teacher who stood in the middle of the room, raised her arms and brought the two large discs of the cymbals together with a mighty clash, every child froze. The music sweeping on around them, they stood absolutely still, the climax of their dance. The lesson was the last in a series of five on the composition of a dance depicting a storm at sea. They were doing a final performance. It was very good. No, it was excellent.

After the powerful movements of their dance, the teacher provided a calm close to the lesson, with children lying relaxed on the hall floor imagining the warm sunlight and breeze of a summer's day. I walked back to the classroom with them. They were excited by the knowledge that they had created something remarkable and they were permitted to chat quietly to each other on their way back by this clever young teacher.

As the last child filed into the room, intent on getting changed, I could not resist motioning the teacher towards me. "I could not have improved on that lesson in any way whatsoever," I said. She smiled, happily understanding the Ofsted speak for 'excellent'.

I walked away down the drab corridor to the final team meeting and knew that I would do the job I was expected to do. I thought how strange it was that I would always remember this school as being the place where my life had changed so much. I was now firmly set on the path of being a school inspector, and incredibly I might have met someone who would come to mean more to me than another career move. What changes, I asked myself would occur the teachers and staff who worked here after we had left and most importantly, what changes for the children? I knew there were no guarantees that things would improve, but at least there would be the opportunity for change, I had to trust that this would be for the better.

Number 113 Bus Stop Stainer Street, Birmingham: One year and six months after Home Farm Primary School went into special measures

Joffrey clutched the bag he was carrying tightly to his chest. He glanced up at his mum and smiled. His Mum smiled back at him. He shifted from one foot to the other, impatient for the bus to arrive. There were several other people waiting this morning. A plump lady arrived, puffing a little because she had run part of the way from her house, afraid she was going to be late.

"Hello Joffrey," she said. "What have you got in that bag?"

"It's bread," he answered. "My mum made it to show them at my school." He spoke his words slowly and carefully so that he knew he said each one right.

"Well, I am sure they're a lucky lot to get your Mum to bake bread for them." She turned to another woman in the bus queue near her," I wouldn't know where to start if someone expected me to bake bread, would you Lisa?" The other woman laughed and shook her head.

The bus came and everyone got on. Joffrey sat holding his precious bread tightly, looking out of the window and watching the familiar streets go by. He knew when it was time to get off.

"Goodbye Joffrey," called the woman as they got off. "Have a good day at school."

"Goodbye," called Joffrey and his Mum.

When they got to school his mother did not stay outside behind the iron railings. She walked into the playground with him. Other Mums and even some dads and grandparents were on the playground and as the children filed into school in their class lines, the adults came in with them. When they walked through the cavernous school doors, they saw Mrs.Johnson, the headteacher. She was smiling and welcoming parents.

"Good morning, good morning. Thank you for coming to Year 5's assembly this morning," she said. "Mrs. Akbar is serving coffee in the hall. The assembly will start at twenty past nine. Oh Mrs. Matabelee, how kind of you to bake some bread." Joffrey and his mother paused for a moment as the headteacher said these few special words to them.

Later on when the hall was packed with children, teachers and parents, Mrs. Johnson stood at the front speaking in a clear loud voice. She thanked the parents for coming.

"The children and Mrs Young have worked very hard on their assembly – I am sure you all know it is about bread, and that it's part of our celebration for the harvest that we in this country enjoy at this time of the year, but which the family of man enjoys in every part of the world at different times. Wherever we live, wherever we come from, we can all give praise for the food that we have to eat. I would like to give a special thank you to the many parents who have gone to the trouble of baking bread for us at home. We can learn so much from you."

When the Year 5's came in, following each other quietly and respectfully on to the small raised platform in front of the whole school, they stood perfectly still. Then at a single command from their teacher they put the things that they were carrying down in front of them. Mrs. Matabelee looked at her child standing so straight and tall, ready to say his few words in English, just like the other children. She had never felt so happy or so proud in all her life.

When the assembly finished everyone clapped. Mrs. Johnson came to the front again and thanked Mrs. Young and the children for a wonderful assembly.

"I thought I knew all there was to know about bread," she said, "but you proved me wrong. Just imagine, people were making bread all those thousands of years ago. Thank you Class 5Y, that was fantastic." She paused and looked around the hall with pride. How different it looked to when she had first seen it just over a year ago. "And now I have something to tell you all. Today is a special day for Home Farm Primary. I have just been given some wonderful news by Her Majesty's Inspectors. Home Farm Primary School has been taken out of Special Measures!" This time the clapping and cheering was deafening, everyone joined in, including Mrs. Matabelee, although she had no idea what it was she was cheering.

Mrs. Johnson held up her hand and the hubbub gradually

subsided. She said how pleased she was that everyone else was pleased and that there was going to be a party later in the term to celebrate, but that all the teachers would find something special for the children to do that day. Then she said that she had one more thing to tell them about. "What a busy day it is today," she laughed, " I just can't let you go though, without sharing with you the message written on this postcard that I received this morning – so strange it should come today of all days." She turned round to where she had left her hymn sheet and other papers and picked up a card. "It reads: 'Dear Home Farm children and staff, this is a picture of the small coastal town in New South Wales where I am now living. Most people here work in the zoo for which the town is famous. It is a nice zoo, though not as big as the one we used to visit at Chester. I go fishing sometimes. I hope you are all well and that all the children are working hard.' And that has been sent all the way across the world to us from Mr. Westcote." When she finished speaking no one was quite sure what they should do. Then the teachers started clapping and everyone joined in. It was a restrained quiet sort of clap.

Mrs. Johnson looked across the room and spotted a smile on the face of Mrs. Miller, her Year 6 teacher who had weathered the storm of special measures incredibly well. She caught her eye and they exchanged a wry smile; they were both thinking the same thing: dear old Mr.Westcote, boring to the end, but how lovely to hear that he was happy and on this day of all days.

Jargon Buster and Acronyms

The world of education loves acronyms and jargon words. Consequently documents for schools and teachers are incomprehensible to the outsider. When school inspections were introduced, inspection generated its own insider vocabulary. Below are a few of the most commonly used terms, some of which you will find in this book.

Attainment Targets: Level descriptors for each subject of the National Curriculum against which children's progress can be assessed.

Co-ordinator: A staff member responsible for a particular subject, or aspect of school life.

DfES: Department for Education and Skills.

Early Years: In some schools this refers to children under school age and in others it includes the children in the Reception class.

HMI: Her Majesty's Inspector.

HMCI: Her Majesty's Chief Inspector.

Key Stage: Key Stage1 children were once called infants and Key Stage 2 were juniors prior to the introduction of the National Curriculum.

Key Issues: A page in an Ofsted report which sets out briefly the main things a school needs to put right.

Lay inspector: This was the title for a team member who was trained to inspect but had had no prior involvement with education during their previous employment.

LEA: Local Education Authority. (Now termed LA, the education part having been incorporated within the umbrella term of Children's Services.)

LO: lunchtime organisers – dinner ladies to anyone over twenty-five.

LOF: Lesson observation form.

PICSI: Pre-Inspection Context and School Indicators – a 30 page document sent annually to each school (superseded by the PANDA.)

PANDA: Performance and Data Analysis document sent annually to each school (superseded by RAISE online – complex statistical analysis of the school's test results.)

Reception: The class children go into at the start of their education prior to their fifth birthday.

RgI: Registered Inspector. These were the people registered by Ofsted to lead an inspection and they were spoken of as 'Reggies'. Stiff assessment and continuous monitoring meant that there was considerable kudos in being a Reggie rather than a teammie. In this book the term 'lead inspector' instead of RgI is used, as this is now the preferred term.

RoCJ: Record of corporate judgement. It is used on inspection to record the agreed findings of the team using a grading system of numbers one to seven.

SATS: Standardised assessment tasks set at the end of Years 2 and 6 in primary schools.

SEN: Special educational needs

SENCO: The member of staff in a school responsible for the children with special educational needs.

SDP: School development plan (which is the same thing as a SIP).

SIP: School improvement plan or school improvement partner.

SMT: Senior management team.

TA: Teaching assistant.

CONTACT US:

You are welcome to contact the Seven Arches Publishing Sales Manager by:

Phone: 0161 612 0866

Email: jane.schaffer@ntlworld.com

Address: 55, Countess Street, Stockport SK2 6HB

Website: http://www.sevenarchespublishing.co.uk

You can order copies of My Teacher Says You're a Witch via any of the above contact routes. You may use the order form opposite if you require.

VISIT OUR WEBSITE TO CHECK OUT OUR PLANS FOR FUTURE PUBLICATIONS AND A DISCOUNT PURCHASE PRICE!

Order Form

Name and Title ....

Address ....

....

Postcode ....

Telephone number...

E-mail...

If you use the post please send a cheque made payable for £7.99 to Seven Arches Publishing.

If you order using phone or email we will ask you to send a cheque on receipt of your order.

On our website you can order copies using your credit or debit card.